The Company of Avalon

Mary Angelon Young

The Summer Country Trilogy

BOOK ONE

Cover photo of Mary Magdalene from Saint Jean de Vedas Church,
Montpellier, France by Mary Angelon Young.

Layout & Design by ZDP Digital Media ~ linkedin.com/in/zacparker

SAORSA PRESS
PO Box 4100
Chino Valley, Arizona
86323 USA

Contents

Contents

Historical Note

During the era of the infamous Tudor king Henry VIII, England was cast into a brutal religious reform that gave rise to a reign of terror referred to by historians as "the Dissolution of the Monasteries." By 1528 Henry had frittered away the significant wealth inherited from his father Henry VII when he assumed the throne. Beleaguered by growing debt and ongoing wars, after twenty-five years of marriage to his Spanish queen, Catherine of Aragon, he had only one living child—a girl named Mary. Obsessed with securing the throne for a Tudor heir, Henry craved a boy child. He devised a plan by which to obtain an annulment of his marriage to Catherine from the Pope, freeing him to marry a lady of the court, the seductive Anne Boleyn, a young woman of ruthless political ambition with whom he was enamored. Henry was certain this match would yield the male heir upon whom he pinned his hopes and schemes.

In 1528, with the reluctant help of his Lord Chancellor, Cardinal Wolsey, Henry petitioned the Pope in Rome to declare his marriage to Catherine null and void based on an absurd rationale. Political pressures and tensions mounted, augmented by the growing movement of

Reform (often violent and ending in the deaths of hundreds of thousands) spearheaded by Martin Luther in Europe, war with France and Spain, and Henry's paranoia, megalomania, and penchant for execution. (The guillotine was the most merciful death; hanging until almost dead then drawing and quartering was far more painful. Worst of all was being burned at the stake. All three were common occurrences.)

Faced with an impossible situation, over twenty abbots of religious houses, including Richard Whiting of Glastonbury Abbey, signed Wolsey's petition to Pope Clement, urging him to dissolve Henry's marriage to Queen Catherine. When the Pope refused the petition, Wolsey was arrested on high treason and—after a drawn-out game of cat and mouse with the king and his calculating, powerful paramour, Anne, a fervent enemy of Wolsey—the former Lord Chancellor died on his way to execution in 1530, some whispered by his own hand.

Wolsey's downfall and demise sent a clear message that reverberated throughout England. The king charged ahead, appointing his old friend and mentor, Sir Thomas More, as his Lord Chancellor. Disregarding warnings from the Pope in Rome, Henry declared himself the head of his own church and divorced Catherine, who had been kept away from court for years. With Catherine effectively side-lined, Henry and Anne were publically married in 1532 in high theatrical style, dressed as King Arthur and Queen Guinevere. Living in guarded seclusion, Catherine died in 1533. She was heartbroken, desperate to secure the future for their legitimate daughter (Princess Mary), and insisted to the end upon her lawful right as Henry's queen.

In 1533, under tremendous pressure, Sir Thomas More refused to sign the Act of Succession, which declared Henry's marriage to Catherine null and void and acknowledged the king's marriage to Anne Boleyn, making her children the legal heirs to the throne. Thomas More drew the king's wrath and was executed for treason in 1535, jolting England into a deeper despair.

Over the next three years Anne Boleyn, like her predecessor, gave birth to only one living child—a girl named Elizabeth. Caught in complex webs of deceit and escalating madness, Anne Boleyn died at the guillotine by Henry's order in May 1536, tainted with shame and ignominy amidst whispers of witchcraft but formally accused of treason and adultery. Each of these stunning deaths—Cardinal Wolsey, Sir Thomas More, and Anne Boleyn, as well as Queen Catherine—is a story in its own right.

This story centers on the dramatic events involving Glastonbury Abbey and its abbot, Richard Whiting, who, along with the abbots of other monasteries, continued to barter their souls, not only to stave off their own deaths but the destruction of their religious houses. Legitimate complaints and accusations of abuses of power and riches on the part of the Catholic Church were used to fuel the juggernaut of Reform against not only corrupt houses but against many religious houses that supported vast numbers of monks and nuns as well as the lay population. The fact was that many religious houses provided the only charity available to the poor, widowed, and indigent of England.

In 1534 Richard Whiting and fifty-one Glastonbury monks signed the king's Act of Succession and soon after signed another edict recognizing royal supremacy in all religious matters. These were acts of submission that cost them dearly in the coin of heartbreak. When the birth of Henry's son Edward by the king's next wife, Jane Seymour, in 1537 did not ameliorate Henry's antagonism toward the Church, it became clear that his greed for the riches of the religious houses was the engine behind the brutal advance of his reform. With a new Lord Chancellor—the reform zealot, Thomas Cromwell—and Thomas Cranmer as the king's new Archbishop of Canterbury, Henry aggressively pursued his course, amassing wealth in pounds, gold, and land from the dissolution of the religious houses to support his opulent, power-mad throne and ill-conceived wars abroad.

In 1538, when our story opens, there had been four years of gruesome violence, torture, and terror since the king's law for royal supremacy in religious matters was passed. John Fisher, Bishop of Rochester, refused to acknowledge the king as the head of the church in England and was executed. Priors John Houghton, Augustine Webster, James Lawrence—and many monks of the Carthusian order—had been tried and executed for treason by the Act of Succession.

These were powerful and complex times. Popular sentiment was split on the subject of religion, faith being ultimately a matter of the heart. Viewed from the vantage point of history, more than anything else, the ordinary person of sixteenth century England—like people in all times and all places—longed for freedom. They longed for religious freedom, the freedom to choose, and the freedom to live without the constant threat of a brutal, arbitrary death at the hands of royal families, corrupt political leaders and religious organizations.

Somerset, England

The abbot sat in the dark, fingers slowly turning the worn vellum leaves of his Bible. His hand, wrinkled and spotted with age, trembled as he squinted at the handwritten text, a single candle shedding no more than a dim aureole of light upon the page. A familiar aching restlessness took him, and his chair grated upon the stone floor as he rose from the desk, walked to the window and opened the latch, pushing out the leaded glass. Cool wet air rushed in as he looked out over the garden, now a black lacuna thick with drifting fog.

His thoughts hovered over the question that had plagued him in these months of struggle, in the miasma of long nights when prayers went unanswered and death danced, jeering, across the landscape of his mind. There were nights when hatred seared his heart, when faith fled before craven images of King Henry, Cromwell, Cranmer—his bitterest enemies. He rubbed a hand across his forehead, pressing fingers deep into sore eyes, then leaned against the stone wall. Did he truly have the strength to live his convictions, to die a gallow's death? The reality of a violent end loomed upon him, for he would certainly not have the peaceful farewell of a long, fruitful life.

When first light illumined the inky darkness, Richard went to the pewter washbowl and splashed his face with water, washing away the grit and strain of the fevered night. Returning to the window, he watched as a brilliant ball of sun painted gold the sea of mist that hovered over the Somerset levels, with the Tor rearing up green and mysterious, glimmering in its midst. Pondering the strange hill, he heaved a sigh from deep within his chest. Relief always came with the rising sun. In the tender ministrations of dawn, his demons fled to their hiding places, and death seemed a small price to pay to affirm those shining truths that purled like a peaceful tide at the shores of his heart. In the reprieve of morning, death whispered sweet words, lured him toward its bright doorway of release.

A rap of knuckles on hard wood broke into his reverie, and he winced slightly at the sound of his chamberlain's voice that came, muffled and grating, through the heavy oaken door of his chambers.

"Tis soon time for Lauds, sir. Will you be needing anything?"

"No, Jack. I will come presently."

His limbs were heavy as he opened the wardrobe and pondered the row of black robes, the mitre and scepter, his chasubles, stoles, and crosier. Pulling out a biretta, he fitted the small four-cornered black hat upon his head and moved across the room toward the door. Thanks be given to the Lady of Light, it was not much longer now before the flame of his life would go out and all of this struggle would be over.

CHAPTER ONE

Glastonbury Abbey
August 1538

Abbot Richard Whiting emerged from the dim interior
of the Lady Chapel into the pearly grey light of afternoon. Blinking, he looked up at stately beech trees that
danced in a restless wind. Small whirlwinds of yellow leaves
scurried under his feet as he passed along the cathedral wall.
The stones of the old church seemed to whisper secrets;
they were dank and mossy and smelled of rain, and, with a
glance at slate clouds that gusted in a seaward sky, he knew a
tempest would arrive before dark.

Moving across the grounds toward his lodge, the abbot
made his way along a worn path through the garden, now
at its peak. Thriving banks of blue delphinium, swaths of
ruddy snapdragons and golden coreopsis spilled from deep
beds, but despite the rich array, the abbot seemed not to
notice the beauty before him but walked head down with
somber, measured steps, his thoughts revolving around
the meeting he had earlier with his great-niece, Magdalyne
Whiting.

Pausing at the edge of the garden, his senses were captured by a fragrance that curled into his awareness. His favorite rose bush was thick with blossoms that hovered heavy-headed and redolent, the color of sunrise. Tomorrow they would be spangled silver with the coming rain. He lingered for moment, bending to touch the shivering petals.

As he turned the corner of the priory, his heavy linen robe flapped in the rising wind and clung to the woolen stockings on his thin legs. A frown creased his forehead as he glimpsed his chamberlain, Jack Horner, holding the door open for him.

"Sir, will you have an early supper served in your rooms?"

"Aye, Jack. I will not sup with the brothers after Vespers. And John Thorne will be joining me." Rubbing his thin arms for warmth, Richard made his way up the worn stone steps and down the corridor to his private chambers.

At the sound of a knock at his door, Richard Whiting turned from the windows that overlooked the garden and cathedral, with the holy hill rising high in the near distance.

"Come in, John." He sighed as his friend and abbey bursar, John Thorne, opened the door and entered the room. Without a word, Richard gestured to the scene below.

Striding across the stone floor to join him, John looked down at a young man in the black garb of a novice, who stood talking with the abbot's great-niece in the garden below.

"Aye, aye," the abbot responded to the unspoken provocation in John's face as he turned to the abbot with arched brows.

"Bold they are, and far too intelligent for their own good in such dangerous times. Soon Colin will have to make the decision whether or not he will take his final vows." A wan smile flickered in the thicket of the abbot's white beard, and his eyes lingered on his friend as they stood side-by-side at the window.

The afternoon light glinted off John Thorne's short iron-grey hair and shone softly from the well-worn heavy linen of his dark cassock. Like the abbot, Thorne wore the simple black garb of a Benedictine monk. Neither the bursar nor the abbot wore their hair tonsured; they had given up that practice ten years before. Instead they usually wore black felt calottes, round caps that fit snug upon the skull. Rather than his ornate chain of office, a simple gold crucifix hung from a heavy chain about Richard's neck, and as he watched John at the window, he fingered the carved bone rosary that he kept in the depths of his pocket.

Finally John stirred.

"Hmm. Yes, I remember how they were, last year at Michaelmas, in Exeter." John's voice was pensive, with only a hint of his usual brash candor and Scottish brogue. "Eyebrows were raised at Langbrook, as I recall. Jesu and Mother Mary, I am loathe for our abbey to lose Colin— though a finer lass than Magdalyne cannot be found. I must admit, seeing them together now brings Margaret to mind. What a time that was, our year on the Isle of Arrain."

His voice had turned wistful, but John smiled at the memory as he glanced at his oldest friend, knowing that Richard remembered quite well, though he listened with interest. The two stood together quietly, lost in thought for

9

the moment, their memories turning to Margaret Hamilton of Kildonan, the catalyst that sent John Thorne to follow his friend, Richard, into a monk's life so many years ago.

John continued, "We never saw one another again after she married my brother. I am glad that we parted as friends."

Decades had passed, then three years ago, after her husband's death, Margaret had sent her youngest grandson, Colin, born and raised in the Scottish isles, to Somerset in England, where he would be further educated under his great-uncle's wing at Glastonbury.

"In a way, I suppose I fell in love all over again, but this time with my gifted great-nephew," John reflected. "He was only twenty years old at the time."

The two friends lingered at the window in silence, each ruminating upon their lives, as men are often compelled to do when time weighs heavy upon them. And yet, their memories were far more pleasant than the tension that hummed beneath the surface of their contemplations. After a time, Richard sighed.

"I daresay there is beauty to be found, even in the dissolution of all that lives then dies." Richard smiled faintly at the irony of his words. "All which has come and then passed—success and failure, riches or poverty, love or hate, faith or doubt—may be transmuted into the gold of wisdom."

A fleeting grin, almost a grimace, accentuated the fine lines of John's face. "Well said! You should keep that eloquence for your next sermon." Turning somber, he added, "I suppose this is the way we old men plow and tend the fields and forests of our inmost selves, making ready for the next season." He shrugged.

"Well, I have no time for regrets. It was my fate to serve God all my life in this monastery, keeping the accounts and overseeing the purchase of geese and cows and pigs and sacks of grain. But, as you say, love is destined for those two. They have been sweethearts since their childhood years on the Isle of Arrain—the place where you and I met our fate, as well."

"Come now, John," Richard chuckled, "you've done a good deal more than buy and sell livestock and barley. You have dealt in land, in gold and silver and precious gems— you have helped to make this the richest monastery in Somerset, maybe even in England."

"With a lot of help from you, sir," John rejoined as he rubbed his bearded chin. "Aye, we've accomplished much with what was passed on to us by our abbot. And that is part of the problem we must now face—that the king wants the riches of this abbey for himself."

"Hnnh," Richard grunted, his lips pressed together in a thin line.

John's words hung in the air between them, tantalizing, but the abbot turned back to the window. Silence spread across the room as afternoon shadows lengthened, until Richard inclined his head toward the pair who walked slowly through the garden below, heads bent close together, toward the wooden door in the transept of the church.

"Sometimes I think they are guided more by the ancient gods than by Blessed Mary," he admitted. "It does not surprise me. Magdalyne is not like her older sister Jane, who is happy at St. Andrew's monastery in Bruges."

John responded thoughtfully, "Aye, the old religion holds sway on Arrain among my people. At best the church

11

is interwoven with their faery faith, their myths, gods and goddesses that thrive to this day in Scotland, Ireland, Cornwall—and north of here, in Cumbria and Wales."

Running his hands through thick white hair, Richard reflected. "Aye, the ancient world is alive here in Somerset as well. How could it not be, with the Tor and the sacred springs, with the legends of Avalon and this holy church founded by Joseph of Arimathea? Many folk in our parish still believe the holy grail is not Christ's chalice but the blessed cauldron of the goddess. This church is filled with the relics of those mysteries. And, there is the tomb in the high altar."

John nodded, pursing his lips. "Aye, and though their bodies were acknowledged by King Edward and his lady, Queen Eleanor—was it two hundred and sixty years ago?— the Reform would have us all scoff at such legends and mysteries, would have us destroy them as frauds."

He sighed heavily then continued, his thoughts unwinding between them, speaking for them both. "'Tis most interesting, indeed. On the one hand, the Reform denies the miraculous, seeking out and destroying false relics, while with the other hand the king reaches his hand toward the treasures of Glastonbury, guarded and protected by our Benedictine fathers for centuries. What are such treasures worth to King Henry? Only the bones, which Henry will use merely to further justify his divine right to rule, bereft of mercy or justice."

Richard said nothing but turned from the window and walked to the table that was laid out with linen, silver knives and forks, platters of cold sliced duck and venison, and bowls of plums, peaches and fresh red currants from the abbey orchards.

"Are you hungry, John? I've asked the cook to bring hot *tisane* and lemon cakes later." He reached for some red currents, tossed a handful in his mouth then frowned slightly, sucking in his cheeks at their tartness.

Richard lifted a heavy pewter pitcher of ale and poured the amber liquid into two cups, then served their trenchers with slices of venison. An intimate quietude mellowed the darkening shadows of the oak-paneled room as the two men ate, while the silence grew as the deeper subject of their meeting demanded its due. A few drops of rain pelted the leaded glass as the wind from the sea brought the storm closer, spurring John to rise and cross the chamber to close the open window. The stone walls and floors of the abbot's priory kept the rooms cool even in the heat of summer, and now a chill seemed to set in along with the first drops of rain. Compared to the lavish and sometimes decadent chambers of most abbots, Richard Whiting's rooms were pristine in their simplicity. Endowed with a fireplace, a few wool rugs, some wooden chairs and the smoothly worn, long oak table where they sat, the one frivolity was a white porcelain vase of sprawling summer flowers that graced the sideboard. In a corner by the window was the abbot's desk, with its stacks of books, wax candles, and the ever-present Bible in Latin. On the wall above the desk hung a crucifix. Waiting for Richard to break the silence, John's eyes rested upon a tapestry of Mary Magdalene kneeling before Jesus to anoint his feet.

"How remarkable it is," Richard gave a wry half smile, "to be caught in the crossfire between the king and

Rome—to have this religious war now, in our elder years, after a lifetime of peace and plenty."

The abbot paused to quaff the last of the ale in his cup as his words sank into the heavy air between them, bringing the reality of their situation into sharp focus. Both men knew with aching certainty that they were likely to pay a heavy price for their convictions. Picking up John's cup with a sigh, the abbot refilled it, set it down, and pushed it toward his friend.

"John, I called you here today from your work over the accounts to speak freely of recent developments. I heard this morning from Jack Horner that even Lady Salisbury has drawn the king's suspicions. So many have died," he leaned forward, spreading one hand upon the table, "beginning with Buckingham. It was stupid of him to plot against Henry for the throne. Wolsey's downfall and death was a terrible blow. And to this day I grieve the execution of Thomas More—though, as you know, his burning of heretics was a sorrow for me. I pray for their souls still."

Richard paused thoughtfully and caressed the gold crucifix that hung about his neck. "Nay, in fact I am disheartened by these barbaric practices that hold sway, condoned by the Holy Church. I have always been considered a liberal by my fellow Catholics."

John Thorne listened, then tossed back the ale in his cup.

"Truth be told, you and I are quiet heretics, Richard. We have been fortunate for many years, left alone here in the West Country by ourselves to worship and live as we do." He stood to check the firebox for tinder.

"Would you like a fire now, Richard? There is a storm on its way."

"Thank you, John, but it's not necessary."

Thorne sat down at the table. Picking up the thread of the conversation, he faced the abbot.

"Sir Thomas More was a complex man. The burnings were a terrible business, and yet his ideas are still inspiring. In the face of the king's madness, it is still hard to believe that Cardinal Wolsey and Thomas More were both Lord Chancellor—the closest to the king!— at the time of their executions. No one is safe." He took a deep breath as he reached to replenish their cups with ale.

Picking up an apple with one hand and a knife with the other, the abbot broke into John's growing rant. "Perhaps it was the sad death of the babe's mother Jane Seymour, only two weeks after his birth a year ago, that has driven Henry further into madness."

John snorted forcefully. "The king is merely ruthless and power mad. His reign is a living nightmare for the people of England. How many have died, how many will die? Everyone lives in fear and horror of being forced to renounce their faith or their lives. Our people are reeling from the tragedies of Catherine of Aragon, God rest her good soul, and the unfortunate Anne Boleyn."

Putting down the apple, Richard bowed his head, the grimace on his face deepening in the growing heat of John's outrage. "You are right John. But let us not speak of Anne Boleyn, lest we conjure her restless, wandering shade, may God rest her soul, and may God protect her innocent child, Elizabeth."

Abbot Whiting genuflected as John Thorne continued, his words clipped and bitter.

"As you say, since Jane Seymour died last year—may she rest in peace!—the king has gotten worse. In his grief, he grows fatter each day. His illnesses eat away at him, like canker sores on a trollop's backside, driving him, in his suffering, to greater madness."

Pausing to take a breath, his eyes rested on the abbot, who shook his head slowly in dismay. Abbot Whiting spoke of these matters only in great necessity, and now, feeling encouraged to speak openly, John plowed the field of his anger.

"If church reform is what the king wants, to cleanse the monasteries of avarice and decadence and the growing fat of lands and money, of false miracles and amulets pandered by corrupt priests, of powerful cardinals and bishops who meddle in political games, surely that could have been accomplished without such bloodshed and destruction. But it's more than that—he wants absolute power, and now he has it. Aye, it's another bloody war in God's name, Richard, and still the Reform rages, proliferating like a plague. The cathedrals are falling to the king's scourge. John Clerk at Wells barely escaped with his life..."

Further emboldened by the abbot's silence, John frowned and forged ahead with growing passion.

"But at what cost? John Clerk had to betray his own faith with conversion and—like all the others—grovel before Cranmer, Cromwell and his commissioners, his minions of evil. The cathedral and abbey at Wells and at Bath have been taken and closed, like all the other monasteries and religious houses that Henry has sacked, destroyed, or shut down. The vast lands and holdings of Wells will be sold to sweeten the king's coffers or given as gifts to his current favorites at court. For all he professes to want religious reform for the masses, the redistribution of the church's wealth does not benefit them. Along with the monasteries, many charities for the poor have been shut down. The people have nowhere to turn. Ours still exist only by the grace of God."

Richard listened, his face unreadable. The sting of the truth reverberated in the room. John Thorne watched as the abbot grew agitated, dragged long, slender fingers through his hair, then stood to pace nervously across the room from the table to the window and back again. Under the monk's robe, his body was thin as a reed but still strong from the force of sheer willpower and natural charisma. How much of this torturous pressure could he endure?

Placing his hands on the table Richard leaned close to John and spoke urgently, lowering his voice to a half-whisper.

"We must prepare for the worst, John. It is only a matter of time before the king's men pound at our door. Henry has already sent Richard Layton here as his commissioner to conduct an investigation. We were fortunate that he could find nothing wrong with our accounts, no possible reason to accuse us.

"That was three years ago, and the time is coming soon when the king will move against us once more. Just as you say, Henry wants the wealth of our abbey, and Cromwell will find an excuse, some way to accuse me of treason and other crimes—and they will threaten to take you and Roger as well. You should both leave here, go back to your families in Scotland and Wales."

The flat of John's hand smacked loudly against the smooth wood surface of the table. His livid face expressed the frustration vibrated between them. Richard did not flinch, but looked steadily at his friend.

"We have spoken too many times about this! I have given my life to this church, and to you as its abbot. You know very well that I am not leaving. If Cromwell takes you to the gallows, he takes me with you."

Taking a deep breath, John rubbed his face with his hands as if warding off a deep exhaustion, then glanced at Richard and shook his head.

"I am weary of hearing this from you, Richard. We are growing old. Our time is passing. Let us at least die with dignity, with our hearts and souls intact." He paused, the fleeting tenderness in his voice giving sway again to the power of his anger.

"I will stand with you, and Roger will as well," John argued. "I am not going to desert you...and I am not giving in to that wretched pig's ass of a diabolical despot who poses as our monarch."

He uttered a curse in Gaelic under his breath. "Would that King James of the Scots could take the throne and restore our church ..."

The abbot stared at his friend as if across an abyss of fire.

"Treason rolls off your tongue like honey from a hive— though it is not particularly sweet," he muttered, then sighed as he rose and walked back to the window.

"If Jack Horner hears you—I am sure he reports directly to Cromwell." Richard stood tall and straight, staring out, hands clasped behind his back. Thorne stood and walked to the abbot's side, placing a hand gently on his shoulder.

"Yes, it is treason. But I mean every word of it and much more, which goes unsaid, as you well know. How many years have we wrestled with this conflict? We have gone beyond trying to forestall Cromwell's hand. With his greedy eye turned in our direction, we must act."

He squeezed the abbot's shoulder then dropped his hand. Richard stared at the bursar, his eyes burning and clear.

"As you say, Benedictines have protected the secrets of this abbey for many years. I agree John—the time has come to take action, to preserve the treasures that lie in the transept of yon great church. The question is, where will we take them?"

Richard did not respond, but looked down through the leaded glass of the window, watching as several monks in black robes, hoods up to shield them from the rain, hurried toward the cathedral to enter at the main door to the nave. When the abbot finally spoke, determination rippled in the set of his shoulders.

"Let us speak no more of this for now. I will leave tonight before Vespers. Roland will bring the carriage around and drive me to Sharpham Manor, where I will spend the next few days. You may join me there tomorrow with Roger, and we will make our plan. Now," he smiled, "the day wears on—it will soon be time for None. The brothers will be gathering, and I shall join them to say mass. Leave me for awhile, would you, old friend?"

With a slight bow John moved toward the door. One hand on the brass knob, he turned to see Richard, the Abbot of Glastonbury Abbey, walk to an oaken wardrobe and carefully remove his chasuble. Breathing deeply through his nose, John closed the door behind him and made his way down the stone corridor.

Magdalyne Whiting reached up to push back curls of hair and drew a hand across her brow, young and smooth despite its apparent worry. Across one arm hung a wicker basket of cut flowers, and she adjusted its weight as she looked up at the tall, dark-haired monk who had called her name as he emerged from behind a high stone wall covered in mounds of climbing rose.

Holding a rake in his hands, he was dressed in the black robe of a novice of the Benedictine order, the monks of Glastonbury Abbey, stewards of the most sacred ground in England. But his habit could not hide the native Scot in him. His piercing grey eyes were at the same time humorous and warm under a fringe of black lashes and the dark arched wings of his brows, now raised in playful question. His full mouth was curved in a half smile as he bantered.

"Why, is it Magdalyne Whiting gracing our church grounds?"

"Colin Thorne!" Her skirts whirled gently as she turned to respond, eyeing the rake in his hand. "Have you left your ink pot and parchments to tend the garden today?

What will your Uncle John say? His talented nephew, wasting time in the garden—much less conversing with a woman, a known heretic herself!"

A luminous smile lit her face as the man came closer and she tilted her head to look up at him. Smiling back, he studied the young woman before him. Modestly attired in a blue woolen dress with a white linen ruff at the neck, she wore about her shoulders a summer cloak the color of red wine and edged with green. Her thick tresses were captured in a knot and further contained beneath a heart-shaped, close-fitting cap edged in embroidery. The stiff little hat could not subdue the unruly chestnut curls that sprang to life, glinting red-gold around her face in the mid-afternoon light.

Clear eyes gazed back at him, candid and unabashed, blue green and transparent as the waters of the Severn Sea. She is beautiful, he thought, a woman fair enough to call a man away from a life of abstinence. Ignoring the rising heat in his loins, Colin admired instead her courage—how she had followed the promptings of her heart to leave the monastery in Bruges and return to England. Seeing her at Michelmas last year, he had been drawn, like a moth to a flame. He knew very well that they had captured the attention of their elders.

"Nay, Mistress Whiting, I am taking a moment away from my parchments and books. I came here to soothe my soul in this peaceful place. It is fate that has chanced our meeting. It has been a long time since we last met."

She laughed lightly as he spoke, but her eyes betrayed a deeper unease. He glanced up at the window in the abbot's chambers.

"Don't worry about your reputation, mistress, no one can see us here—except possibly your uncle!" He chuckled, leaning the rake against the wall with a glance up at the abbot's priory.

"You are bold indeed, Colin Thorne. It's not my reputation that I worry for but yours. Just because I left the monastery..."

He shrugged off her concern and gestured toward the church.

"May I accompany you, Maddy?"

His familiar use of her childhood name grazed across her heart like a passing comet. Suddenly confused, she nodded hesitantly, glancing up at him as they fell into step.

"We meet again in dark times, Colin." Walking slowly, Colin leaned in to listen as Maddy spoke in a low voice.

"The king's dissolution of the monasteries has progressed this past year. Uncle Richard told me this morning that Lady Salisbury may be arrested under the Act of Attainment. The king will have her executed for treason without a trial. And, most recently, the cathedral of Wells has fallen." She stopped for a moment to glance up at him.

"We knew it was coming," he responded, "Who can blame the abbot of Wells—that he chose not to die but to live and preserve his church as best he can?"

She sighed and held her hand out, palm up, to catch the raindrops that grew in number as she spoke.

"I am terribly worried for Uncle Richard, and for your uncle. Glastonbury is one of the last strongholds of the Church, and one of the most powerful—certainly the most revered." She muttered fiercely under her breath. "King

Henry is evil. His greed and murderous avarice knows no bounds."

Colin's grey eyes held hers. "As you say, these are hard times, and it is not only our abbot who will suffer at the king's hand, but all who stand with him."

Her eyes roved over the sculpted stone arches of the cathedral. "I grew up loving this abbey. I stayed here often with my uncle and played as a child in this garden, attended the midnight mass at Christmastide when the thorn tree blooms, and at Easter. The monks allowed me to help with chores, arranging flowers and such, sweeping and dusting the shrines. They accepted me as their own because of their love for my uncle."

She gazed toward the Tor that rose to the south of the church, some distance away. "I fear for his life. Uncle Richard will not convert—not ever. He will not give way to the king's demands. I fear that these long centuries of Glastonbury Abbey with its history and secrets, and indeed the world as we have known it, are coming to an end."

Moving on, they fell back into step.

"I share your concern, Maddy, not only for the abbot but for my uncle as well. John Thorne and our sacristan, Roger James, will not give in. They will stand beside Abba, come what may."

His eyes lingered on hers, growing serious. "We stand on the threshold of a new order, ushered in on a tide of blood."

She nodded once, lifting her face to the rain. "Would that Nimuë, the Lady of the Lake, could come to help us in these days of peril, as she did long ago for our king and queen."

With a sigh he gestured toward the chapel. "Ah, but the rain is coming harder now. Come, let us go to pray."

The backs of their hands touched lightly as they moved away toward a large wooden door at the southern transept. The cavern of the cathedral echoed with sonorous notes of the immense organ that called the monks to afternoon prayers. Two young monks, Angus and William, had finished setting and lighting fresh candles around the high altar where a golden sheen lit the polished black marble of the tomb. They glanced at Colin then at Maddy with curiosity, interest, and a hint of vague consternation. As they moved away toward the nave, the air was tinged with excitement—a special mass would be given within the hour by the abbot himself.

With a nod to the young monks, Colin approached the shrine with Maddy. Rooted and ancient, the immense sepulcher was enigmatic in its silence. Surrounded by stone vases filled with flowers from the abbey garden, it was banked with a wild riot of color and fragrance. The top of the tomb was wreathed with fresh-cut branches, laden with clusters of orange berries from the hawthorn trees that grew in the back of the church.

Stopping before the tomb, they stood suspended in the rare atmosphere that permeated the surrounding niche, where the walls were hung with tapestries of the great king, his queen and knights.

The light of the candles sparkled in drops of rain caught in Maddy's hair as she lifted handfuls of blue larkspur and snapdragon from her basket, then leaned over to place them on top, in the center of the tomb. She bowed her head, running her hands over the smooth cold surface of the stone, her fingertips caressing the words engraved in Latin:

Here lies interred the renowned King Arthur and
his queen, on the Isle of Avalon.

Colin waited in silence while she finished her prayers. As she raised her head, he took her arm to usher her down the aisle of the church toward the nave. He hesitated, then pulled her into an alcove with a sudden and urgent whisper.

"I have missed you sorely, Maddy. Why have you not answered my letters?" His somber voice penetrated into her heart. She turned to face him, pausing to consider.

"Colin, I do not wish to encourage you. I have left the monastic life, but that does not mean you should."

He smiled, but his hand trembled as he took hers and held it, opening the fingers and stroking the soft skin there. Lifting it gingerly, he kissed the inner palm. Looking up at her, his eyes gleamed in the soft light of the alcoves.

"It is time for mass. Let us speak of this again at Michaelmas, in two months. In the meantime, I will write to you, and I will wait each day, hoping for a letter to arrive."

His eyes held hers for seconds that ticked into moments, until he released her hand just as Brother Angus appeared. The smile that spread across the monk's flushed cheeks soon fell to hesitance as he registered the looks upon the faces of the novice and the abbot's niece.

"Time for mass, Colin," the young Irish monk reminded, his words crisp. "Are ye not to sing today?" Recovering his usual jolly demeanor, Angus then turned to Maddy. "Are ye stayin' with us a few days, Mistress Whiting?"

"I will be present for mass," she replied with a smile, adjusting her cloak about her shoulders. "Then I leave with my uncle for Sharpham Manor. I depart from there for Exeter, early in the morning. Now I will stay a few more moments with the king and his queen, before I come to our Lady."

With a quiet, embarrassed glance at Colin, she forced herself to turn away and walk with deliberate calm back to the king's shrine. Placing her hands upon the cold stone, she bowed her head, but her attention was on the receding footsteps of the two men as they echoed between the vast stony silences of the church.

CHAPTER TWO

Exeter
October 1538

A heavy wooden sideboard was set with crisp white linen cloths and adorned with bowls of autumn chrysanthemums. Fat wax tapers burned bright in silver candelabras, adding to the ambient light of the late afternoon sun that slanted through the room's paned western windows.

Crusty round loaves, fresh from the oven, had been set out in baskets for a feast soon to be enjoyed by the Michaelmas gathering at Langbrook Crossing in Exeter, the ancestral home of James and Elizabeth Whiting. People had come from all over the great estate and beyond to celebrate this year's harvest, the bounty of garden, field, and barnyard. Abbot Richard Whiting—along with fellow monks Roger James and John Thorne, and the bursar's nephew, Colin— had arrived the night before from Glastonbury to join in the festivities with the exuberant Whiting family, their friends and tenants.

Elizabeth Whiting stopped her ceaseless tasks to gaze out the window for a moment at Magdalyne, who was sitting with Colin in the autumn garden beneath the trees, her festive green dress in pronounced counterpoint to the black novitiate robe he wore. She had watched as Maddy went outside earlier for a breath of fresh air, then as Colin quickly followed. Now, washed in the last rays of the sun, they were limned in gold, and she could see their breath pluming white in the chill October air. The magnetic attraction between them could be seen even at a distance—surely it was obvious to all. She glanced around at her husband, the abbot, and John Thorne, who were deep in conversation together.

Elizabeth secretly hoped they would find their way together. She remembered well how, as children, she had seen how their eyes shone as they invented games in excited, animated conversations of innocent play. With her other daughter, Jane, in the monastery, the potential for grand-children finally appeared on the horizon of her life, a pleas-ing arrangement altogether. She remembered how, even after Magdalyne made her novitiate in Bruges and Colin made his at Glastonbury, their letters never ceased to fly across the salt waters of the channel. When they met again last year in Exeter, when John Thorne and his nephew Colin had joined the Whiting family for Michaelmas, the two young people were deep in converse.

James and Elizabeth had watched that night, suspect-ing there was a deeper chemistry at work. They had kept their thoughts to themselves, not wanting to see Colin renounce his upcoming vows, but nonetheless, they would be pleased to see one of their two girls marry well and know the joys of love and family, rather than live monastic lives of solitude, asceticism, and renunciation.

Watching her daughter, Elizabeth sighed. Mayhap Maddy would be blessed with a happiness that she had never known, though she had grown to deeply cherish the loving and kind husband she had discovered over the years in James. She wiped a grease-smeared hand on her apron and smiled to herself. She had always tried to show equal love to her daughters, but in her heart she favored Maddy. With a smile of satisfaction that revealed deep dimples, Elizabeth moved briskly toward the kitchen.

While the women of the family chatted or scurried about busy with food and overseeing the servants, the men stood with glasses of wine or ale in hand, lingering near a sideboard laden with sweetmeats and rounds of white cheese. Slicing a thick chunk, James Whiting, father of Magdalyne, moved away from the table to stand beside his uncle by a window.

"Uncle, what do you think the king's next move will be?" His voice was low as he leaned into the abbot.

Glancing sharply at his nephew, Richard looked around at the family and friends who basked in the gaiety of the occasion. Despite the felicitous mood, there was an underlying hum of anxiety that permeated everything in these desperate times. His sharp eyes lingered on Elizabeth, who bustled in and out of the kitchen giving orders to Matilde, the cook.

"Whatever it is, I pray God to keep them all safe."

His response was offered with a grim smile. The elder man then turned toward his nephew and continued, speaking somberly.

"The teachings of Martin Luther are raging on the continent. It's gone far beyond Germany. He continues to keep everyone stirred up, antagonizing the Pope and—though Luther may not intend it—encouraging Henry in his madness. It seems he never stops expounding; the man is unquestionably brilliant. Truth be told, I think Luther has very wise commentaries on many subjects." He shrugged. "Aye, some say I'm a heretic, but I am true to my faith. The point is that, unfortunately, our king feels vindicated by Luther's arguments."

Richard laughed softly, attempting to bring levity to the weighty heft of their conversation. John Thorne walked over, stopping to pour a glass of the sweet golden wine that had recently arrived from France. Always quick to sense an opening to express his radical views, John glanced from the abbot to their host, James.

"So, have you heard that the king is moving against our old friend, Henry Courtenay? Once again he attacks his own close kin, and this time it is Lord Exeter! I have heard that it is just a matter of time before Courtenay is attained and thrown into the London Tower."

James rubbed a dark beard that glinted red in the late afternoon light.

"'Tis a tragedy. The so-called 'Exeter Conspiracy' wasn't even started by Courtenay. We saw it happen here, how the commoners clamored for Lord Exeter to claim himself heir apparent and prevent the king's children from taking the throne after his death." James shrugged. "Though surely the king's death is far from imminent, even if his excesses are legendary—everyone knows that Henry Tudor eats and drinks himself into a sickness from which he will never recover."

Richard drained his glass before he responded thoughtfully. "People don't want the king's policies to continue beyond his death, but that hope alone is sedition. Many are true to the faith of their fathers and forefathers—and many who embrace the Church of England do not want the Catholics who are faithful to Rome to be punished and oppressed."

He sighed. "The whole thing begs the question of religious tolerance. Why not have a reformed church and the Catholic church? When Henry dies, with a different monarchy there might be some possibility of peace."

James glanced around uneasily. "Courtenay is close to the throne, related to both the Yorks and the Tudors. He is the first cousin of the king, grandson of King Edward IV, first cousin to Margaret, Queen Consort—he certainly has a righteous claim to the throne."

John Thorne wagged his head in consternation. "Ah, what a complicated weave, the bloodlines of the royal families, their changing liaisons, betrayals, the subterfuge and intrigue." He raised his glass to Richard. "And all we wanted was the simple life of a monk."

John took in Richard Whiting's calm exterior with a wry smile as he continued, his words tinged with humor and yet burdened with implication. "What irony! Now we find ourselves embroiled in the madness of it all. Tis strange indeed, how fate has its way with us."

The abbot sighed. "Henry Courtenay has been a friend of Glastonbury for many years."

James listened attentively as he watched his wife hustle about the burgeoning table before he responded. "His wife,

Gertrude Blount, is loyal to Rome. She was a great supporter and friend of Henry's queen, Catherine of Aragon. It's known that they corresponded until Queen Catherine's death. Now it is not only Henry Courtenay but also his wife Gertrude and their son Edward who are under attack. Many people hate the king and would do anything to see him brought down. That's how something like the Exeter Conspiracy comes to pass, casting the king's evil eye on Courtenay."

Lifing his wineglass to his lips, James glanced at his uncle. "We live in hard times, and there is danger for us all. Glastonbury is next." Lowering his voice, he added, "And you, Uncle? What will you do?"

Richard raised his brows. "It is the mighty struggle of my soul to determine exactly that, James."

Just then Maddy and Colin came bursting in the front door, faces flushed from the chill autumn weather, to make their way into the large room where everyone was gathered for the feast. Twilight was soon to settle upon the surrounding fields and forests, and they sought the warmth of the fire and the companionship of family before the evening festivities began. Richard and John exchanged a glance as James turned to his uncle.

"They have always been drawn together, Uncle, even as children. Should Elizabeth and I forbid Maddy to be with him?"

"No, James. It is in God's hands." Richard returned. John Thorne snorted and pursed his lips.

"Well, I am not beyond speaking to the young man involved," he growled. Richard's eyes fell upon John in somber reflection.

"Go easy, John. We cannot, and should not, dictate the seasons of the heart."

Seeing the three men talking together, Colin made his way toward them while Magdalyne joined her mother at the table and was quickly whisked away to the kitchen. Joining his uncle, the abbot, and Magdalyne's father, Colin looked at them with speculation.

"Your conversation appears quite deep. You must be talking about our king and Cromwell—and Glastonbury Abbey."

While Richard smiled at the young monk, John shuffled uneasily, tossing back the spirits in his cup, and James looked over the guests who quaffed ale and wine in spirited conversations. Roger James, sacristan of the abbey, was absorbed in conversation with James's nephew, Ben Pritchard, and his wife Anne. Other members of the family were gathered near the fireplaces that crackled with bright flames at either end of the great hall. They talked in animated tones, or stood near the long table, watching with anticipation as the servants came and went and Elizabeth worked with Magdalyne to arrange the food.

Matilde and two other maid servants whisked in heavy pewter platters of steaming meats—roasted fowl, pork, and venison—and placed them upon the long table beside bowls of cooked apples, sausages and plums floating in heavy syrup and tureens of dumplings swimming in duck fat and butter. Elizabeth carried a porcelain bowl of leeks in cream, set it down, then turned to the waiting assembly. The servants gathered along the wall near the kitchen door. After the guests were served they too would join in the feast, sitting at a table set for them near the kitchen door—a custom upheld by the Whiting household for generations.

"The table is ready!" Elizabeth smiled broadly, speaking over the din to capture their attention. "Let us give thanks for all of our blessings and especially for this most bounteous harvest. Uncle Richard, would you lead us in a prayer?"

Richard bowed in her direction then began. "Lord Jesus, all things are in your hands. You made heaven and earth and everything in them. Who can stand against your majesty? God of our fathers and mothers, have mercy on your people, as the enemies of the spirit would have us lose our souls. You are omnipotent. If you want to save your people, no one can fight your will…"

No one missed the meaning of the abbot's words, and silence thickened in the room as he paused. A woman sniffled and others wiped tears from their eyes. Richard's voice deepened with a passion shared by all as his supplication on their behalf grew in power.

"Blessed Mary, our problems are many. Listen to our prayers and receive our gratitude for the many blessings you bestow upon us at this time of abundant harvest. Forgive our sins. Punish us not, as we may deserve, but show mercy. Turn our sorrows into joys, and allow us to praise Your Holy Name now and forever. Amen"

Making the sign of the cross, Richard opened his eyes and saw many in the room genuflecting with glistening eyes. The prayer had been a spontaneous outpouring that expressed the burdens that pressed upon them. Shared glances spoke wordlessly—all they held dear was no more than a bauble hanging by a slender thread from the fingers of King Henry's hand. Worst of all, perhaps, was that Abbot Whiting might well lose his life.

Moments ticked by, counted by the old grandfather clock, during which the gathering sat frozen as winter stone. Finally, James tapped his crystal wineglass and called out, "God has seen fit to give us a harvest such as we have not seen in many a year! Let us enjoy the bounty of the feast!" Relieved, the gathering roused to jubilant action as Elizabeth ushered them to the table.

The Whiting family was known for their robust table, and the guests were not disappointed. New dishes were brought out and platters were replenished, plates refilled. Hot steaming mugs of cider and mulled wine were served with spiced apples and sweet cakes, sticky with honey, cinnamon, and oranges from Spain, and a creamy pudding laced with cherries dried from summer's harvest. Ale flowed and cups were filled and refilled, faces grew more flushed and eyes glittered with the fullness of the feast.

As the merriment swelled they called for Magdalyne to play the harpsichord, which she did with dexterity and *joie d'vivre*, leading them into singing many of the old harvest songs, ballads of love gained and loss, and of the ending of the year. Standing beside the harpsichord with cup in hand, Colin made a request that caught on quickly.

"Maddy, sing the song of Arthur's birth. You sing it well—it's become a Langbrook tradition at Michaelmas." Everyone chimed in, begging for the ballad of the great king.

"First," her mother insisted, "you must tell the story. Then sing the song."

Voices were raised with enthusiasm at this idea. "Tales of Arthur and the Knights! Gwenivere and Lancelot! Do tell the tale!"

Maddy raised her chin and looked around, her cheeks ruddy with joy and the inner heat of the wine. "Just one story, there are so many! This is the story of Arthur's birth." She flung a bright smile toward Colin.

"Once there was a beautiful young woman, Ygraine, who was married to an older man—Gorlois, the Duke of Cornwall. They lived at the castle Tintagel, on the high cliffs overlooking the sea. She was a Celt by birth but she also carried within her the ancient faery blood of Avalon."

At the mention of Avalon, hushed sounds of awe and murmured excitement flowed around the room as the crowd leaned in to listen.

"Gorlois was a vassal of the old king, Ambrosius Aurelius, who killed the traitor Vortigern and beat the invading Saxons back for a time. But when Ambrosius died, his brother Uther became the king.

"Now, this was an event foretold by the druid, Myrrdin Emrys—the sorcerer known to most as Merlin, the very one who prophesied that Uther's son would be a great leader—a king who could bring them all together to secure the land of Briton." She looked around at her audience, drawing them in with her gaze.

"When Uther Pendragon was crowned, all the vassals and dukes and petty kings were called to a meeting in London to attend the coronation and swear their fealty, as Uther's aim was to unite them all against the Saxon invaders."

Maddy's storytelling skill was at its height as she plied the craft in the great hall that, despite the cold and rainy weather, had become hot with the blazing fireplaces and the heat of bodies pressed close together. Their faces were flushed from ale and whiskey and high spirits as they pressed close to hear every word.

"But it was not to be this simple! In a gathering of kings and nobles in London town of old, Uther saw Ygraine, who stood next to her husband, the aging knight, Gorlois. Raw desire overcame Uther, though he said it was love at first sight, as the bards say, for in that moment, his destiny caught him by the throat. He was helpless to do anything other than its bidding. Seeking Ygraine out in a secret meeting, he told her that he wanted to marry her. She protested, saying, 'No sire, for I am already married, to Gorlois. We have two children.' "

With a knowing look around at the gathering, Maddy cried out dramatically. "Uther would not take no for an answer. Ah, but the song tells the story well!"

And then she began to sing, her fingers moving with deft precision on the keys of the harpsichord. The flare of the candelabra glinted on her chestnut hair, bringing out its red lights as her voice sailed out across the hall.

> *'To horse! to horse! my noble lord,'*
> *Thus spake the fair Ygraine,*
> *'Ride hard—ride fast all through the night,*
> *Nor stay, nor slack the rein.'*
>
> *'Now why such haste to leave the Court?'*
> *The Duke of Cornwall cried.*

'Ah me,' she said, 'King Uther wills
Thy wife should be his bride.>

Fast, fast they rode all through the night,
Nor stayed, nor slacked the rein,
Until the towers of Tintagel
Rose shining o'er the plain.

But on the morrow, messengers
Came riding from the King:
'Uther Pendragon bids the Duke
Himself and wife to bring

Back to fair London town.' — Unto
The King this answer gave:
'Nor self nor wife shall tread his halls
So long as either live.>

She paused the song to embellish the story, telling how Uther devised a plan with Merlin. They would come at night to Tintagel, where Merlin would cast a glamour to make Uther appear as Gorlois, not only to the guard at the caste gate, but to Ygraine.

"Merlin's magic was strong and sure, and that very night the mists rose up in a thick fog when Uther appeared at the gates of Tintagel. 'Is that you, sire?' The wary guard asked, unsure of the man swathed in hooded cloak and mists alike. When Merlin raised his hand to abide the spell, the guard greeted Uther warmly, saying, 'Tis you indeed!' and sent him up to the room of his mistress."

Maddy shook her head, her face showing dismay. "Before Ygraine knew it was not her lord who had visited her that night, a child had been conceived."

And when her baby boy was born,
*   In cloth of gold with state*
'Twas given to a beggar-man,
*   Who waited at the gate.*

But this was Merlin, in disguise
*   Of beggar old and grey,*
The great enchanter, Merlin hight,
*   Who bore the babe away....*

The listeners sat rapt, drinking in every word of the familiar song and reliving the legend once again, their minds and hearts absorbed with vivid images of Merlin, Ygraine, and Uther Pendragon.

The next verses recounted how the hapless Gorlois, Duke of Cornwall, was ruthlessly sent by Uther to battle, where he was killed in a hopeless skirmish with the Saxons, freeing Ygraine to marry Uther. The son of their union, a boy named Arthur, was taken by Merlin at a very young age to be fostered by Ector, a nobleman both Celt and Roman, and was raised as a son alongside Ector's own son, Cai. Maddy's voice was sure and rich as she deftly wove the tale.

"It was Ygraine's two daughters, Morgause, the eldest, and Morgan, who objected most to these dramatic events. Morgause was sent away to Orkney in the far north of Alba, where she would marry King Lot, while Morgan was sent to Avalon to train as a priestess. But that," Maddy explained, "is another story!"

She made a little bow, smiling as they clapped and shouted for more.

"Sing of the Tuatha de Danaan!" Someone called out, spurring on a spate of begging for the legendary tales of Ireland, Wales and Scotland. Maddy laughed gaily.

"My cousin will have to play. Anne is the expert in the ballads of the Irish and the Welsh." She smiled as she rose from the harpsichord.

Anne blushed to the roots of her fair hair at the compliment. She had been standing beside Magdalyne, and they had sung in beautiful harmony on many of the verses, just as they had since they were small children. First cousins and best friends, the two young women smiled at each other, clasping hands briefly as Anne slipped into the seat at the harpsichord to cheers and applaud.

As the group joined in the songs and the merriment swelled toward a peak, lutes were taken out and tuned, while one of the tenants, a big man with curly brown hair brought out his fiddle, calling for Colin—the Scotsman among them, along with his uncle John Thorne—to step up and sing. Then the dancing began in high spirits, fortified by a free flow of cider, wine, and ale.

Hours later the fires in the big hall were burning low, and only a few candles illumined its shadowy corners. Remnants of the feast had been carried away by Matilde and the other servants. All of the tenants and some of the aunts, uncles, and cousins who lived within close range or on the estate lands had left by carriage or on horseback to arrive at their homes before midnight. Others were staying overnight in the large household of James and Elizabeth, and as Elizabeth saw to the needs of guests and oversaw the ceaseless activities of the kitchen servants, sleepy children were trundled off to bed.

A deep quiet had settled over the big house, while in James's study the hearth blazed, piled high with wood. Outside a fine mist fell in the chill October night while inside a small group of his family and friends gathered around the warmth of the fire. A well-aged whiskey from the highlands had been brought out by James, and the flames cast a play of light that flickered upon the rich wood wainscot of the wall and the many shelves of James's precious books—remnants of his teaching years at the university in Oxford. Deep in discussion of what pressed in upon them most, Colin argued.

"The evidence that Courtenay was involved in what Cromwell calls the 'Exeter Conspiracy' is scant at best. Isn't it obvious that Courtenay has been set up by Cromwall?"

John Thorne nodded thoughtfully in agreement. "Cromwell detests the Marquess, Lord Exeter. Everyone knows they are enemies—they certainly vied for the king's attention, and to wield his power, for many years."

James poured a round of libations as he added his view to the discussion. "Courtenay is the most powerful landowner here in the west country. Although he has long been known as the king's man, he is also sympathetic with the tenants who work his land. When I saw him this summer past, he spoke of his sorrow at their sufferings, and his own growing outrage at the king's crimes."

Sitting with Anne beside the fire, Magdalyne shifted her weight on the settee, one hand resting of the embroidered green bodice of her gown. "Both clerics and laity have been turned out of their lands and homes," she interjected. "The suffering is not only physical but spiritual. In the recent dissolution of Saint Nicholas Friary, here in Exeter, hundreds of monks have been put out on the streets. And now, the plague is back in London...have you heard?"

Seeing that Colin was watching her intently, with quiet regard, James glanced at his daughter. Her dark blue eyes shone in the candlelight as she looked at her great uncle, eyebrows raised in question. The curve of her cheek and brow were beautiful, but there was more than beauty to this extraordinary young woman. She had always been unusual, of a brilliant intellect. James thought of Sir Thomas More, who had stood against prevailing custom to advocate for the education of women in their society. Sir Thomas had been an inspiration for James and Elizabeth, who educated their daughters and encouraged them to grow in beauty and intellect. They had supported Maddy's unconventional passion for mythology and ancient traditions, her amazing capacity with language—French, Greek, and Latin were three of the several languages she spoke and wrote well.

The monastery in Bruges had seemed the only place where Magdalyne and her sister Jane might live free from the crippling roles forced upon women in England and all of Europe. But it soon became clear that Magdalyne could not be shut away within those stone walls. Her pulse beat in sync with the urgency of their times; James pondered the uneasy feeling that his daughter somehow had a part to play in the unfolding of it all. In truth James would be relieved when Maddy was finally joined with a good husband, one who could provide for her. He said a silent prayer that his gifted daughter would flourish in her own right as the lady of a manor, somewhere far from Glastonbury and the drama that would assuredly play out there. His hopes for her safety made the dire circumstances all the more poignant, and his thoughts were broken by Colin, who was speaking with an authority that seemed, to James, more of a Scottish laird than a novice of Glastonbury.

"But of course the king was in a fury when he learned about the banner that was hung at St Keverne in Cornwall, demanding that King Henry name Lord Exeter his heir apparent, which would effectively disinherit his own children. The very thought of such a thing was heresy, and incited the people to revolt. Then Courtenay, Lord Exeter himself, was found in correspondence with Reginald Pole in Rome."

Maddy frowned in consternation. "If Glastonbury Abbey, the largest and oldest ecclesiastical estate in England, falls to the king's scourge, many more will be made homeless, penniless, hopelessly lost."

Listening, James pursed his lips. "The Marquess hates Cromwell and his religious reform, even though Courtenay has long been at the right hand of the king. Of course his wife Gertrude is a staunch Catholic, and Courtenay's family alignment with the Poles and his correspondence with Cardinal Reginald Pole in Rome has not helped his case."

Ben Pritchard stirred the fire with the iron, levied a thick oak log upon the flames, then stood to face the group.

"I heard that he wrote a will on September 25, just a month ago," Ben submitted. He shot a worried glance John

Thorne, who brooded with a glass of spirits in his hand.

"He must be preparing for the worst," Thorne muttered, tilting the golden liquor in his cup to his lips.

Just then a commotion attracted their attention. Rupert, the household butler, appeared at the door with a disheveled man of about twenty years.

"My a-apologies, sir," the young man stammered to James Whiting, who had jumped up from his seat and started toward the study door.

"Edward Courtenay! For God's sake, come in, man! What in heaven's name are you doing here at this time of night?" James reached out to embrace the young man, who raked cold, trembling fingers through his windblown blonde hair.

"Thank you, Rupert." James glanced over his shoulder at the butler as he gestured for Edward to take a seat. Leaving unobtrusively, Rupert closed the door as Ben Pritchard stood up and offered his chair, but the young man declined. He was flushed and wet from the rain and breathless from riding fast through the night. Obviously distraught, he appeared to have his emotions under fierce control.

"I cannot stay long, sir. Please allow me to warm my hands at your fire and deliver my news, then I must ride straightaway to Cornwall, where my father is staying, hoping to ride out this political storm. I am riding against the tide to warn him—we must flee to France as soon as possible. We have a safe haven in Bretagne, with a distant relative there."

"Ah, then the worst has come to pass for your father, Lord Exeter," James Whiting sighed heavily.

Edward Courtenay nodded, "It is true. I have heard that the king is now moving against the conspiracy in Rome involving Reginald Pole. Sir Geoffrey Pole, the younger brother of the Cardinal, came to London with the news that a Catholic conspiracy was fomenting a new uprising. Cromwell has accused both Poles of spearheading this conspiracy, and he has convinced the king that my father is part of it. He accuses my father of treason and complicity with the Poles and will act against him very soon!"

"By God! We were just speaking of your father's situation!" James Whiting breathed out forcefully, his whole body tense. A stunned silence descended as the news sank in.

Looking at James and then to Abbot Whiting, the son of Lord Exeter reached out a hand. "You have been allies of my father, and I wanted you to know, so you can determine your own course of action. I heard from reliable sources that the king is turning his attention toward Glastonbury after he arrests Lord Exeter and his wife—and possibly me as well. I felt it was urgent that your family know, for the sake of Glastonbury Abbey."

Edward gripped a pair of dank leather gloves in his hand, looking as if he would bolt immediately. His face was creased with lines of worry as he stood by the roaring fire, which had been replenished with wood by Rupert before he slipped out the door.

Magdalyne had listened from her place beside Anne, and now she leaned forward. "At least accept one glass of whisky or wine to warm you for the journey ahead."

"I will accept your hospitality, mistress, and if I may impose upon you further?"

He turned back toward James, who responded quickly, "Yes, anything!"

"May I leave my horse here and take one of yours? She is winded from the desperate pace I am keeping."

"Of course, most certainly." James glanced at Ben Pritchard. "Ben, would you speak with Rupert?"

"Right away," Ben answered, jumping from his seat to open the heavy wooden door to the study.

John Thorne poured a glass of whiskey and pressed it into Edward's trembling hand. He eagerly drank, then downed the rest in a gulp.

"My son, shall we pray together?" Richard asked gently.

"Yes, Abbot, I would be most grateful," Edward answered, a mute appeal stamped upon his young face. He stared, looking from one to the next of them, some of whom he had known since he was a small child who visited Langbrook Manor, traveling on occasion with his father.

Patting Edward gently on the shoulder, Richard moved to stand beside him at the fire while others bowed their heads.

"Stand by the Courtenay family, Lord, and be merciful in every way. Let true justice prevail. If it be Your Will, let the king come to know compunction, remorse, let his heart be changed, moved by the suffering of others. We ask for mercy in Your Name, and in the Name of our holy Mother Mary, whose compassion for her children never fails to succor us in times of darkness."

Rain spattered in a sporadic rhythm on the windows, and a branch scratched across the thick glass. Their hearts beat together in silence for the passing of some moments, until Abbot Whiting stirred and took the young man in his arms to hold him close.

Released, Edward stepped back to face the abbot. "Thank you, Father. I must go. I pray you all safe journeys in the days ahead. Think of me and my family. Pray for us." His last words were spoken in solemn haste as he moved toward the door, which opened to reveal Rupert.

"Your horse is ready, sir." He pressed a wrapped packet of meat and bread into the young man's hands. Tucking the victuals into his doublet, and without further ado, Edward was gone. Stunned, they looked at each other, faces awash with feeling. A messenger of doom had visited then vanished into thin air, leaving them desolate with a foreboding sense of things to come.

They were too tired and overwhelmed to speak of it further. Richard was already making ready to leave with John and Roger. The abbot turned at the library door and said gently, "Let us not speak further tonight. In the morning we will the grace of the rising sun to strengthen us. Then we three will depart for Glastonbury."

Colin looked sharply at Magdalyne, his face flushed with emotion as he searched her face. Seeing her drawn and etched with worry, he swallowed hard, his gray eyes shadowed, then stood to accompany the monks of Glastonbury as they took their leave.

With a glance at Ben, who nodded in silent agreement, Anne turned to Magdalyne.

"Come, Maddy. Ben will escort us upstairs to our rooms. Let us retire for the night."

It was still dark when Maddy heard the first eruption of a cock's crow, signal to the coming dawn. She had been wakeful for hours, unable to sleep. With some relief, she pushed back the heavy quilts and rose up from bed to wrap herself in a woolen robe. Shivering, she pulled a thick shawl about her shoulders, slipped her feet into lamb's wool shoes, and padded downstairs to the kitchen, where she found the coals from last night's fire banked and smoldering. Heaping them with tinder and then chunks of wood, she brought the fire quickly to a blaze.

Her hair hung in a long braid down her back, and she smoothed back the strands that curled around her face. Filling the kettle with water from a bucket, she hung it over the fire. The door creaked, startling her, and she turned to see Colin standing in the shadows, face illumined by the flicker of the fire. He stared at her with eyes as dark as a winter storm.

"Maddy," he called lightly.

She pulled the shawl tight around her and jutted her chin out with a sharp inbreath.

"Colin, what are you doing here?"

"I couldn't sleep. But you know well why I am here."

His eyes deepened as he reached out for her. "You and I cannot sleep because we long for each other."

She lifted her free hand to place it upon his arm and admonish with a slight push, "Colin! Have you no shame? You are a monk, pledged to the monastery..."

"Not yet, Maddy." He came closer to slip an arm around her waist and draw her near. Planting a fervent kiss upon her cheek, one kiss led to another, and pulling her closer, his lips sought the warm softness of her neck as he whispered, "I have no shame…"

Her hands were warm upon his solid chest, and she felt the beating of his heart beneath her palms as she softened against him.

"*Cariad*," he whispered, pulling her close, breath hot on her skin as his lips found the hidden places of her neck, where rich blood flowed just beneath his lips. "Jesu, I have missed you this past year!"

"Colin! The house is waking, someone could walk in at any moment." Torn between yes and no, she struggled feebly to be released, but she was held firmly by strong arms.

"Maddy, Maddy! One word from you, and we will marry. I will gladly renounce my novitiate and make you Lady of Kildonan."

"I told you last year—I will not be the reason for you to end your novitiate. You must know that you want to relinquish your vows, with or without me."

"That is far too reasonable," he muttered as he caught her face in his hands, kissing her cheeks, her forehead. Her body was pinned against the stone wall of the kitchen by the length and strength of his. Despite her protests, candlelight gilded her features and sparkled in her eyes as he leaned in to press his lips against hers.

"What better reason than this? Say yes, Maddy, before I leave this morning for Glastonbury!"

Warmth flowed, honey from a hive, from his body to hers, and she felt her resolve melt beneath the pressure of his hands that roved now, across her shoulders, down her back to her waist. With a rush of breath she leaned into him, giving sway to the sweet flame that surged through her.

The sound of voices jolted them from their absorption, and they jumped apart just as the maid, Mathilde, pushed open the door. Elizabeth was close behind, midstride and issuing directions for beginning the meal they would prepare for the guests who lay sleeping in the bedrooms of the rambling old manor. Smoothing back her hair with shaking hands, Maddy fell into a coughing fit while Colin dropped his hands from her waist and stepped back.

"Mistress Whiting!" He bowed slightly, offering Elizabeth the winning charm of a flushed smile. "I bid you good morning. The cock's crow woke me, and Maddy and I chanced to run into each other, in search of hot *tisane* at this early hour."

Elizabeth stood still, eyes lingering over her disheveled daughter and the young man in the black cassock of a novice, who stood apparently unabashed before her.

"Chance, indeed." She turned toward the serving girl. "Start the bread first, Mathilde," she instructed, eyes glued to Colin. "We will serve it hot with honey when everyone comes down, along with apple compote."

She turned to her daughter. "Maddy, please go upstairs and come back in proper attire. At least Colin knows he must come to the kitchen in his cassock and not his nightdress!" Turning her back on them she hid the smile that spread behind her hand.

CHAPTER THREE

Glastonbury
November 1538

Richard Whiting came in from the garden stamping his feet to shake off the rain before he climbed the stairs to his chambers. Drops of water glistened on the shoulders of his black robes as he opened the paneled oak door to his study.

Moments later Jack Horner rustled down the stone corridor toward the abbot's chambers, a grim expression on his face. Stopping abruptly at the thick wooden door, he rapped his knuckles against it.

"Come in," Richard Whiting called from within. Horner opened the door and saw the abbot sitting, his head bent over a large Bible that lay open on the polished surface of his desk. Several candles burned against the waning afternoon light. Outside the rain poured in an incessant thrum, as it had for days.

"Yes, Jack, what is it?"

"Sir, I am the unfortunate bearer of bad news." The spare, angular man spoke in a raspy, whining voice. He opened his mouth then closed it, pausing, as if reluctant to continue.

"What is it, man? Don't just stand there," Richard urged his steward to speak.

"A messenger on horseback, sent by your nephew in Exeter. Sir James Whiting sends news that Henry Courtenay—Lord Exeter, that is—his wife and son Edward were arrested yesterday by Cromwell's men who took them, in chains, to the Tower in London. Courtenay will surely be hanged for treason, and soon."

Richard stood, grating his chair across the stone floor. Walking to the window, he looked out over the cloister garden toward the Lady Chapel and crossed himself. He whispered under his breath, "Mother Mary be with them!"

After a few tense moments, the abbot clasped his hands behind his back and faced his steward.

"Is there anything else, Jack?"

"Sir James expects Courtenay will be hanged very quickly," the steward reiterated dolefully. "And perhaps you have heard," his whining tone quickened to spurious, "there is gossip among the monks about the novice, Colin Thorne, and, um, Mistress Whiting. Some of the monks wonder what you are going to do."

"Oh?" Richard stared coldly at his chamberlain, watching as the man wrung his hands, his head sticking out over his chest, rather like a turtle in the river, Richard thought dimly. The man had an uncanny knack for irritating those around him. The abbot shook his head to dispel such thoughts and turned to warm himself at the fire.

"As you know, Jack, every novice has the right to affirm or disaffirm his vows at the end of his novitiate. What Colin Thorne does is not your concern. What Mistress Whiting does is certainly not your business. Take this as a warning: Anyone who dares to discuss my niece in any way is subject to disciplinary measures."

Jack hastened to bow, hands fluttering as he reached for the doorknob, hesitating. Richard turned back to the fire with a sigh. As annoying as it was, Jack Horner was only a brief distraction from the heartache that had become his companion day and night. Silence crept like a fog through the room, which grew colder despite the flames that leapt brightly in the fireplace. Moving back to his desk, Abbot Whiting peered at his steward.

"You can leave me now, Jack. Oh, and Jack, would you send only hot milk with a little honey for my supper? I will take it in two hours."

"But sir, you haven't eaten all day," he objected, his tone turning obsequious again, "and you are quite soaked by the rain," Jack eyed the tendrils of wet hair and the damp patches on the abbot's black robe.

"Never mind, it's nothing," the abbot responded kindly. Equanimity restored, his blue eyes glistened in the soft light as he softened his brisk directives with, "It was raining on the way back from afternoon prayers. I will stand by the fire to dry. Oh, and Jack, would you ask John Thorne to come to my chambers within the hour? You can send some food for him, whatever the cook has, along with the hot milk."

Closing the door behind him, Jack Horner stood in the corridor inwardly fuming. The abbot never confided in him, his chamberlain, the person who should be closest to him, but he talked about everything with that unpleasant Scot, that arrogant, secretive keeper of books, John Thorne! They were fools to go against Cromwell and the king. At least he would save himself from the coming tide.

Muttering and frowning, the little man scuttled down the hallway toward the kitchens. After he ordered the abbot's supper, he would go to the chapel study, where Thorne would probably be in his office writing out accounts in the last of the dying light, before evening set in.

When Thorne arrived he was bursting with the news of Lord Exeter's arrest. "Ah yes," Richard smiled, fingering the pages of the book in his hand. "I thought Jack would be unable to leave it for me to tell you. The man is meddlesome, to say the least. I despair that he will ever have discipline of mind or speech. He has resisted me all these years, even while he has placed me on a pedestal in his mind. To my misfortune, I am his obsession—an obsession that I fear has turned toward revenge." He stood before the fire, hands held over the flames.

A grimace passed briefly over Thorne's face. "I know he is one of the burdens you bear, Richard. For the hundredth time, why in God's name don't you replace him? As abbot you should have a steward who is trustworthy, who is good company for you—who brings some wisdom to the task of serving Glastonbury's abbot!"

Richard shook his head slowly in response, eyebrows raised, as if he too was perplexed by the whole situation.

"He also informed me of gossip about your nephew, Colin Thorne, and my niece."

John burst out, "Christ and Holy Mary! We don't have time for such nonsense! You put him in his place, I assume." Richard suppressed a smile and inclined his head to listen with arched brows while John raged on.

"He is only going to get in the way of what we have to do, interfering and poking his inquisitive nose into things he should not know about. But worse than that, Richard, I do not trust the man. I saw him in the village last week, talking to strangers. They looked like the king's men."

"Last week?" Richard's keen eyes narrowed as he gazed at Thorne.

"Yes, a few days ago. I mentioned it to you, but you were so absorbed that day, I didn't have the heart to press the issue."

"Well, there's nothing to be done about it now. I have a plan for Jack, to get him out of the way. Is Roger coming?"

"He'll be here at any time," John answered. He had hardly uttered the words when a light rap came at the door.

"Come in," Richard called. The door opened and Roger James, sacristan of the abbey, walked in. Younger than the other two men by twenty years, James had tonsured brown hair and beard cropped close to his head. He was short, slender and quick with an austere face, long narrow nose and dark eyes. Every inch a monk, he could seem fore-boding, but his face lit up with joy when he smiled. Like Abbot Whiting and John Thorne, he was much loved by the

Benedictine monks of Glastonbury—with the exception of the steward, Jack Horner, who made it clear that he did not care for anyone other than the abbot.

"There is ample food, Roger, if you are hungry." John Thorne gestured to the platter of cold meat and plain brown bread on the table. A pitcher of mead sat beside it with mugs. The abbot's cup of hot milk was empty and long cold.

"Nay, I am not hungry tonight," Roger smiled. "I am fasting for some days."

John growled, "Really? You and Richard are two peas in a pod. How am I going to keep you both alive to fulfill our mission if you don't eat? Oh well," he laughed darkly, "you will be saints soon enough, if the king has his way about it."

"Very humorous, John," Richard intoned with a frown, although he could not suppress a half smile.

"Well, some humor is needed in dire situations," John rejoined, "since we will probably all be dead within a year."

Roger's face was grim as he walked to the fire to warm his hands. The abbot sighed and, sitting down, indicated seats for the other two.

"Alright, let's attend to business. John, would you check to be sure there is no one outside the door? I cannot trust my steward not to eavesdrop." When John had closed the door to the hallway and joined them at the fireside, Richard Whiting looked from one to the other.

"The king accuses us of hiding a treasure in the coin of the realm—gold, of course, silver and jewels," he began, "but we know that our real treasure is not temporal. Aye, there are pounds and gold ingots in our keeping, but we know the real treasures of Glastonbury are the relics of the king and queen and the many books of antiquity that we harbor, held in secret for centuries, obscured to the uninitiated. And of course, the relics brought by Joseph of Arimathea."

Roger James frowned. "Tis known that Cromwell and King Henry are destroying relics from the churches and abbeys they have closed. The Reform considers most relics no more than superstitious bunkum used by unscrupulous priests to squeeze money from the poor, and it's true that some of them are. Such things have been wrongly used—we know too well that there are good and bad men in every walk of life, including within the Church. Even so, religious relics have helped to sustain the faith of the common supplicant before God's throne. All that being said, the artifacts we protect are treasures of a different nature"

Agreement was written upon the men's faces; John Thorne pursed his lips, a scowl upon his brow. The abbot sighed and murmured, "Well said, Roger." Richard stirred to stretch his back then settled against the hard oak chair.

"And so it falls upon us to protect that treasure," he asserted, "to preserve it for generations to come. Indeed, this is a sacred trust passed to me by Abbot Bere, given to him by John Selwood who was abbot before him, and the abbot before him. Aye, Richard Bere set an example for us all. He was my teacher and preceptor. I often feel he is with me still."

"I have waited many months to hear you speak so, Richard," Roger held out a hand, palm up, his excitement visibly growing. "And so, we must move as much of our treasure as we can manage," he urged. "But who will we ask to help us, and where should the relics go? They must be placed somewhere in safety, at least until Glastonbury is secure again, if it ever is."

He looked from Richard to John, then back to the abbot again. "Into whose hands do we entrust these artifacts, who will not take advantage in some way, or steal them outright?"

John took a deep breath. "I have given this much consideration. At first thought, it seemed that the Sinclair family of Lothian might help us—that at least the bones of the king and queen would best be kept at Rosslyn."

Roger nodded in agreement. "Yes, I remember well this place. We traveled there more than ten years ago as pilgrims, before these terrible times came upon us. I met with the sacristan there, and we spoke of the care for precious relics, which is certainly something we have in common. Rosslyn Chapel is a holy place that captures spirit in stone—a masterpiece, indeed. It is said the Sinclairs built their chapel on Templar wealth. Many pilgrims go there yearly, and we would have to take the Sinclair family into our confidence. It may seem the obvious choice, but is it wise? Once our treasures are in their hands, would we ever get them back?"

John pressed his lips together. "That is the question. The Sinclairs were connected to the Templars and other secret societies of France and greater Europe—the esoteric brotherhoods, holders of secrets of antiquity. They are sympathetic, they would help us, yes, because our treasure is rare and valuable. But can they be trusted?"

Roger nodded. "What do you say, Richard?

The abbot had sat gazing into the fire, deep in thought. Glancing up, he responded.

"The persecution of the Templars was terrible, their grand masters and many of the knights brutally assassinated, burned at the stake. Of course, it's said that they drew this to themselves, with the way they wielded wealth and power—too often abused, by most accounts. It was unwise to become such a threat to the royal families of Europe, not to mention the Holy See. It was not so long ago that Jacques de Molay—their grand master—was burned at the stake in Paris."

John Thorne muttered, "The memory stays fresh, even two hundred years later."

"Indeed," Roger James nodded in solemn agreement.

"Of the hidden Templars," Richard continued, "it is hard to say. What is their true purpose? The secrecy around them is legend, and that is as it should be, considering the past. But things are whispered about them. Of course the Holy Father in Rome has long washed his hands of the Templars and such keepers of pagan secrets."

The abbot's face lit briefly with a conspiratorial smile. "Somehow we have managed to carry on without the Pope interfering with our own secrets! Ah well. Perhaps it is heresy even to think of inviting such a liaison. But on a more practical level, I believe our treasures could easily disappear into their hidden shrines. In fact, I do not doubt that these societies could make some attempt to steal the treasures from us. Mother Mary as my witness, it has happened before!"

Silence filled the space as they pondered Richard's words. John held his hands before the flames. "Aye, what you say rings true, Richard. And The Sinclair family is powerfully aligned with the Scottish throne. They are allies of King James, may he be blessed."

He picked up a small log to toss on the flames. "The Sinclair family has blood ties and bonds of power in France as well. We know that King Henry despises and fears the French. No, I think the Sinclairs will remain unscathed by our English king. Regardless of his supreme arrogance, Henry is not ready for a full-scale war with the rebellious Scots and our Stewart king."

Roger frowned. "No, he is far too busy dealing with his own house!"

Standing to pace the room with hands clasped behind his back, Richard pursued his thoughts.

"If not Rosslyn Chapel, what of the Sinclair castle in the far north of Scotland—Girnigoe, in the wilds of the highlands on the sea, near Orkney. It is a stronghold that lies far from London and the king's arm. I traveled there many years ago and remember it well. But..."

"There is also a problem with this idea." John settled on a bench and crossed his legs. "The young Earl of Caithness, George Sinclair, who is still a boy. He lives miles away from Orkney in Lothian, at Castle Rosslyn, where he is educated by a man I once knew—a scholar named Duncan Meldrum. A harsh and vicious person, as I recall. He served as seneschal and advisor to George's father, John Sinclair. These people are known to my family on Arrain."

Taking a seat at the table beside Roger, the abbot leaned forward, chin resting in his hand, as Thorne continued.

"Traveling many years ago with my grandfather, the old laird, Geoffrey Thorne, I met John Sinclair, and Duncan

Meldrum as well. And I remember when the Earl died in the Battle of Somersdale in Orkney. It was almost ten years ago. His son, George, must be twelve years old now. Soon to take up the leadership of the clan, I suppose."

He paused to take a deep breath. "Sadly, it's known that many highlanders start exacting their cruelties upon the world at a very young age. I know too much about the Sinclair clan and their lairds, who are known to be quite ruthless, even vicious. The Sinclairs learned from their French ancestors, you know."

When John's droll commentary elicited only the raised eyebrows of the abbot, he got to his point. "Although Rosslyn Chapel, or even Girnigoe, their castle on the northern coast, may be good choices of places to preserve treasures, I say we should not trust the Sinclair family. As you said, Richard, there have been past attempts to steal our treasures, and it's highly possible that the Sinclairs and their friends were behind it."

Looking to his fellow conspirators, Richard tapped his fingers lightly on the table, the other hand pulling gently at his beard.

"So, we cannot turn to the Sinclairs for help—for many reasons, including perhaps the glaring fact that it is simply too obvious. But most of all, once the treasure is in their hands, then we have relinquished stewardship. Glastonbury Abbey has been entrusted with these treasures for over a thousand years—they are meant to be here, near the Tor and the hidden realm of Avalon. I still have some small hope that, God willing, the treasures can be returned to Somerset someday."

Tapping his fingertips together in thought, Richard fell silent. With a curious glance at John Thorne, Roger broached the question that hovered in the thick atmosphere of the chamber.

"Richard, you speak of the hidden realm of Avalon. Do you believe that Avalon still exists?"

"Indeed I do, Roger," the abbot asserted. "I not only believe in it, I know it to be true. Yonder Tor is the mystic doorway to that realm. "

Looking at his sacristan, Richard smiled. "You know very well that I am a true Christian, but this old heart harbors a deep vision. I have learned from Blessed Mary that God the Father, in his great love, takes many forms to reach the hearts of human beings in this world. Far from heresy, this is the true gospel of Jesus—that his Father in heaven is a God of love and mercy."

He weighed the words he would speak next before continuing.

"I have walked upon the Tor many times over the years, Roger. Sometimes I imagine it as Ynys Witrin, the Isle of Glass, when the Tor was still surrounded by its tidal lake."

John Thorne smiled behind his beard, pleased to hear his friend speaking openly the secrets of his heart, usually kept guarded. He glanced at Roger, who listened avidly as Richard reflected with rare candor.

"I was first drawn to the Tor forty years ago, when I was a young teacher in the claustral school of the abbey. I often walked on the Tor in the afternoon, making my way up to St. Michael's tower for solitude. One day when the fog came swift and unexpected, I got lost—evening was coming on fast, the shadows grew deep and purple as the heather, and rain began to fall. Wandering in circles, I was drenched by a steady downfall, and as twilight further obscured my view, I became disoriented and fearful. That was the first time I sensed a powerful presence on the Tor. As I stumbled and searched through the fog and mist, a faint form appeared to me. She guided me back to the abbey through a blinding, foggy rain with night coming on."

"She?" Roger queried, his interest piqued.

"Yes, *she*. I call her the Lady of Light. She led me to a place where I could see the path again. It was a miracle that I found my way back to the abbey. At first I was surprised, maybe even shocked. My mind could not grasp or encompass what had happened. I even tried to deny my own experience. But I contemplated that experience in the months and years that followed. What I discovered was a revelation.

"Since then, I have gone back to the Tor many times. St. Michael's tower on the top of the great hill has been one of my favorite places of prayer. But there is another place on the Tor where I go to contemplate, which overlooks the sacred spring whose waters run red, at the base of the hill. There I often sense the same loving presence of the Lady. And here is the real surprise—that she is not different than the presence I perceive in the Lady Chapel, when I kneel before our Lady, Saint Mary Magdalene."

Richard's chest and shoulders rose and fell with his breath, but his blue eyes burned steady and did not leave Roger's.

"Who is she?" Roger asked.

"It is impossible to say, for all this is a great mystery. But I sense that she is connected to the ancient Lady of the Lake, Nimuë, known also as Viviane—and somehow she belongs as well to Blessed Mary, as I said. More, I will not venture to say." Richard went silent, his eyes landing upon the lively dance of flames in the fireplace.

"You have given me much to think about, Richard." Roger's smile transformed the austerity of his face. "I will contemplate it with joy, as your words strike a similar chord in my own heart."

Clearing his throat, Roger spoke thoughtfully. "I grew up in Wales hearing the legends that were brought to life by Geoffroy of Monmouth and the French writer, Chrétien de Troyes."

John Thorne pursed his lips and gave a brief nod of accord. Richard's eyes settled on Roger, his head inclined toward the younger monk.

"But most of all, there were many winter nights by the fire when my Welsh grandmothers and grandfathers told the stories of ancient Cymru, of gods and goddesses and epic heroes like Arthur. These are to this day passed down over countless generations. It was their stories that lit the fire of my passion for sacred objects of antiquity and led me to be sacristan here at Glastonbury.

"By all appearances my grandsires were Catholic by faith, but if you scratched the surface of their hearts, you found a Celt, alive and well. For them, Avalon and Annwyn, faeries, gods and goddesses were as real as you and me sitting here, talking together. As real as the fact that, if you put your hand into that fire, you will get burned."

John Thorne's robes rustled as he folded his arms across his chest, crossed one leg over the other, and grumbled. "Aye. As real as King Henry, sitting in London stuffing his bloated face with roast pig, French wine, and cake."

Outside, the darkness pressed in. Rain splashed and dripped on the windows as Roger fell silent and John picked up the thread of their thoughts.

"What you say is true for my people on Arrain as well, and all over Scotland, especially in the highlands. Christians at first glance, but an ancient spirit lives in the blood, in the heart and soul of our people. That spirit is alive in the land—in the mountains and hills and islands, in the lochs and burns, the forests and moors."

"Well then," Roger surmised, "it may be that very spirit to which we entrust Glastonbury's treasures! Wales is too close to Somerset, but you must know of many remote places in the land of your youth, John, where such a secret can be kept."

Rain lashed harder at the windows and the fire popped loudly. They drifted in a pensive silence for a few moments before John responded.

"Actually, Roger, what you say makes me think of one place that might work, on the Isle of Arrain, where my family serves as regents in the Hamilton stronghold of Lochranza, and Colin's grandmother—a Hamilton herself—is Lady of Kildonan.

"The island is a rugged place where druids once worshipped, and even more ancient tribes lived among the standing stones there. They inhabited the isle with the druids and priestesses, long before the Irish *gaels* came to set themselves up as the kings of Dalriata, in Alba of olden times."

Interest piqued, Richard looked keenly at John. "I know Arrain well, but tell us more about the place of which you speak."

"There are legends that say Merlin spent time in Scotland a thousand years ago, on Arrain as well as in the highlands, during the time when Avalon could still be broached by boat across the lake."

Roger pondered the idea aloud. "The Isle of Arrain. Isn't that the island where the early Christians lived off the western coast, on a small islet called the Holy Isle? It was settled by Saint Molaise. I've heard many tales of that place. I believe that Arrain is not far from the place called Dunadd, where, as you say, the Irish came, a thousand years ago."

John shrugged. "Yes, there are many places in Scotland, where secrets are well kept. But, what I have in mind would necessarily involve Colin. And he would need help."

The abbot brightened visibly. He stood and began to pace, as John and Roger had seen him do many times when he was getting an idea.

"Arrain, and the Holy Isle, and Dunadd near Kilmartin, where the Gaels came over the sea from Ireland to establish their kingdom of Dalriata. I remember it all well—we went there as young lads, before our vows. Yes, John, go on."

"Well, as you know there are sea caves and wild places on Arrain where something could be hidden, until it can be moved to a safer place, or returned to Glastonbury when this madness passes. Even King Henry will die, sooner or later."

Richard gave his friend an affectionate glance. "I take your meaning and understand it well. We must entrust the secrets of Glastonbury to those who will carry on after we are gone, when Glastonbury is free from this religious war, who can return them to their rightful place, here in Somerset."

Roger nodded in agreement. "It sounds feasible. And Colin will be eager to help."

"'Tis decided that he will not take his final vows. He has told me that if Maddy says yes, he will leave to marry her as soon as her family allows. But even if she says no—and she won't—he will not take the vows." As he spoke, John glanced from Roger to Richard. "Colin will have many good ideas—he always does. If indeed he does handfast with Magdalyne, it will inevitably involve her too."

Richard exhaled sharply with a terse nod. "The risks are grave. I wish it could be otherwise, but I fear this is a destiny written in their stars."

John caught up with Richard as he walked out the Magdalene Gate toward the Glastonbury Tribunal in the middle of the town. The sun shone in fits and starts through fast moving clouds, and Richard shielded his eyes from the glare as he walked slowly with Father Rowland at his side.

"Richard! On your way to the Tribunal?" John called out, falling into step with the two monks.

"Yes," Richard huffed, slightly out of breath and coming to a stop. "I am to judge several cases in less than thirty minutes—including one I have been putting off, with our tenant, George Welton. Actually, I am dreading it. The man is a liar, and I will have to judge against him. It is not a good time for such a thing."

With a nod to Rowland, John took Richard's arm, indicating the record book he carried under one arm. "Aye, I am to testify in that case, in fact. I will accompany you, Richard—if I may?"

John glanced at the younger monk for a brief second. Rowland was clean and neat as always, his tonsure perfectly shaven, leaving a fringed circle of light brown hair. As Roger James' assistant sacristan, Rowland was considered a senior monk, though he was considerably younger. He had come to the monastery ten years before, born and raised in Cornwall and called to monastic life. He was a good man, and John prayed that he would be saved in some way from the ordeal ahead, even though he was one of the monks who was privy to the greater secrets of the abbey.

Twenty minutes later, the abbot sat behind a heavy wooden podium on a dais, a curried and powdered wig on his head, a red tippet worn as a stole over his long black silk judiciary gown. As presiding judge at the tribunal court in Glastonbury, where local residents came to settle disputes and where cases were heard and adjudicated, Abbot Richard Whiting had served as judiciary in cases for the past fifteen years. He had a reputation of being fair, which meant that he did not always deliver the hoped-for verdict, but he was trusted by the local populace.

The case of George Welton was not uncommon; it was a dispute that Welton, a tenant who farmed lands belonging to Glastonbury Abbey, had brought against the abbey and its accounts. John Thorne watched, amazed at Richard's patience as Welton laid out his case.

"In good faith I sold six fine shoats to yon church, and the abbey cook, Brother Edward, he did swindle me by far," the man swore, wiping his mouth with the back of one hand.

John listened, his ears growing red at the man's prevarications. When the man stepped down, he was called to testify as abbey bursar.

"This man sold Brother Edward three pigs, not six, and they were not shoats but spindly half-dead tough old sows that had not been properly fattened. He was paid well despite the fact that he did not deliver what we had asked for. Our accounts will show exactly that."

Welton jumped to his feet to fling harsh words into the space while an older man, also awaiting his case, yelled out, "Georgie Welton, ye're a known liar and cheat! Shut yer mouth, man!"

When Richard did not decree in the man's favor, Welton raged.

"Anyone can see ye're favoring yer own, abbot! Whiting is no fit judge, he's a traitor to the king!"

The crowd gasped in shock at the insult, just as the doors were thrown open and six soldiers burst in carrying lances. Their captain strode forward to the judge's podium, holding out an official paper that Richard took into his hands. Unrolling it, he saw that it bore the seal of the Lord Chancellor, Thomas Cromwell. John watched as Richard's face registered shock as he read the edict, relieving the

Abbot of Glastonbury from his judiciary duties, then quickly gained control of himself as he looked up at the waiting captain.

"Please convey to the Lord Chancellor that I have received his command and will comply."

The plumed feather in the officer's hat trembled, belying his brash and overconfident demeanor. Like his men, he wore the short red cloak of the king's guard; the captain's cloak and doublet, however, was decorated with gold and embossed with emblems of the Crown: the red rose of the House of Tudor and three golden lions. The room froze with tension as the captain lifted his chin and two of his men surged toward the podium, hands upon the swords sheathed at their sides.

"The Lord Chancellor commands this effective now. You are no longer judge over this Tribunal. You are ordered to depart this place immediately!" The captain's voice, raised to a shout, reverberated around the room.

Inhaling deeply, Richard collected his things, and as he stepped down from the podium to go to the judiciary's chambers, the captain moved to block the way while the soldiers stamped the butts of their lances on the stone floor, their swords clanging at their knees.

"You are not allowed to go to the chambers first," the captain barked again. "If we must remove you now by force, we will do so."

"I knew it!" George Welton groused, loud enough to be heard throughout the chamber. "Ye get what ye deserve, ye high and mighty abbot. I'll see ye hang for treason yet, and rejoice at it!"

"Shut yer face, Welton," a woman shouted bravely amidst a muffled outcry of protest. The abbot wiped beads of sweat from his face with a linen handkerchief and turned toward the front door of the Tribunal. John and Rowland moved swiftly to his side and led him, with labored breath, through a pressing crowd. People crossed themselves and whispered anxiously; some of the women wiped away tears. As soon as they were on the street, John gave vent to his fury, his voice hoarse with emotion.

"My God! Now Cromwell has taken away another of your rights as Abbot of Glastonbury. The evil bastard!" Rowland and John exchanged a strained glance.

Richard's face was drawn and pale as he looked quickly at John. "Speak of it no more, John. Just help me get to my chambers. I must rest."

CHAPTER FOUR

Glastonbury Christmastide 1538

On December 14, only days before the Elizabeth and James Whiting and their daughter Maddy would arrive from Langbrook Crossing to celebrate the handfasting of Maddy and Colin just before Christmastide, another messenger arrived from Exeter. This one asked directly for the abbot and refused to talk with an offended Jack Horner, who officiously announced his arrival.

"It's perfectly alright," Richard soothed his fuming steward, who stood rigid in the abbot's chambers, "it gives me a good reason to get outside. I've been inside all day, and I need some fresh air. Send him to me in the garden cloister in ten minutes."

It was early afternoon, and a clear day. Stepping outside, the abbot walked the garden path toward the central cloister, where he stood basking in soothing rays of bright sun. It dazzled his eyes and sparkled in the tips of winter grass that grew lush and green in contrast to the stark sculptures of trees, bare of leaves and standing naked in the cold garden. A flock of winter birds settled in their branches. They twittered and cheeped as the messenger approached the abbot with awe stamped upon his face.

"Abbot, sir. Father," he hesitated. The lad, not more than sixteen years old, coughed and paused, then bowed at the waist. Drawn up to his full height of six feet, Abbot Whiting was both a reassuring and an imposing figure.

"Yes, my son, go on... What is the news?"

"Sir James Whiting has sent me to tell you that Lord Exeter, Henry Courtenay, was found guilty of treason on the third of December and decapitated by sword three days ago, on December ninth."

The youngster's message rushed out, ending with a gulp. The abbot did not flinch but breathed in the chill air that shimmered with the boy's shocking words.

"Blessed Mary, have mercy on the soul of Henry Courtenay," Richard uttered, crossing himself. A moment passed as the abbot looked out over the garden, eyes filling with tears. Then, facing the lad, he asked, "What is your name?"

"William Chauncey."

"Very well, William. Now go to yon kitchen and tell the cook that I sent you. You are to have a plentiful hot meal and a good night's sleep before you return to Exeter. Over there." Richard pointed toward a large stone refectory on the other side of the cathedral. "'Tis the square building with the four chimneys, you see? Thank you for the message, my son. God bless you."

With a bow the boy bounded away toward the impressive monastery kitchen. The abbot watched him go, then turned slowly toward the church to walk through the archway of a high stone wall that cloistered the garden, and on toward the ornate oaken door on the side of the chapel at the front of the cathedral proper.

Near the door grew an unusually large hawthorn tree, its gnarled roots covered with moss and contained within a low stone holding wall. As usual for the time of year, it was covered with buds that would burst into white blossoms as Christmas drew near. Glancing at the tree, the abbot made a mental note that it would soon be time to send a branch of the blossoming thorn tree to King Henry, as he had done at Christmastime every year of his abbotship, and every abbot had done before him for their monarch for uncountable generations.

Pausing to look at an inscription carved in the stone wall—*Jesus, Maria*—Richard's fingers traced the ancient script. Moving on, the heavy door of the Lady Chapel opened with a creak and, entering the hushed gloom, the abbot was enveloped with the thick atmosphere of sanctity that suffused this most hallowed place of the Benedictines. He walked slowly across the floor, noticing with satisfaction that the paving stones were swept clean and adorned with fresh rushes.

Passing the shrines of Saint Patrick of Ireland and Saint Indracht, he genuflected as he said a prayer for the holy men and saints buried in graves and shrines throughout the church—former abbots and great unsung saints of his order—as well as countless monks who were interred in the gardens and yards that surrounded the cathedral.

The abbot moved toward the stone stairs that led down into the crypt below, called the Joseph Chapel—the great project of Richard Bere, his predecessor, whose body lay cold in the recesses of the crypt, not far from the shrine that drew Richard now. On one end of the shrine stood a wooden sculpture of Joseph of Arimathea, founder of their church and champion of the family of Jesus. Pondering the life of the saint, Richard ran a hand over the smooth sculpted folds of the saint's robe, feeling the satin of the wood.

On the other side of the altar stood another wooden sculpture; this one was obviously feminine. The artist's rendering of Mary Magdalene, carved from the trunk of an apple tree, was dark with the smooth patina of great antiquity. Her bare feet were worn smooth from the loving touch of pilgrims who had come to worship her over the centuries. She held in one slender, expressive hand an amphora, suggesting the spikenard oil used to anoint the feet of the king. The other delicate hand was poised in the air, the first finger pointing up toward heaven. A skull rested at her feet, signifying her presence at the crucifixion.

All about the altar were packages wrapped in cloth and bundles of grain or dried flowers and herbs were propped against the bottom of the stone alter or against the walls nearby. Children's shoes, old boots, canes and crutches were clustered around the altar, the walls lined with small plaques in stone or wood, chiseled with names and dates— testimony of prayers answered and miracles attributed to the Lady of Light, as the abbot called her—their Lady of Glastonbury Abbey.

Swaths of smoke twined and disappeared into the air where candles burned brightly at the shrine. A pungent smell of frankincense clung to the tapestries that hung on surrounding walls. The abbot stopped before the shrine, hands resting upon its hard stone surface. He looked up at a large oil painting of Mary holding the baby Jesus in her arms. Like many of the sacred artifacts that resided in Glastonbury Abbey, the painting was most unusual. No one knew how old it was, or who the artist had been. Its surface was cracked with age, and yet the oil colors remained vivid and true.

Richard's eyes roved lovingly over the mystic landscape in which Mother Mary was portrayed. She stood upon a path that led to a distant peak where a crown glowed, emitting rays of gold. The artist had imagined Mary, dressed in blue and white and gold, on her way to the mountaintop, but she turned around with her child in arms to bestow a blessing on the viewer.

In the distance behind her stood another woman dressed in an ocher gown, wearing a long red cloak. Her hair was black and twined in a braid that hung over one shoulder and down to her knees. The alabaster jar was held in one hand and a skull in the other. Mary Magdalene looked at Mother Mary and the baby Jesus as if she waited for them to resume their journey. About the heads of all three shone coronas of light.

With a sigh, Richard bent his head over clasped hands that rested in intimate repose upon the black stone of the altar. His whispered prayer was faint yet fervent, springing from a certainty as bitter, cold, and deep as a highland loch, and so profound it could hardly be voiced. The abbot's breath misted faintly in the chill atmosphere of the shrine, and his whispered prayer could be heard by none but the Blessed Lady to whom he now spoke.

"Beloved Mary, Lady of Light, you have blessed me with a long life. Somehow, you have brought me through the worst night of my soul, in which a great darkness comes for me. You know my heart better than I do. It is the Will of God that I shall die soon. I entrust myself into our savior's hands, and still, my heart weighs heavy with the care of this church and all who take shelter within its sanctuary—the living and the dead.

"Guide me, Blessed Mother and Lady of Light. Give me strength to bear what must be borne and the wisdom to act as I am called into action. I ask it, in the name of our Lord, Jesus Christ."

Falling into a deep quietude, he was cradled by a formless presence that melted the icy stone in his heart. Certain that all he had said, and that which he had not said, had been heard by the divinity that suffused the crypt, finally he stirred and crossed himself. He rested the palms of his hands on the flat stone of the shrine for another moment, then turned away to walk across the hexagonal tiles of the floor, up the stairs, through the Lady Chapel and out the door, into the rare sunlight of the late autumn day.

"It is magnificent, is it not?" James Whiting spoke quietly to his wife, Elizabeth, as she gazed up at the majesty of the cathedral. Taking her elbow, he guided her across the paved stone floor and out the nave, maneuvering through a fervent crowd that pressed in on all sides. The church after mass was cloaked in evening shadow but ablaze on this night with candles and draped with holly, ivy, fir and pine boughs. The aromas of heavy incense, evergreen and human bodies in close proximity permeated the air.

"Yes, it is glorious," Elizabeth agreed, "but I will be happy for a breath of cold fresh air."

The church burned bright at this time each year, when so many traveled from the surrounding countryside and villages to throng the cathedral with worshippers. The Whiting family had sat in their customary place in the nave through liturgy and chants, singing hymns and taking communion to finally receive what they were most eager for—the abbot's sermon, given at sunset mass on the eve of Christ's birth.

This year the abbot had spoken of charity, kindness, and the need for compassion in the troubled time in which they found themselves. He exhorted his listeners to pray for their king and his minister, Cromwell, so that all hearts might be softened by the power of Christ's love. People had listened avidly, stirring now and then and muttering, for commoner and gentry alike feared and hated the king and his chief minister. Finally Richard ended with a prayer, asking for strength and guidance in the coming year, for health and prosperity for all, and for peace and magnanimity to reign in England. Elizabeth sighed, recalling the eloquence of the abbot's words. If only it was possible that the king could have a change of heart.

Three days before, on the winter solstice, the Whitings' daughter Elizabeth Magdalyne Whiting handfasted with Colin Hamilton Thorne at Glastonbury Abbey, one day after Colin ceremonially ended his novitiate, declaring before a council of the abbot and his senior monks that he would not take his final vows. Rather than a sad occasion, a lively gathering came together that night at Sharpham Manor—the abbot's private manor house at Sharpham Park, a mile away from the abbey—to celebrate Colin's new life. His friends, the young monks Angus and William, attended as well, smiling and pouring libations.

Maddy's eyes gleamed as she gazed at Colin, appearing tall and slender in the clothes he had worn upon his arrival in Glastonbury three years before—a padded doublet over a linen shirt with woolen hose and heavy boots, a belted Hamilton plaid draped over it all. Now her hand rested upon his arm as the newly joined couple walked behind James and Elizabeth on their way after mass to dinner with Richard Whiting, John Thorne, and Roger James. Tomorrow the family would move back to Sharpham Manor, but for tonight they supped in the abbot's chambers in the great abbey. As they grew near to the cathedral door, Maddy leaned forward and whispered to her mother, "Colin and I will go for a moment to the King and Queen. We will meet you in abba's quarters."

Standing before the black stone sarcophagus, Magdalyne's eyes roved over the scene. Candles burned, wreathed in heavy smoke, while people nudged her, surging against the shrine. Some wept or whispered avid prayers while others stood solemnly to carefully lay or gently toss small bundles of glossy green holly thick with red berries or branches of the white-blooming hawthorn. Others stood mute, caressing the cold black marble. Sprigs of mistletoe adorned a large arrangement of green winter boughs—fir and pine and cedar—on the flat stone top of the shrine.

"We must go," Colin whispered in her ear after a few moments, pulling her away. She gazed up at the painting of Arthur, gleaming hair the color of wheat, a golden circlet, inset with dark gems, set about his forehead. On one side stood his queen, long dark hair with chestnut highlights, eyes the color of dusk. Her cloak was pinned with a well-fashioned brooch, a golden stag within Celtic knots. On her forehead was a slender crown of gold inset with moonstones. On the other side stood a tall dark knight with midnight eyes and brown hair that waved to his shoulders. One hand rested on the sword that hung at his side in its scabbard, and the other held a vessel finely crafted of silver and gold encrusted with gleaming jewels.

Gazing at the tableau, she whispered to Colin. "Such mystery surrounds them. There are many different versions of their legend, mostly with Lancelot and Gwenivere betraying the king, and yet this painting shows them together in harmony. When I contemplate the lord and his lady and their first knight, it always seems to me that they answer me as one. And in this painting, it is Lancelot who holds the grail—but he is not separate from the king and queen."

They stood in silent absorption, taking in the images until Colin stirred, his hand at her back. "'Tis a rare painting, to be sure, *cariad*. The artist had a vision to which he was true in its making."

Taking her arm to move away from the shrine and threading a path through the other pilgrims, he leaned down to whisper in her ear.

"I suspect it is to them that this night, and perhaps the months ahead, will be dedicated."

As Elizabeth and James Whiting walked in silence through the chill December air, their faces betrayed the worry that ate at their hearts. Richard had warned his nephew the day before of the serious nature of the discussion that awaited them on this night. Making their way across the frozen garden, they walked up the abbot's stairs and down the cold stone hallway, dimly lit with burning sconces, toward his chambers. At the sound of their knock the door opened, and there stood Roger James, his beatific face exuding a warm welcome.

"Come in, come in!" Richard called from within the chamber.

Inside the large stone fireplace was heaped with wood that blazed in a merry fire. A modest feast was laid out on the table—stewed venison with turnips and carrots, crusty mutton pies, loaves of fresh brown bread, a mound of pale butter in a bowl, and a pot of thick honey from the abbey's beehives. Pewter bowls, trenchers, and wooden spoons were laid out, while flagons of red wine, some steaming and spiced, stood ready upon the sideboard beside hunks of cheese and a bowl of apples. A glass decanter holding the amber liquor of stronger spirits reflected the light of the silver candelabra that burned with a score of flames.

"Nephew, niece, welcome on this fine Christmas feast!" Richard came forward to take the hands of James and

Elizabeth. "I hope you are hungry, for the cook has lavished us with a grand repast, once again." He gestured to the table and its contents.

"Colin and Magdalyne are on their way," Elizabeth offered. "They stopped to pay respects to the Lord and Lady."

Taking this in somberly, Richard replied. "Good. They are exactly the subject of our gathering tonight." Elizabeth and James exchanged a glance, taking the seat indicated by John Thorne, who sat upon a hassock near the fire.

Talking quietly of the weather, which would soon turn to snow, moments later another knock came at the door, and Roger ushered in the young couple. Greetings were exchanged, then without further ado they turned their attention to the feast that lay before them.

When they had eaten and sat with cups of wine or spirits in hand, Roger stood and moved to the fire, throwing two more logs upon its crackling flames. John Thorne went to the door, opened it and looked outside, then closed it and resumed his place by the hearth. Richard moved to a chair beside the fire, where he warmed his long slender hands.

John and Richard were close in age, though the abbot was older and seemed more advanced in years than his friend. To Magdalyne, her uncle appeared more ancient than ever. His aquiline profile, blue eyes and shaggy white hair conveyed the wisdom that years of prayer and dedication had honed in his visage. He stood tall, but with a slight stoop to his shoulders that spoke of the many burdens he had borne—the weight of responsibility, discipline, and dedication. Her heart went out to him, and she sensed that, somehow, this night would be a crucial turning point. Together, they would walk through a doorway, and their lives would never be the same.

"We have asked you to come tonight," the abbot began, "for a reason that is more important, in some ways, than the Christmastide we celebrate together again this year. We have waited, hoping for a reprieve, praying that God will intervene, that the king will have a change of heart. Now, we must speak of the dire situation that forces us to remove the treasures of Glastonbury to a safe haven.

"Like so many others, Lord Exeter is dead, and we do not know what will come of his wife Blanche or Edward, his son. The king's folly holds sway and continues on a path of destruction and wanton murder. And yet, too many words of speculation have already been spoken about the dangers of our situation—finally the time has come to act." Their eyes fastened upon the abbot as he continued with a glance at Roger and then John.

"The king has made it clear through Cromwell, his Lord Chancellor, that he wants our abbey's gold and land. We know that his eye is on our others treasures. Our stewardship of these relics weighs upon us. We must keep them out of the clutches of the Reform and whatever fate might await them there.

"We have considered safe places where the relics of Glastonbury might be hidden until this religious war is over, and we have come to a decision," he glanced at John and then Roger, "but our plan must be fully supported by you all, for it involves Colin and Maddy and could put everyone in our families in danger."

Looking at his father-in-law and receiving an affirmative nod, Colin spoke first. "With the agreement of James and Elizabeth, of course, Maddy and I will do whatever is needed. What is your plan?"

Richard nodded slowly, deeply touched by the resolve he saw in the face of the young man. Looking around and seeing the faces that turned to him in trust and trepidation, Richard's heart quailed with pity. Speechless, he held out a hand, inviting John to explain.

"After some deliberation," John began, "we decided that the safest place to hide the relics is on the Isle of Arrain, perhaps near your family stronghold at Kildonan, Colin, where you will soon be laird."

Colin's face grew somber as he angled his head to one side, listening.

"It must be done soon, no later than midsummer," John added. "We have heard that King Henry will move against Glastonbury next year, certainly by autumn." He looked around at the small group, his eyes landing back on Colin.

"Magdalyne and I planned to go to Exeter after Christmastide. We thought to travel to Arrain in the summer," Colin commented thoughtfully, "but that is too late for this plan to work. We will need to leave sooner to arrange a place where the relics may be safely established and protected from the harsh elements of our isle—the sea, storms, winds, cold."

They listened raptly as Colin spoke. "The island is both beautiful and rugged. Our lands and the stronghold of Kildonan is a place where our people carry memories of druids and the ancient tribes that worshipped at the standing stones of Machrie Moor, long before the Irish came to our shores.

"Most people are of the Catholic faith, but in truth, in many ways they are still pagan. There is nothing that goes unnoticed by the sharp eyes of the island dwellers. They have no love of the English king—their political loyalty is with King James of Scotland. They will help us in any way they can."

John chuckled from his place by the fire. "He is as bold in his treason as me, Richard."

"Hmm," Richard replied with a glint of amusement. "Yes, we have been forced to plot directly against the king. I am growing accustomed to being an accomplice to such treasons. So be it."

Maddy's skirts rustled as she moved to pull a woolen shawl around her shoulders. Sensing she had something to add, Richard turned toward her with a questioning look.

"This involves you as well, Magdalyne. What do you say?"

Her thick unruly hair glinted red in the light of the sconces, barely held in place by a close-fitting blue velvet cap. She looked around at her family.

"When my heart called me to leave the monastery in Bruges, I sensed it had something to do with these terrible times in England. And now, I have a feeling in my bones that this is right." She locked eyes with her mother, who sat quietly beside James.

"I accept this responsibility," she said simply, "but Colin and I will need help to transport the relics—I remember the harsh roads going north through Wales to Scotland. And then we must cross the sea to the isle."

Leaning forward, Maddy submitted her idea. "Ben and Anne Pritchard are in Exeter, we will see them in January when we arrive at Langbrook Manor. They are our closest kin and dearest friends. We hoped they would join us in Arrain next summer, when Ben will leave his post at Oxford. Their hearts are with Glastonbury Abbey, and with the lord and lady. They will help us. Allow us to confide in them." She glanced again at her mother, whose face was blanched and drawn.

Turning toward Roger James, Colin was already forging into practical questions. "How many wagons will we need—two?"

"Yes, at least two wagons. For the king's and queen's bones, for books and other relics..." Roger's voice trailed off as his eyes flickered briefly toward the abbot and Thorne, who stood side by side at the fire.

"There is no time to waste," Colin asserted briskly. "Maddy is right. We need the help of our trusted friends. We must leave for Arrain no later than the Feast of Saint Brigid, at the beginning of February. We will need to find the right place, perhaps a cave, one that does not fill with seawater at high tide, like those on the coasts. We may need a stone mason to build a crypt.

"It will take some time—and will most certainly involve the liegemen of Kildonan. My man, Geleis, is completely trustworthy and will most certainly help. And our family—my sister Jennet and her husband, Broderick—live at Kildonan, along with my grandmother. They will be with us in this. We can be ready before midsummer to transport the relics to Arrain."

John Thorne moved from his place by the fire to lift the crystal decanter from the oak table. Offering the strong spirit, he poured libations for the men and Magdalyne. Elizabeth declined with a demurring shake of her head.

"What about your brother, Nathanial Thorne?" John asked. "How will he respond to this undertaking?"

Colin shrugged. "My older brother Nathanial lives in England. He teaches at Oxford and has no interest in Kildonan. He has passed the lairdship on to me. It is my grandmother, Margaret, who must agree, for she is fiercely protective of Kildonan—and of me," he chuckled.

"To my memory," John remarked dryly, "you have always had a way with your grandmother. When she sent you here, her letter of introduction made it clear that you were her greatest treasure. "

With a glance at Richard, he explained. "I think the death of her husband Thomas, my brother, left her in a permanent state of grief. I will send a personal letter to her with you. Perhaps it will help as well."

He frowned as he lifted the decanter. "Aye, this calls for a wee dram." He poured the ruddy liquor into his cup and then into Colin's, offering it around again.

"The islanders will be celebrating Imbolc at that time, while we celebrate the Feast of Saint Brigid here at Glastonbury," John continued.

Richard had been silent through much of the discussion. Now he turned to his nephew.

"And what of you, James? And you, Elizabeth? What do my nephew and niece say to this plan that involves your daughter and Colin, and now includes your ward, Anne, and her husband Ben?"

Elizabeth's lips had been pressed in a thin line as she listened to the conversation. She gripped her husband's hand, knuckles white, as he covered hers with his own and patted it gently. She wiped a tear from her eye to no avail, as it was followed by several more.

"Fear clutches at my heart," Elizabeth's breath rushed out, "and I cannot yet give my blessing for Maddy to walk headlong into danger."

She looked around at the group.

"This plan puts all of our families in danger, and most of all Maddy and Colin, as your direct kin. Cromwell will look in our direction when he knows the treasures are gone. In truth, we are already in danger."

She turned toward Richard. "At this moment I fear most for your life, Richard, and for John Thorne and Roger James. Richard, you have been the spiritual guide of our family for many years...even before Abbot Bere passed away and you took on the abbotship."

She paused, and Richard did not take his eyes from hers as he considered her words.

"You are a good and generous woman, Elizabeth, and a wise one as well," Richard's words finally came, somber and measured. "And you are right. There is danger, very serious danger, in all of these plans. What other choice to we have? Allow the relics to fall into the king's hands, into Cromwell's hands? Into the hands of the new church? And to what use? They will destroy most of them, but Henry and Cromwell will use the bones of the King and Queen to their own advantage.

"In truth, I would rather the treasure be in the hands of those who worship the pagan gods of old ..."

His words trailed into emptiness but his blue eyes were soft as he gazed at his niece. "Elizabeth, I ask you to pray for me. Perhaps you will find it in your heart to give your blessing, for I sense that the hearts of Colin and Maddy are already set upon this quest." He paused, his voice suffused with the power of his conviction.

"I do not know how the dissolution of our abbey will take shape, but I do know that I will not surrender this church." Richard stood before the fire, his hands clasped behind his back. The gathering curves of his long robes hung in folds to the floor and curled slightly upon the smooth stone. The dark wool fabric was worn to a sheen that glinted in the mellow light of candles and fireplace. They waited for him to continue, and after a while, he mused, "I am an old man. I have lived a long life, served my Lord, been blessed with so much."

Facing them, he lifted his arms, palms up. "Yes, my life is at stake, but truly I am much more concerned with Maddy and Colin, with you, Elizabeth and James, with the Pritchard family, with all who live at Kildonan and will become accomplices in this task of treason.

"I am more concerned with the monks of Glastonbury who have dedicated their lives to this church. Small pensions will, perhaps, be granted to them, but that hardly assuages their souls of the great losses this dissolution will incur. They will lose all they hold dear. My prayers are for all of you, who must carry on."

He turned toward Roger and John, who stood at

his left side. "I have begged these two madmen to leave Glastonbury Abbey. But they will not. They insist on standing with me. And stand to the end, I will."

Seeing the stain of anguish upon their faces, he sighed heavily then mustered a faint smile.

"Please, do not worry for me. My time has come. I know it with every bone of my body. I am following God's Will as best as I can understand. You will need to accept whatever may come to pass. What happens to the relics is now more important than any one of us." He paused, taking a deep breath. "Now, let us say goodnight, and meet again on the morrow."

His words sank into their hearts as silence gathered about them like a caul thick as lamb's wool. After some moments, James rose to retrieve Elizabeth's cloak from a peg by the door, making plans with Roger to meet with everyone in the morning at the Magdalene Gate. Their carriages would be waiting for them to make the short trip to Sharpham Manor, the abbot's country house, where they would spend the next days together before departing for Exeter.

CHAPTER FIVE

Scotland
January 1539

Sea birds swooped in lazy circles calling their plaintive cries as Maddy watched the breakers roll in from a restless, blue-gray sea that surged across the sandy shore. From the windswept bare rocky shores of Argyll where she stood, she could see the mountainous hump and distant wild shores of the island—Arrain—across the salty waters of the Firth of Clyde.

"We canna cross at high tide," Colin was saying, speaking close to her ear as the wind whipped their hair and clothes, whisking his words away to the sky. "We must wait, Maddy, so says the *aiseig*." Seeing her quizzical look, he explained. "The *aiseig* is the boatman, love."

She moved closer to Colin's warmth, and he circled her waist with his arm to pull her close in response. The incoming tide filled the bright air with mist, and his dark hair, pulled back into a queue, was speckled with drops that shone silver in the morning light. Smiling into her eyes, he leaned in to kiss her warmly on the lips. His grey eyes reflected the sea, while hers remained the color of the sky, now hidden behind thick blankets of cloud. It was late January, the coldest time of the year in Ayrshire, and she shivered, knowing that at least their destination—the southern tip of the Isle of Arrain—might be slightly warmer, renowned as it was for pleasant winds. Still, she smiled grimly to herself, knowing it would be cold.

Her eyes roved the horizon then rested on the boat—a sturdy karve, built in the ancient style of the Vikings—that was anchored near the shore of the tiny harbour of Ayr near the Castle Culzean. The karve had one mast and sail and would suffice for the four of them and the boatman, but they would need to stable their horses in Ayr at the inn where they had slept last night, then retrieve them upon their return from Arrain, in two weeks thence. Watching the karve bob and float easily upon the incoming flux from the Irish Sea to the south, her mind flooded with impressions of their hasty journey north from Exeter after Christmastide.

They had traveled by horseback with Anne and Ben, making their way across Somerset to Wells and Bath and on into Wales, where they skirted the Cambrian Mountains and Snowdonia, with its mythic escarpment of Dinas Emrys to the west. They felt the magnetic pull of the legendary place where Merlin once envisioned two dragons or *vermes*—one red and one white—sleeping coiled about the underground spring-fed pool. But there was no time to journey into ancient Gwynedd. Instead they moved steadily toward the thriving fort of Carlisle in Cumbria, at the border between England and Scotland, and finally into the highlands.

From Carlisle they quickened their pace whenever possible until they reached Dumfries and finally Ayr, the town on the western coast of Argyll from which they would set out to the Isle of Arrain. With the winter weather slowing their pace, it had taken more than a fortnight to make the trip. Along the way Colin's brogue had gotten thicker with each passing league. Maddy smiled to hear traces of his native Scots coming out, and she listened with a careful ear to understand the Gaelic he interspersed, knowing she would soon be an inhabitant of this mysterious and ancient land, which she had loved so well as a child.

"When the tide turns, in two hours, the wind will be in our favor. Then we will set sail for Arrain." Colin turned toward Ben and Anne, who stood beside them on the strand. "The crossing is fast, and if we are lucky, we will arrive at Kildonan before dark. With God's grace, my message arrived two weeks ago, and they are prepared for our coming."

The sea crossing was harder than Colin had hoped. The winds were not in their favor, making the karve heave and buck upon the waves. As their boat sailed toward the shore, to the north they saw the small hump of land called the Holy Isle, where a monastery had been established long ago by Saint Molaise. Little more than a bare mountain, it reared up in pooling drifts of fog that flowed about its rocky peak.

Although the *aiseig* landed the boat with a seasoned mariner's skill, the sun was already dipping behind massive cloudbanks to the west as they came ashore the island. After a long conversation in Gaelic with the boatman, who explained where they might find the transport they would need to reach Kildonan, along with some supper and a night's rest, Colin lead the weary party through a drizzling rain toward a wayfarer's inn—a large stone house not far from the bay.

As they gratefully relished a simple but hot and nourishing meal of stewed barley and fish provided by the innkeeper's wife, a misty darkness seeped into the landscape. After supper the mistress led them to a windy, damp stone barn where they spent a restless night on beds of dried heather and grass. They woke before dawn and loaded a wagon hitched to two horses, which they had managed to procure from the fisherman with a silver coin and a promise to return them in a fortnight, then set off down a rutted rocky lane that was little more than a well-worn footpath leading south.

Three hours later they descended a hill, and the castle keep, perched on its promontory overlooking the Irish Sea to the south, came into view. The sky was awash with color and light that played across a sparkling sea, majestic cloudbanks, and the fierce beauty of a land that was both green and austere. Maddy drew a deep breath, surprised by how her heart opened with sudden joy. The intermingling of countless shades of blue, green, gray, and brown interspersed with brilliant splashes of yellow gorse produced a visual panorama that halted the progress of the four companions as they paused to gaze in awe at the beauty of each direction in turn.

The vista across the water toward the village of Ayr and its surrounding landscape, from which they had come, was just as magnificent. To the south below the castle lay a sweep of white sand and a tiny village enclave of thatched-roof stone huts huddled amidst tumbled rocks, sea grasses, and wild oats. Several pathways led to the windswept beach, where one could cross a small expanse of water to an islet—a strip of rocky land that washed bare just above the blue-green waters of the sea.

"It's called Pladda," Colin explained as Anne and Ben stretched their necks to take in the views, exclaiming over the tiny island. "And there, to the southwest, rises Ailsa Craig. It looks like a pyramid, does it not?"

Colin continued. "To the west is the Kintyre peninsula and, beyond that, Ireland. To the north from here on Arrain is Goatfell Mountain—a wild place mostly cloaked in mists."

With a shake of the reins and a click of his tongue, Colin spurred the horses onward. Minutes later they rolled to a stop in the outer courtyard of the castle, where a blacksmith stood working over a forge in one of the sheds and another man curried horses in a stable. Despite the chilly air, two women washed laundry in a tub with reddened, chapped hands, taking advantage of the sun that shone sporadically through a light rain. Eager to come down from the wagon, Maddy and Anne adjusted their cloaks, smoothed their skirts and wrapped thick woolen shawls tighter around heads and shoulders just as a woman with a long black braid and gray eyes came running out.

"Colin! *Bràthair!*"

Throwing her arms around her brother, she squeezed hard then leaned back and reached up to tousle his shaggy black hair.

"You are here, safe and whole!" She laughed with satisfaction. "Come, Broderick is at the shore, bringing in our dinner, and Mòrai is waiting beside the fire. We saw you coming down the hills, and you can imagine she is eager to see your face."

She turned to Maddy with a broad smile and twined her arms about the other woman's waist.

"*Piuthar*! At last, we are now truly kin, just as we always wished to be as wee lassies, so many years ago!"

Returning the hug with a warm embrace, Maddy leaned back with a happy grin. "Jennet! It does my heart good to see you, sister! And this is my dear cousin, Anne Pritchard, and her husband, Ben, from Exeter. We will have much to discuss when Broderick returns, and I am as anxious to see Grandmother Margaret, the *màthair mhor* of this family, as she is to see her grandson."

The young women bent their heads close together and chatted affectionately as they walked into the first floor of the stone keep with Anne and Ben following. Colin lagged behind to greet a gaggle of men and women, whom he had known all his life, as they dropped their work and crowded around him. Their joy was evident as they clapped him on the back and exclaimed at how he had changed these past three years. Indeed, they were unabashed in their joy to have their young laird, who had grown into a fine man, back among them—and no longer a monk but a married man who had brought his lady with him. After some moments he extracted himself.

"Mòrai Margaret will be needing to see me now. *Bidh mi a 'tilleadh agus bidh sinn a' co-roinn bheag drama!*"

While the men cheered at the idea of sharing cup of whiskey with their laird, a man with curly dark hair and seawater eyes had walked around the corner, a bright smile wreathed upon his rugged, noble face. Geleis Blackwater stood grinning patiently, hands resting on the sporran that hung over his kilt, as Colin extricated himself and then turned toward him with open arms.

"Geleis! *Beannachdan charaid*! *M 'fhear-dàimh...*"

Taking the man in a warm embrace, Colin muttered, "My God, man, how I have missed you!"

"And you are a sight for sore eyes as well, Colin."

He pounded Colin's back with affection then looked around cautiously, lowering his voice.

"I received your letter. It was fine news, to hear you were no longer monk but husband, my brother! It suits me fine, for sure. You could not find a better girl than Magdalyne, indeed. As to what brings you here so soon, I ken tis a matter of grave importance."

"That's right. As soon as I have greeted Mòrai, I will come to find you. After supper we will all talk. Now, I must go to her," he smiled, "she will be waiting."

"*Mo chridhe tha glad*," Margaret Hamilton Thorne's rich, deep voice rasped a little as she stood imperiously, cane in one hand, "to see you again, Colin. Indeed," she admitted, looking up into his eyes as he moved close to embrace her, "*mo ghaoil an gille... Nay, mo duine làidir breagha.*"

Colin chuckled lightly and muttered, "Yes, a married man well grown." Enveloping her slender body in his arms, Colin kissed her on each cheek then stood back to look into her eyes.

"Mòrai, you are beautiful as ever!"

"Pah," she laughed, obviously pleased. "You must be mad, or very kind, *a chiall mo chridhe*. You'll just have time to change into your kilt for dinner."

Every inch a matriarch, Margaret Thorne came from a long line of Hamiltons, the family who had served as regents for the Stewarts—the royal family of Scotland—who had been the lords of Arrain since King James III appointed the lands and castles in 1406. Indeed, the Hamilton family had been lairds at Lochranza, Kildonan and Brodick castles on Arrain for well over a hundred years, coming from their estates on the Scottish mainland.

As Colin led Anne and Ben to their rooms, they passed numerous paintings of ancestors—Stewarts, Hamiltons, Blackwaters and Thornes—which graced the stone walls along with trophies of war and intimidating if rusted weapons. The couples stopped to gaze upon a series of rare tapestries depicting mythological scenes. First, it was Leda and the divine swan, Zeus in disguise, his beak closed upon her bare nipple, her head thrown back in ecstasy. Then the old Celtic gods came into view: Blodeuwedd with her flower maidens helping Ceridwen tend the cauldron of plenty. In another scene a wild-eyed and fierce Morrigan presided, a black-winged harbinger over a field of battle, while Manannan rose from vaulting waves to protect a warship that struggled in a stormy sea.

Knowing the light would soon dissipate into another winter night of mists and primeval spirits and unknown powers, the young couples gathered around the Hamilton matriarch for an early supper in the great hall, where two fireplaces blazed and sconces burned, shedding a flickering, orange-gold glow upon the room. Margaret Thorne sat upon a high-backed velvet chair with arms and legs carved in a cunning design of stags, a gnarled whitebeam cane resting at her side. Her thick, once-black hair was now white, braided, wound about her head, and fastened with a thin, long hairpin inlaid with gold and silver. She wore a gown of fine, dark blue wool with tufted sleeves, its slits showing sea-green insets of silk. About her neck hung three long strands of sea pearls that gleamed opalescent in the candlelight.

Wrapped around her shoulders was a woolen shawl in the rich Hamilton clan colors—a complex plaid of deep seagreen, red, and blue with a thin white stripe—and draped over the chair was a fine cape of dark seal pelts, its edges embroidered with seed pearls. Dressed for dinner in a kilt and belted plaid, Geleis Blackwater stood at her back, awaiting the moment when Lady Hamilton's attention might turn his way from the stream of commands she issued to the serving maids who hustled about, carrying steaming bowls and platters to the heavy wood table where they would soon sit to dine.

"How fine you are!" Maddy exclaimed, holding a hand out toward Colin as he appeared wearing a Hamilton kilt with a sporran of horsehide and hair. His jacket was green velvet over the fine linen of his shirt, and around his neck was a silver chain of office, beaten and wrought into a thistle design. With his dark hair and eyes, his height and stature, the sight of him turned their heads.

"Here Colin, pour everyone a *beag drama seo càin spiorad*," Margaret instructed as he leaned down to kiss her soft cheek. "We must strengthen our hearts for this occasion. As I understand it, there is much to discuss, and my interest is piqued, indeed!"

She smiled kindly and reached a hand out to Maddy, drawing her in close to sit hand in hand as Colin moved to the sideboard and lifted a glass decanter filled with whiskey. Pouring into six silver cups, he commented for the benefit of Ben and Anne.

"This spirit is distilled here on Arrain, in the northwest of the island near Machrie Moor. Tis said to be the best in Scotland—but of course, you would get some argument about that!" He chuckled as he poured. "Geleis goes there twice a year to trade the oats and barley we grow on our hillsides and the dried herring, caught and cured here at Kildonan, for this fine spirit."

Handing cups first to Margaret then to Maddy and Anne, he poured libations for Ben and Geleis and then one for himself.

"To reunions...and to mysteries!"

He raised his cup, lips pressed together in a tight smile as his thoughts turned toward John Thorne, Abbot Richard Whiting, and Roger James, and to the plight of the monks of Glastonbury. For awhile they spoke of the journey from Exeter, then Margaret turned her piercing eyes on Ben and Anne. Learning that Ben was older than the others and was also recently married, she expressed her congratulations and then her curiosity.

"And how did you come to know the Whiting family of Somerset?"

With enthusiasm, Ben Pritchard explained, answering her questions with care. Assistant professor to James Whiting at Oxford for ten years, he had been a regular visitor at Langbrook Crossing near Exeter. It was there that Ben had met the niece of Elizabeth Whiting, Anne Gifford. After the death of her parents, Anne was fostered as a girl of ten at Langbrook, welcomed into the family and educated with Maddy and Jane.

Upon their meeting two years ago, love had blossomed between Ben and Anne, and they were handfasted in the summer past, a few months before Colin and Maddy. Now Ben was a tutor and grammarian for boys and a few girls of privilege in Exeter—until he embarked on this quest when James Whiting and Colin Thorne had asked him to come. Margaret listened with interest then turned toward Colin.

"Yes, your quest, Colin. We are anxious to know, exactly what *is* it?"

When Colin took a deep breath, she changed course. "But here is Broderick, coming in with Jennet, and I see that Kenna has our supper laid out. I fear it grows cold … à table, tout de suite!"

Her grandson stepped forward to take her arm and help her to the table, dressed with formal linen, silver spoons and knives. Tall tapers burned brightly in candelabras, their light glinting off crystal goblets. Taking her seat at one end, Margaret looked in satisfaction at the supper that awaited their pleasure. Platters of venison, a stew of lobster and prawns—caught that day by the fishermen of

Kildonan—cooked with cream and watercress, were laid out along with butter, cheese, and warm barley bread.

Broderick and Colin came together with an embrace, happy to be reunited, while each one at the table was seated. As laird, Colin's place was at the opposite end, facing his grandmother; as liegeman, Geleis sat at her right. After Margaret and Colin, each one was served in turn by Kenna, the serving maid. Waiting for their *màthair mhor* to begin, the hungry travelers dug into plates and bowls of the rich meal before them.

"This wine comes from France," Margaret laughed gaily, picking up the decanter and serving Maddy, who sat at her right side next to Jennet and Broderick.

"We are quite lucky to have such pleasures. As you may know, my younger brother, James Hamilton, is the second Earl of Arrain. His residence is north of here at Brodick Castle, but he spends most of his time," she laughed easily, "in Glasgow, Edinborough, London, and Paris. As you know, he is also the Duke of Chatellerault." She snorted, lifting her shoulders in an offhand gesture as she continued.

"He has always been more concerned with his political ambitions than with the simple life of this island. *Mais c'est bon pour moi*, and for our humble branch of the family. By the grace of the Stewarts and the Hamiltons, we are the *glèidhidh* of this fine *chaisteal*, Kildonan, a holy place where Saint Donnan lived for a time, long ago. After he left to wander, some of his monks continued to live here. The isle off the eastern shore, near the bay where you landed, is called the Holy Isle. 'Tis the place where Saint Molaise, who we know as Laisren, had a monastery for a time, almost a thousand years ago.

"We have always lived close to the magic of this island. There is a *càin* spirit that dwells here, pervading sky, earth, sea. The seals know it—we have many that live along the rocky shores and islets of Arrain. When you see the rolling of the giant whales, the leaping of dolphins, the herds of red deer bounding across the moors, you will feel it." She nodded to Ben and Anne. "But, as fine as it is here, we may also enjoy the rewards of James' pursuits in this great world!"

She lifted her goblet to them, tasted and pursed her lips to savor the wine. A contemplative moment spanned the table until Anne broke the silence.

"Arrain is more beautiful that I could have imagined, and as you describe the wildlife, the hunting must be quite rich."

"'Tis true," Brodick answered. "As Mòrai said, the lobster and prawns we are enjoying on this chilly winter night were caught today in our waters. Vast herds of red deer roam the land—thence the venison on yon platter." With keen pride and a glance at Geleis, his hunting partner, he gestured to the rows of antlers, many of them with twelve points each, that hung on the stone walls of the chamber.

"We have red squirrels and golden eagles aplenty. And off the coasts you will see seals, otters, and whales in season. Goatfell Mountain and all the northern climes of this island is a rugged highland. Here in the south we have the green rolling hills and wild moorland, kissed by the warm winds that come off the great ocean."

Jennet's eyes sparkled with enthusiasm. "Aye, in fact this land grows many wild herbs, both edible and good for medicine. Even in the winter we have scores of wildflowers that bloom, especially the yellow gorse, which you see all around here—it flowers from November through the spring. Of course on the hills and in the glens of Arrain, you'll find an abundance of bracken, heather, and the blessed bilberry—which is good for so many ailments."

Margaret listened with pride. "Jennet is a fine herbalist and healer. She tends to all here in Kildonan with her draughts and potions. She inherited the gift from her namesake, my sister Jennet," she crossed herself, "may Mother Mary protect her and God rest her soul. And Broderick keeps our table rich with meat and fish, among many other things."

Their love of the island was palpable as they spoke of its beauty and plentiful life, until Margaret's words grew more serious.

"The winter is long and dark and we are often chilled to the bone. This is our great privation. But if you are lucky and know how to read, we have a library here at Kildonan, stocked with books in English, Gaelic, Latin, French, Greek, German and even some in Spanish. My father, Gordon Hamilton and my youngest brother, Richard, who was laird here after my father, both had a passion for reading and learning. Of course the library was greatly enhanced by my dear husband Thomas Thorne, who was a fine scholar himself, much like you, Colin, and your great-uncle John Thorne—which brings us to the subject at hand."

Taking a moment to look around the table at her family and guests to determine that all had finished their supper, she suggested, "Let us move close to the fire."

Colin rose and helped her from the table to her chair, where she wrapped herself in the sealskin cape while Broderick moved to pile the fire high with wood. Kenna came and went, removing the food from the table and checking the sconces and candles, replacing some with fresh tapers while the rest of the group settled around Margaret on a long divan, chairs or hassocks.

"Geleis, would you pour the libations for us?"

Margaret called to her liegeman who, with a slight bow, walked to the sideboard and poured cups of whiskey for the men and port wine for the women. Colin settled near his grandmother to tell the long tale of their purpose for arriving at Kildonan six months sooner than they were expected.

Their task had taken on the deeper nuance of a spiritual quest, and as Colin laid bare the hard facts—the terrible suffering inflicted as the monasteries, friaries, and abbeys were dissolved in the reform madness of the English king; Henry's religious war with the Pope in Rome; the deaths by accusation of treason; the plight of Glastonbury Abbey, and the impending threat to Richard Whiting, Roger James, and John Thorne—Margaret's face grew sad and drawn.

The Hamilton matriarch sat still as stone during his lengthy narrative, asking a penetrating question now and then to clarify. Maddy told the story of the great treasures of Glastonbury Abbey—with an emphasis on the bones of King Arthur and his queen—and along with Ben and Anne, they drew the picture in detail. Jennet, Broderick, and Geleis listened and absorbed, asking questions now and then. It was overwhelming, and yet their hearts were captured and, after two hours, the tale was told.

Finally Margaret spoke at length, her words heavy with sorrow. "We have followed with dread the terrible news of King Henry's religious reform, his dead queens, and the closing of the religious houses, and of the deaths and executions, the burning of heretics by Thomas More—and then his own death! We have heard many tales of the horrors that have transpired these past ten years. I have prayed often for the priests, the monks and nuns, for Henry's wives and those who have come under the executioner's blade, and for the souls of the persecutors as well. Now he strikes closer to home indeed. Glastonbury is dear to our hearts."

Looking at Margaret and then around the table, Geleis spoke for all.

"Aye, Colin, we are all with you. Now we need to make a plan."

Broderick rose to tend the fire. "It is uncanny, Colin, is it not, the way the bones were found—what, three hundred-and-fifty years ago?—by the Benedictine monks of the abbey."

He stirred the coals and dropped a thick log upon glowing embers, then continued. "You said it was a giant of a man laid out, then the smaller bones of a woman with threads of golden hair, supposedly the queen, folded up at his feet. Verra strange, indeed—golden hair, not like the queen in the tapestry on the third floor of this castle."

Maddy, Anne and Ben all looked as one toward Broderick. With brows raised in surprise, Colin responded.

"I had forgotten that tapestry of Arthur with Gwenivere and Lancelot. But now that you mention it, yes, of course. In fact, it reminds me of a painting that hangs on the wall of the king's shrine in the abbey. In both the painting and our tapestry, Gwenivere has long dark hair, just as you always imagine her, Maddy. We must have seen that painting many times as children, playing there..."

Margaret interrupted with a rap of her cane, a glimmer of smile playing on her face. She moved her cane from one side of the chair to lean her hands on its knobby top end.

"Though you were told not to! That part of the castle is old and in disrepair. It was dangerous even then, twelve years ago. We should move that tapestry and display it elsewhere." Margaret moved restlessly in her chair, her smile disappearing.

"I remember Richard Whiting so well...I knew him as a young man, and I have heard that he has grown into a true man of God during his years as Glastonbury's abbot. I ken he is a saint, if ever there was one. And John Blackwater Thorne," she paused wistfully, "I remember him like it was yesterday. These sad tidings tear at my heart." Margaret drifted into silence while they remained quiet, sensing she had more to say.

"We three were friends, and with my sister Alva and my brother, we could not be parted in our young days! It was my brother and John Thorne who taught me to read.

"John and I were sweethearts once. We would have married, but I saw that he was destined for the church, that he would follow Richard Whiting anywhere, even into the jaws of death. And then his brother stole my heart away. God grant my beloved husband, Thomas Blackwater Thorne, to rest in the arms of Saint Mary and her son Jesus." She crossed herself, jostling the pearls upon her breast to shine in the candlelight. "May they protect dear John Thorne."

After a moment, Colin turned toward Geleis and Broderick. "What do ye propose, Geleis? Broderick? Do ye ken a place to hide the relics of the king and queen? Until we can find a better hiding place, or take them back when all this is over."

Geleis cocked his head to one side and, resting his chin on his knuckles, then replied. "Aye, well now, there is the King's Cave, where James Bruce hid two centuries ago, before he went to fight for the freedom of Scotland. But it's too well-known for my tastes. And verra wet. There is another cave, on the west coast, where we might arrange it to be dry enough, at least for a while. Tis a holy place, where our Celtic Christian faith took root almost ten centuries ago, not so far from the ancient cairns and standing stones. But the bones and relics will need a place less wet and wild than a cave on Arrain, Colin."

"Tis true," Broderick agreed. "Perhaps for a year or two we can safeguard the relics, then we should move them or they will molder and crumble in the sea air."

The problem was apparent to all. Colin suggested hopefully, "In a year or two this ordeal may have passed. The abbot's plan is to return the relics to their rightful place—Glastonbury—when we can. Geleis, how long does it take to get to the place you have in mind?"

Looking to Brodick for confirmation, Geleis replied. "Well Colin, I am thinking not of a sea cave but of a hidden cave inland, on Goatfell, where very few are brave enough to wander. It's an easy journey of two days, going north across the moors. Then it gets rough, ascending into the highlands of this isle. Traveling fast, we can go and return in five, six days. Then you can see for yourself."

It was soon determined that Colin and Geleis would depart in the morning. They would spend the first night at Brodick Castle, then continue on to Goatfell. With well-stoked fires burning bright and Kenna coming in to replenish both candles and whiskey in the decanter, they relaxed into a lively round of stories about Arthur and Gwenivere and her paramour, Lancelot—legends they knew and loved. Everyone grew quietly attentive as Margaret recounted a surprising version of the tale.

"When I was a growing girl, coming up on Arrain and in our family home near Glasgow, I heard many songs and stories of Arthur and his knights, and of Gwenhyfar, in the old language. It was the Welsh folktales—from the ancient people of Cymru—that my grandmothers knew best. For them it was Gwenhyfar who carried the royal blood and not her battle hero, Arthur. He married her to obtain the loyalty of Cymry chieftains and nobles and to inherit, as her bride gift, the legendary Round Table, where Arthur's knights sat in counsel.

"My mother's mother grew up in the lowland wilds of Wales. She was called Briallen—a name she inherited from her Welsh grandmother, who remembered all the old folktales. Ye ken, people here on Arrain worship the old gods and goddesses—and ken many of the Welsh legends as well. It's a fact," Margaret continued with growing enthusiasm, "in two days' time our people will celebrate Imbolc in Kildonan village below, even as we also celebrate the Feast of St. Brigit in the chapel with our priest, Father Gordon.

"My *seanmhàthair* Briallen once told me an interesting fable about *an righ agus banrich*. She said that all the elders in her line knew that Gwenhyfar was the first wife and true queen of Arthur Pendragon, but Gwenhyfar was driven into exile with Lancelot. They narrowly escaped death when the other knights turned against them, and they disappeared, spirited away by the faerie forces of the place called Avalon, where the priestesses in those days still had the knowledge of old magic. Somehow Myrddin and Nimuë, who we know as Merlin and Vivianne—and the sorceress Morgan le Fay— had something to do with it.

"As the story went, the search for the grail, told in the legends of the Frenchman, Chrétein de Troyes, was a fabrication that hid the truth of Lancelot's exile with the queen. Once they were gone, Arthur married another woman, a very young girl from the shores of Cornwall, where he was born at Tintagel. Her name was Winifred—a Roman version of Gwenivere, and of course the English form of the Welsh name, Gwenhyfar. A mere child, Winifred was said to have golden hair and eyes the color of the great sea. She charmed the king, and kept his bed warm. Still, it's told that Arthur died without a worthy successor—though he had illegitimate children by other women. Some say Briton still awaits the return of a true Pendragon king."

She paused in remembrance, holding her audience spellbound in the mood she had cast, its mystery augmented by the play of shadow and light from the flames that crackled and leapt in the fireplace.

"And here may be the most interesting thing of all. My grandmother said that she once heard a legend that told of

Gwenhyfar and Lancelot coming to Alba—indeed, to this very island—when they left Arthur's court and the Summer Country."

Maddy took in a sharp breath and glanced at Colin, who raised his black-winged brows in surprise. Ben and Anne exchanged looks as well, but it was Jennet who intervened, seeing that her grandmother grew tired.

"Maybe that is why we have the tapestry of a king and queen from Welsh legend here at Kildonan itself! Tis a verra grand mystery, *n'est ce pas*? But it's growing late, and Mòrai, you should sleep soon. Let me take you to your chamber. We will talk more of these things in the days ahead. *Bràthair*..."

She smiled at Colin, who rose to help Margaret from her chair as the other men stood respectfully. They were all weary, and it was time for them to retire.

Maddy was happy to see that Kenna had made their chamber ready—a cheerful fire burned on the hearth and the bedclothes were turned back. She stood beside the fire, leaning into Colin's solid length as they warmed themselves for a few moments, until she stirred and mused, "What a story your grandmother told. I did not know you had Welsh ancestors, Colin. It is another bond we share. Do you think it is possible that the bones of Arthur are drawn into exile, in a way, to reunite with his queen and first knight in the land where they found refuge?"

"Anything is possible, Maddy. Many of the folk in these parts are of mingled blood—Gaels from Ireland and Wales and Alba, as well as Roman and Viking blood that mixed in hundreds of years ago. There is even a bit of the French

Gaels intermingled here, through the Hamilton line. I dinna ken this story before tonight, and I will have to dwell on it before I can answer."

He moved to take up a flat iron pan with a lid and a long handle, filled it with burning coals from the fire, then warmed the bed before they crawled in. Shedding their clothes, they quickly burrowed close to share warmth. As Colin pulled the linen coverlet and heavy woolen blankets up over their shoulders and settled beside her, Maddy smiled into his eyes.

"*Mo chridhe*," he breathed softly, stroking her face and pulling her closer to kiss her cheek. "Are you tired?"

With a sigh of contentment she replied, "Yes, *mo gràidh*, but I am not too tired to love you. Who would believe that our former discipline could avail us so well," Maddy chuckled, "all those hours of vigil and liturgy, when we were too exhausted to see straight!"

She stretched with pleasure as his lips traveled, warm and moist, down the length of her throat to explore the deeper hollows of her neck and shoulders. Swiftly unbuttoning her gown and pulling the linen aside to caress her breasts with firm and sure hands, he shifted her weight to wrestle the linen nightdress up around her hips, freeing her body to explore further. He reached the gushing spring between her legs with a moan.

"Magdalyne, my heart. *'Se mo ghràdh gu bràth*."

Pulling him closer, she whispered, "Tell me what that means, darling. I want to learn everything about you, to discover all your secrets." She nuzzled his neck, pressing against his chest and inflaming his desire with each silken caress of her flesh against his.

"I said, 'my love is forever.' And this I ken to be true, Maddy," he returned, his voice growing hoarse with passion, "that we will have a fine life together, beyond the adversity of the quest and the sorrows we share."

"Yes," she replied, afloat in the current that flowed between them. "Love endures even the worst of trials. Terrible times may be upon us and those we love, but for now, husband," she breathed deep, stroking his thighs and then gently taking his sex, warm and hard, into her hand, "come to me."

CHAPTER SIX

Glastonbury
June 1539

It was a blustery day in early June when Colin and Maddy arrived in Glastonbury with Geleis, Ben and Anne. Tired but content to be in the safe harbor of the abbey, they were warmly met by John Thorne, who had received the news by messenger the day before that his nephew would arrive at midday.

"Sharpham Manor is not far," John said as they sat around the large table in the refectory eating bowls of hot soup provided by the cook, Brother Edward. "Richard went two days ago, before we heard news of your arrival. He plans to stay in residence there, where it's quiet, for the rest of Lent. We can easily make it there before dark, if the women are not too tired and you are willing. It is north of here, and if we leave soon, we may arrive before the storm breaks."

John paused, and after a while Maddy asked, "We are not too tired, John. And I'm anxious to see Uncle Richard. How is he?"

"The abbot isna well," he replied after some hesitation.

"What do you mean, 'not well'?" Maddy plied, her brow puckered. "Is he ill or..."

Colin's uncle rubbed his forehead with long, tapered fingers. "Aye. His heart pounds uncontrollable in his chest, and he is given to weak spells. Brother Raffe is giving him substantial doses of bilberry and hawthorn," he sighed, "but if you ask me, his heart 'tis nigh broken, Maddy. Richard isna a young man, ye ken. But at the same time, he is holding up as well as can be expected, considering the terrible weight he bears."

His cropped hair and beard shone iron gray in the dull light of the refectory, which made the dark smudges on the tender skin beneath his eyes more pronounced.

Shifting in his seat, John's speech reverted from a Scots brogue to his more usual clipped English, "And now he's fasting all but one meal a day for Lent, and eating only a scant bit of fish. He will refuse red meat, wine, and sweet cakes until Easter has passed, in almost two weeks' time."

He gave a rueful snort. "I, on the other hand, have never been as stalwart in my religious observances as our blessed abbot."

With a frown, John admitted, "Truth be told, there is a heavy burden on us all, and it falls especially hard on Richard. Roger and myself, and some of the other monks who understand what is at stake, we try to take as much of the weight from his back as we can. Henry and Cromwell will burn in hell for all the suffering they have caused!"

Colin reached out a hand to grasp his uncle's shoulder.

A pained moment of silence waxed between them until John relaxed.

"Well, it's all in God's hands. As soon as we are finished here, we shall go. It will do Richard good to see you all—especially you, bonnie Magdalyne—and hear the news you've brought."

With John Thorne on horseback and the two wagons drawn by teams, their reins wielded by Colin and Geleis, they rolled into the yard of Sharpham Park Manor at the end of a long day. The wind was beginning to blow, spurring the women to clutch their cloaks and pull their hoods down as they hoisted their voluminous skirts and lifted bags to run into the house, while the men quickly unloaded the wagons. They were greeted at the door by sandy-haired, plump Father William, who jumped in to help Colin and Ben while Geleis unharnessed the horses and saw them to the stables where they were taken over by Johan, the stableman.

Sharpham Park Manor was a fine but modest half-timbered house built of stone and plastered with wattle and daub, its tile roof a display of the abbey's wealth. Located on one of the many vast domains and parks owned by the abbey, the house was originally built by Richard Bere, the previous abbot, as a place of retreat for the abbots of Glastonbury. During the past fifteen years it had become an important place of refuge for Richard Whiting, who within moments came walking down the stairs from his rooms on the second floor to greet them in the parlour.

He had grown noticeably thinner since they saw him last, four months before, and his shock of thick white hair brushed his collarbones in a haphazard but endearing way. His blue eyes were bright and alert, flicking this way and that to take them all in as he walked eagerly toward them with the help of a cane.

Magdalyne ran to her uncle and took his hand to raise it to her lips for a kiss. Patting her back gently, he leaned in to kiss her cheek, and, with a beaming smile, his gaze lingered on her face as if he gauged her state of happiness. Satisfied with what he saw, he then moved his eyes toward Colin, who stood waiting reverently.

"Colin! Maddy!" Tears welled in his blue eyes as the abbot stood between the two, holding them close in an embrace. "My eyes are blessed to have the sight of you." Ben and Anne approached to receive the abbot's blessing and finally, Colin motioned to Geleis to come forward.

"Abbot Whiting," Geleis bowed low to kiss the ruby ring on the elder's hand.

Resting a hand on Geleis' head for a brief moment of benediction, Richard then pulled the young Scot up for an embrace. "I am most pleased to meet you, Geleis. Colin has spoken well of you, my son, and I am thankful for your help in the great task before us. And I quite admire your kilt. It has been many years since I have been in Scotland. Come," he invited warmly.

Gesturing to chairs, a low couch and bench near the fireplace, the abbot looked around at all, his eyes lingering on John Thorne.

"Let us sit comfortably here in the parlour. We can speak freely at Sharpham Manor—I keep my troublesome steward Jack Horner away from here, busy with very important tasks around our estates, and William and Angus will never speak a word of anything they might hear. In fact, they will be helping us a great deal in the weeks ahead."

He moved to a table near the fire that burned low in a flagstone hearth, and as they settled on chairs around him, a short, stocky monk with red-gold hair, ruddy cheeks and blue-gray eyes came in the room through a door that Maddy remembered as the way to the kitchen and buttery, where food was stored.

Richard smiled with genuine pleasure. "Ah, and here is Father Angus now, just in time to tell us when we might have supper on this stormy spring night."

Angus flushed to the roots of his red hair, casting a shy smile at Colin with a nod of his head. He took in the group before him, seeming to take a mental count. "Aye, tis a fine stew of monkfish, spring onions and sweet peas from the garden that we'll be sharin' in two hours' time. William and I have also made spiced bread pudding with wild honey and last fall's apples. Now if you'll excuse me, Abba, Father John, Mistress Maddy, Colin, and all, I shall learn your names at another time." With an amiable nod to the three newcomers, he disappeared back into the kitchen.

"Angus loves to cook," Richard mused. "And I love the way he cooks—simple food for monks and common folk. It's not his usual job, and so he is as happy as a pig in sunshine at the moment. In fact, he and William are assistants to Roger James, our sacristan as you know, who will arrive at Sharpham next week. But now, two hours' time is just long enough for you to tell us everything about your journey. First of all, how is Margaret Thorne? And your sister, young Jennet?"

As Colin plunged into a detailed description of his indomitable grandmother and her remembrances of Richard Whiting and John Thorne, her heartfelt support of their task and her sorrow at the necessity for it, John grew thoughtful. Rising from his chair, the bursar of Glastonbury Abbey walked to the sideboard and poured whiskey into a cup. Turning, he offered it to Richard.

"Nay, but thank you, John. Please offer a cup of spirits to everyone else." The men gratefully accepted, while Maddy and Anne declined.

"Perhaps we'll partake in a little wine with dinner," Maddy ventured, smiling at Ann. John inclined his head, making a mental note to ask William to bring two bottles of their best Muscadet from the brewery for evening supper.

Richard and John listened attentively as Colin and Geleis described the cave they had found on Goatfell Mountain, and the stonemason who was already making plans for the cairn he would build to protect the boxes containing the bones of the king and his queen and any other artifacts.

"Ah yes, Goatfell Mountain." John ruminated, squinting at Richard to recall the memory. "We went there as young men—do ye remember? It was a hunting trip, and we stayed for many days, exploring the terrain."

"Yes," Richard recalled. "It was quite unforgettable. I remember Goatfell as rugged and quite formidable, its horny summits cloaked in mists—a true highland landscape. Very few brave its more remote reaches. At any pace, it's your decision, Colin, Geleis, and it sounds like a good one."

John turned toward Colin, prodding him about their earlier conversation. "You said that Margaret told a folktale about *an righ agus banrich*. Will ye share it with us?"

Between the five young people, they relayed the story of Arthur and his second queen of the golden hair, then the extraordinary tale of Gwenhyfar and Lancelot traveling to Alba and living in exile on the Isle of Arrain.

"Yes, I recall Margaret's father telling a tale once about that tapestry," John exclaimed with an uncharacteristic excitement. "He said it had been passed down in the family from their Welsh ancestors in the lowlands, through a kinswoman named Briallen. If the old tale is true, then Arthur's bones will go to the place where Gwenhyfar and Lancelot took refuge. Maybe they will be reunited, after all."

"I had the same idea, Uncle John," Maddy remarked with satisfaction. "It is a romantic notion, for sure, but who knows? Sometimes the truth is strange indeed."

A moment of silence pooled the air. Thick woolen drapes covered the latticed windows to insulate against the cold, but even so they could hear the spring wind that howled outside in counterpoint to the popping and crackling of the fire. Rich smells drifted into the oak paneled parlour from the kitchen as Father William came and went, attending to the heavy oaken dining table that he made ready for their supper.

"You have brought us interesting and hopeful news, indeed," John ventured. "Being on the road for so long, you may not know that on January 12 this year King Francis of France signed a treaty with Charles V, the Holy Roman Emperor—that is, Charles I of Spain, who was once an ally of our country but is no longer, thanks to Henry's annulment of his marriage to Catherine of Aragon, close kinswoman of Charles. They have agreed to make no further alliances with England. They are sick to death of Henry's abuses, his war with the Holy Father in Rome, his brutal attack on his own people and Catherine, his lawful wife, and his ruthless reform movement."

John's voice grew weary. "Whether this treaty is good for England remains to be seen. It has incurred Henry's ire, to be sure. Just last month Canterbury Cathedral was forced to surrender and revert to its previous status as a college of secular canons. Again Cromwell is bearing down on the religious houses of England."

He recounted the news that Bolton Abbey, Colchester and Newstead Abbeys, St. Albans, York and Hartland were all falling prey to the dissolution of their monasteries. Beaulieu Abbey would soon go down. Thousands more monks and nuns were being turned out on the streets of villages and towns.

"Some monks receive pensions but often the nuns are given nothing." He stood and walked to the sideboard. "Many are being forced into begging. And now Glastonbury hangs in the balance. We are suspended by a fine thread that could be cut at any moment."

As John refilled their cups with whisky, Geleis asked, "Do ye ken any news of the king's commissioners coming again to Glastonbury?"

"No. Most likely they will come in surprise," Richard answered. "But I have heard from our illustrious bursar," he glanced at John with a flicker of a smile, "who has his own sources—fortunately, he does not tell me who or what they are—that they will probably move against us in the fall, after Henry has made his summer progress from Windsor Castle to Hampton Court and back to Whitehall."

Richard paused, then added, "Right now the king is busy playing with his little son—may God bless young Edward. He still grieves the untimely death of Jane Seymour two years ago, who finally gave him the son he craved. But Cromwell and his ministers pressure him to marry again, and as soon as possible, so we heard. Cromwell is offering Anne of Cleves as our future queen."

John pressed his lips together, biting back a bitter comment, then regarded Ben with a wry smile.

"And so, sir, ye have been brought into a mighty struggle. This is surely a long way from Oxford!"

Ben leaned back in his chair. "Indeed, Father John, I used to teach in Oxford, and my subject was the history of England. I spent many a long hour discoursing on the legends of Arthur and the knights of the Round Table, and the works of Geoffrey of Monmouth and Chrétein de Troyes. The quest to safeguard the precious relics of this abbey has the call of destiny for me. I am proud to be here tonight with you all." He raised his cup to toast the two elders and then the rest of the group.

"And you, Anne, are you afraid of the dangers that lay ahead?" Richard turned to the young woman who sat quietly beside Maddy.

"Nay, I am not afraid. I am willing to die, if necessary. May be that there is a warrior woman among my Welsh ancestors, who seeks to live through me." She laughed lightly and pushed ruddy gold curls away from her face. "My line goes back to ancient Cymru on my father's side. As a small child he took me and my mother to Dinas Affaron and Dinas Emrys, where he told me the story of the two dragons that are said to sleep there, according to the vision of Myrrdin Emrys, that is Merlin, of course."

Maddy encouraged her. "Sing a little of that verse, Anne, the one about Beowulf and the dragon. Go on, stand and sing." With a reassuring smile from Ben, Anne stood and began to sing in a fine alto voice.

Then Beowulf came as king this broad realm to rule
and he ruled it well fifty winters,
a wise old prince, warding his land,
until One began in the dark of night,
a Dragon, to rage. In the grave on the hill
a hoard it guarded, in the stone-barrow steep.
A straight path reached it, unknown to mortals...

It is he, who, blazing, seeks burial mounds,
He, the smooth, the spiteful dragon
that flies throughout the night!
Enveloped in flame, all men fear him greatly...

Her voice was melodious and confident, and Maddy squeezed her hand as Anne sat down, giving a little curtsy when they clapped in appreciation.

"Sometimes I wonder if Merlin's story did not inspire the writers of *Beowulf*, penned only two hundred years after Merlin's time." Ben commented, smiling at his wife with pride.

Anne smoothed her skirt and settled as she settled back into the chair. "As a child, I learned all the verses in *Beowulf* concerning Grendel the dragon from my father. Now I only remember those few lines."

"Your father and mother would be very proud of you today, Anne," Richard offered. "I knew them both well."

She beamed, her face bright and lively. "And I thank you for your kind words, Abba. I take them as a great blessing indeed."

"Ah! Here is Angus, come to call us to supper." Richard stood and moved toward the long wooden table, set for nine, while Angus carried in a tureen of stew and William brought wine and bread. The travelers were hungry, and they welcomed their steaming bowls, generously ladled by Angus, with sounds of contentment. Lifting their spoons, no one spoke for a few moments, a sure sign that they were pleased to devour the nourishing country supper laid out before them.

Afterward they gathered again on chairs and stools around the stone hearth of the fireplace. The rain had retreated a little, and when John opened the window a crack for a draft of fresh spring air, they could smell the salt tides that wafted in the evening, hear the dripping of branches in the manor garden.

Colin ventured, "Uncle John, we brought a gift for you. A small cask of Arrain's finest whiskey, which I ken you would relish. It was stored in the brewery when we arrived. Shall I bring it inside and pour ye a wee taste?"

John's face brightened. "Aye, by the sweet Lord Jesus, a fine gift, and I thank ye—it's a well known fact that Arrain makes the best whiskey in all of Scotland!" He cajoled, bragging unrestrained with a wink to Geleis.

While Geleis and Ben brought the whiskey to the kitchen and opened the cask, Maddy took a stool to sit beside her uncle. Taking his hand in her own, she looked into his face with a smile, reaching out to touch his long, unruly hair.

"Uncle Richard, who cuts your hair? I would not mind taking the scissors in my own hands to polish you up a bit. I do a fair job for Colin, don't I, darling?" She smiled at her husband, who had just walked in with a decanter of amber spirits, which he handed to John. He put a hand to his own black hair that was neatly pulled back into a queue and tied with a strip of black ribbon.

"Aye, she's handy indeed, Abba," he offered. "She can give you a good trim without taking your whole scalp!"

Richard chuckled. "I would say yes, but William has cut my hair for many years. It is a job I do not think he means to give up—but it's my fault, not his, my dear, that it's grown so long. In a way, I just cannot be bothered with sitting for the scissors to do their job."

Moving about the room to serve the whiskey, John picked up the thread with a wry comment. "Richard is rather distracted these days, niece, as you can imagine. But I ken verra well that you want to take care of him. We all do."

Looking at the abbot, Ben asked, "Sir, would you tell us something of your life? How you came to a monk's vows, how you came to Glastonbury Abbey, and how you became the abbot here?"

Richard had settled into his chair beside the fire and watched as Colin hefted two big logs on top of the coals.

The young people settled around him, while John Thorne stood leaning against the fireplace at his left side. He encouraged, "Tis a good story, Richard, if you feel up to it. I would rather enjoy hearing it as well," he drawled, "though I know it already, like the back of my hand."

Richard smiled, "Well, you can help me, as it is true that you played a big role in it all, and still do, John Arthur Thorne."

Ben and Anne exchanged looks of amazement. "Your name is Arthur?" Ben asked, incredulous.

"Indeed, yes it is," John admitted. "It's my spiritual name, which replaced the name of my ancestors, Blackwater—in our family we are given plenty of names, aren't we, Colin?"

Colin said nothing, but his eyes sparkled as he sipped the Arrain whiskey.

John continued with a conspiratorial wink. "Given the story you told us tonight about Arthur's second wife, Winifred, 'tis amazing indeed that Roger James is Welsh, and his spiritual name is Winfrid," he paused for effect. "Not exact, but close!"

Their burst of laughter was equal parts release and awe at the extraordinary circumstances in which they found themselves, embroiled in a plot against the king of such magnitude and spiritual depths that they could not fully grasp the far-reaching implications of it all. The laughter subsided slowly, and John looked at Richard, raising his cup in a salute and urging him to continue.

"Well, to make a very long story as short as possible, I was born in the year of our Lord 1460, not so far from

Glastonbury, in the hamlet of Wrington. My family was well-educated gentry, my grandfather having amassed a small fortune as a spice merchant. As a boy I was predisposed toward language and history, and I attended the claustral school here at Glastonbury. I was a fast learner, and could comprehend Greek, Latin, and French with some ease. The stories of the Bible intrigued me, and I studied the Old and New Testaments with a passion. I found myself as a young man of twenty sent by the abbey to study in Cambridge. It was there, a few years later, that I met this rascal Scot," he flashed a glance at John, "and we became fast friends.

"That year we traveled together to his native place in Scotland on the Isle of Arrain, where his family were regents under the Stewart clan at the castle Lochranza. At that time, John was madly in love with Margaret Hamilton, and his heart yearned for her so, we had to make the journey to Arrain, and then to *Cill Donnain*, which we know as Kildonan, in Kilmory on the southern end of the isle. Of course, I was most eager to travel, and to see the beauty of Caledonia and her islands, of which I had heard so much."

Richard spoke softly, a pastiche of vivid memories fleeting across his face.

"It was on a hunting trip with Margaret's father to Goatfell Mountain that we met a holy man, a highland monk named Father Donaidh Macleod, a cousin of Margaret, who befriended us. Being young and adventurous, we decided to travel on foot with the good father, and it was he who took us to Birchburn Blackwaterfoot on the western shores of the island, and to Machrie Moor to the standing stones and cairns, and the king's cave on the coast nearby—holy places where he said a monastery called Aileach was once founded by the Irish saint named Brendan, a thousand years ago. He taught us a very old Irish poem, called *Agallamh na Senorach*. Do you remember it, John?"

"Aye, that I do," John declared, clearing his throat to sing in a warm, rich baritone.

> *Arrain nan Aighean lomadh*
> *Arrain of the many stags,*
> *the sea strikes against her shoulders*
> *A company of men can feed well there*
> *blues spears reddened among her boulders*
> *Merry hinds are on her hills*
> *juicy berries are there for food*
> *Refreshing water in her streams*
> *with nuts aplenty in her wood*

Maddy burst out in exclamation. "That's a haunting melody, fit for the bagpipes most certainly—you play them, don't you Geleis?" Responding with a self-deprecating shrug, the young Scotsman blushed a pleasing shade of rose.

"Aye, he plays them verra well!" Colin intervened.

"We will entice you to play for us when we return to Arrain. Perhaps Anne and I can learn to sing it whilst you play." Maddy finished with a smile.

Colin faced the abbot. "And what happened then, Abba?"

Richard had fallen silent and seemed to wander in the inner world of his memories. With a start, he looked up at Colin.

"Well, I had an experience there that changed my life, in a stone circle overlooking the salt water to the west. 'Tis quite hard to say exactly what happened. But I saw a shining form that I could only recognize as Mother Mary. She came to me from the sparkling waters of Kilbrannon Sound and opened my heart with her love. I fell to my knees, transfixed, in the high heather of ancient Machrie Moor."

He paused, his chin dropping toward his chest. John picked up the story as Richard's gaze fastened upon the fire.

"Aye, Father Macleod and I found him like that, sunk into the grass on his knees, his face shining like the sun that was soon to set over the Kintyre Peninsula, just across the water from where we stood. I remember well, it was so green and almost balmy that day, and the summer wildflowers were in bloom on the moor.

"He was in quite a state, and all he could say was, 'Tis Mary, the star of the sea, beloved Mary!' We sat with him until, after awhile, he grew very serene and calm. Twilight came, and it was a moonlit night that shone the way as we trudged south across the moors to the stone barn of a kind farmer, where we slept. Richard dinna utter another word. Even then, as a lad, my intuition served me true enough to know that he would never be the same."

Taking a sip of whiskey, John smacked his lips together in satisfaction before he continued.

"We returned to Kildonan for a time after that, and Margaret could see a change had come over Richard. It was clear to us all that he had been transformed. He was not quite ready for the Benedictines, for we were young and our studies called to us, and we soon returned to Cambridge. A few years after that, Richard received his degree as doctor of theology and philosophy. Mine came later, as he was older than me and had been at his studies longer.

"Back in university, Richard became more inward, spending long hours in prayer at the church, talking with the priests there. Time passed, and the next year we returned to Arrain. It was then I discovered that Margaret had become enamored with my older brother, Thomas, and they planned to be handfasted. It was a sad time for me, but I ken Margaret could see the way of things the year before, when we came back to Kildonan after our sojourn in the hills and moors among the stones with Father Macleod— that my soul was following the same path as the soul of Richard Whiting. His conversion had touched my heart as well, and that is the way it was. We have much to thank Father Macleod for, though we never saw him again. We were called to this life through him."

With a wave of his hand, the abbot resumed the telling of the story.

"In the end it was for the best, as we can see how well it all turned out, for here we are, with you all. After I received my doctorate, I taught at the abbey school, here in Glastonbury. Time went by, and finally the inner call became so strong that, some years later, I received my habit as a novice Benedictine from John Selwood, who at the time was Abbot of Glastonbury, the church of my childhood. A few years later John Thorne received his own habit from Abbot John.

"We spent many years working hard, living the Benedictine Rule, doing our duty here at Glastonbury

Abbey. Whenever we were free we went to Langbrook in Exeter to visit my brother's family—my nephew, James Whiting, for whom I had a great fondness. I had a particular affection for James's young daughters, Maddy and Jane, and their cousin Anne," Richard chuckled as he glanced at Maddy and then Anne.

"From a very young age, you wanted to come to Glastonbury, Maddy. How you loved this place! You spent hours as a child picking flowers for the shrine of the king and queen, and asked me time and again for their story, and the stories of the many other relics at the abbey."

Richard stopped to reflect. They waited as he drank the last drops of water from his cup. After a moment, he continued.

"John Selwood passed away and Richard Bere became our abbot. There was never a finer spiritual guide than Abbot Bere, with his passionate love for Blessed Mary and our Saint Joseph of Arimathea. I was made chamberlain by Abbot Bere, who also appointed John as assistant to the bursar.

"Abbot Bere was a noble man of God, a man of great vision and foresight—I loved him as an elder brother or a father. We were all bereft when he died. None of the brothers of the Benedictine Order at Glastonbury could bear to name a successor, when we grieved so deeply we did not think we could ever carry on without our abbot.

"And so we asked Cardinal Wolsey to name a new abbot. After some deliberation, to my surprise, he picked me."

Richard concluded with a flourish of his hand. His smile of genuine disbelief carried a glimpse of the charm of his personality, now softened to the gentle light of his elder years.

"I still sometimes wonder at his choice, nonetheless..."

John interposed with a laugh. "Don't listen to him. I will tell you the real story. Cardinal Wolsey interviewed the abbey monks. He heard nothing but praise for Richard Whiting, a pure soul and a wise monk, as well as a most capable administrator of abbey business. Wolsey decided to take a vote of all the monks, and not a single hand was raised against Richard. The brothers were relieved and gladdened by Cardinal Wolsey's choice, for Richard was loved and respected by all. These past sixteen years he has become the true spiritual father of this holy place and all who live and pray and seek shelter here. The young monks would follow him into death, hell or wherever he might need to go."

"But I'll not take them with me!" Richard intervened with sudden vehemence. "It's a harsh enough fate to be carrying you and Roger James on my shoulders in this. For it's into death and the heavenly spheres—hopefully not hell—that I am going."

With his strong declaration came a silence emphasized by the pop and hiss of burning logs. The abbot's words evoked the spectres that waited in the shadowy corners of the room, opening a chasm of sorrow that gaped wide within their hearts. The realities they faced lurched suddenly upon them, overshadowing their spirits. It was John Thorne who jolted them from their contemplation when he coughed loudly, looking around at the company.

"And so," John began, "we come around to the horrors we face. Glastonbury's past is mired in legends, fantastic tales, and fragments of arcana. The king and his religious zealots, Cromwell and Cranmer and all the rest, are eager to have not only Glastonbury's immense wealth and lands, but its spiritual treasures as well. They know very well that our treasures are genuine—not fakes fashioned to bolster the faith of the poor and downtrodden."

"That bring us to another very long story," Richard pushed himself up from his seat by the fire, "but it is time for me to retire. When you are ready to sleep, Colin will show you upstairs, where the married couples each have a room. Geleis, you will share a room with Angus and William. Tomorrow, after you are well rested, we will take the next step, and we will answer all of your questions as best we can."

CHAPTER SEVEN

Sharpham Manor
June 1539

The next day when the abbot came downstairs from his afternoon rest, he gathered them around, John at his side. He seemed relaxed as he shepherded them into the garden behind the house to sit beneath an arbor bursting with early June roses. Above the sky was pale blue, and birds sang and chirped around them, oblivious to the weight of their gathering.

"Before we can easily speak of our relics, you must learn the inner secrets of our abbey, passed down to us across hundreds of years by the Company of Avalon, as the monks of Glastonbury who have carried this obligation are called. It was a task imparted to us directly by John Selwood and Richard Bere, and to them by a long line of abbots who came before them.

" 'Tis a long story indeed, much of it known by you, Colin and Maddy. But for Geleis, Ben and Anne, let us begin at the beginning, with Joseph of Arimathea and a small group of disciples who were sent here from Gaul by Philip, the

Apostle of Christ, only ten years after the crucifixion. At that time, Joseph was already a sage, advanced in years, but still fit enough to make the journey across land and sea."

John Thorne's audience was spellbound as he told the legend of Joseph of Arimathea, who had brought Jesus as a lad with him to Briton, traveling on business as a merchant of the tin that was mined in the south of Wales, just north of Somerset. Briton was known, even then, as a rich source of ore, and not only tin but gold, silver, and copper. The Romans were also interested in the riches of the Summer Country and soon built a hill fort, Caer Glas, near an unusual Tor that rose high in the flood plain.

Some years later, after the crucifixion, Joseph came back with his companions. They were received by the Celtic king, Aviragus, who looked kindly upon these men and women of God. Aviragus sent them to Ynis Witrin, the holy Isle of Glass and the most sacred place in Briton. There, Aviragus granted land to Joseph, and on that land was planted the seed that would grow over the centuries into the abbey of Glastonbury.

"At that time Ynis Witrin was a vast shallow lake," John explained, "with the Tor its dominant feature and smaller hills that protruded like islands from a landscape of supernatural beauty and mystery, caused by the constant fogs and mists of tides and floods from the Severn Sea. The tribal people of the area, the Dumnonii, lived here in a wattle and daub lake village constructed of timber poles covered with straw and clay."

When John lifted his cup to drink, Ben spoke with flushed excitement, the scholar in him inspired to add, "The

138

druids and local people believed the Tor was the entryway to *Annwyn*, their mythical Otherworld, which the Irish Celts call *Tir na nog*. The deepest hallows of Avalon reverberated from this magical dimension within the Tor itself, known to common folk as the land of the dead, or the place of the faeries."

John nodded briskly. "Aye, in those times folk moved about in corracles or *currachs*—small round boats made of lashed willow boughs and well-tanned and oiled hides that carried them across the shallow lake or on the moving tidal streams. The villagers and druids also made their way by foot on a labyrinth of pathways—raised timber tracks. Upon these wooden planks one could walk just above the constantly changing levels of the shallow lake. There the Dumnonii thrived, intermingling with druids, hermit sages, and the priestesses who lived around the Tor in a hidden enclave called Avalon."

Even those who knew the history well were captivated as John unfolded the story of Avalon. Centuries before the druids and Dumnonii tribes of the region, the sacred landscape of the Tor was inhabited by priestesses and sorcerers connected to those known as the Old Ones, who came and went from the mystic realm of Avalon. Indeed Avalon was the sacred place where an ancient, primordial goddess was worshipped upon the Tor, where spiritual knowledge and power had been preserved since the archaic mists of time.

Avalon was ruled by a high priestess, known as the Lady of the Lake, and it was one of these who welcomed Joseph of Arimathea and the disciples of Jesus to establish the first church, built of osiers wattled together, not far from the Tor.

"I sometimes imagine Saint Joseph and his band arriving when the apple trees were blooming on the Tor and their petals filled the air, enchanting and opening the hearts of the early Christians." John smiled at his own poetic rendering of the tale.

Ben queried thoughtfully, "But the Christians and the pagans did not get along. Our histories tell us that the pagans were persecuted by the Roman Christians. What is the story as you know it?"

Enthusiasm piqued, John's face was flushed as he continued. "The secret lore, passed down by our abbots, tells that for generations the disciples of Jesus and the denizens of Avalon co-existed in peace and mutual respect. The Tor was largely the domain of the priestesses. The inner mysteries of Jesus and his ministry, as it was taught by Saint Joseph, meshed well with the ancient knowledge of the priestesses.

"It's hard to imagine, in our world today, when even those of Christian faith murder, execute, persecute one another. Aye, it was that very mingling of Christianity with the Isle of Avalon that would, hundreds of years later, become Glastonbury Abbey."

John paused to gauge the response of his listeners. Their excitement was evident to all as he explained that the split between them came later, seeded by the zealot monk known as Saint Patrick, who traveled through and lived in Ynis Witrin in the early or mid-fifth century. The schism happened over time, as the monks became more rigid, following the orthodox dictates of the Church in Rome.

Richard had been quietly listening. Finally he roused up and interjected, "Joseph's companions worshipped a deity that was both God and Goddess, thus it was that Joseph's sect lived in harmony with the Celtic priestesses of old and the druids as well, for it was the Mother Goddess to whom they turned in prayer and supplication. What they had in common was a great love for the Sacred Heart of the Cosmos, exemplified for those early Christians by Mary, the mother of Jesus, and Mary the Magdalene, the dearest companion, the wife of Jesus, who became the patron saint of Glastonbury."

Anne gasped at this revelation, covering her mouth with one hand. Recovering her aplomb, she gasped, one hand to her heart, "Truly, our reverence for Mary Magdalene was brought to Briton by Joseph of Arimathea?"

John answered. "This is, in fact, the core secret guarded by the Company of Avalon. To us, it is understood that Mary of Magdalene was the closest and dearest to Jesus, but this knowledge was suppressed in the years after the crucifixion, when the Church was guided by the Apostle Peter and, later, his followers who became the religious authorities of Rome."

Ben stood up and paced the arbour, unable to contain himself.

"I once heard an old scholar of Oxford speak in a lecture," he looked from to another as he spoke candidly, "and he told us that there are many places in France, cathedrals and basilicas and monasteries, where this knowledge was also preserved. He himself had traveled there and seen these marvels! The folktales of southern France say that Mary Magdalene took refuge there, in the mountainous region of the south where she lived among the Celtic Gauls in a cave on a high escarpment."

Colin nodded in agreement. "Aye, tis known to the Company of Avalon that she went into exile to preserve her life and the life of her children. In France she continued to minister to the people, and she traveled north, to ancient Briton and Alba. She was known as a great healer. Over the years the truth was distorted, possibly even by some of the disciples of Jesus. Across the centuries, the importance of her role—and the truth of her relationship to Jesus—was removed from the gospels."

Maddy sat throughout the revelations in silent absorption. She turned to Richard with a quizzical look. "Abba, would you say more about how Joseph and his companions were accepted by the people of Avalon and Ynis Witrin?"

Richard stroked his beard as he began. "In ancient Briton, the denizens of Ynis Witrin—Avalon and the wise ones among the Celts—recognized both Mary, mother of Jesus, and Mary, the wife of Jesus, as the goddess incarnate. For them, this was natural, as the goddess was known to the Celts in many forms, with many names across Briton and Wales, or Cymru, as well as Alba and Erin, or Ireland. She was worshipped as Brighid, as Bloeduedd, and as Arianrhod. She was feared as Morrigan. And perhaps she was loved most of all as Ceridwen. They understood that the Lady of the Lake not only represented her but also embodied her."

With eyebrows raised in excitement, Anne glanced at Maddy, who squeezed her hand reassuringly.

"It's just as we knew in our hearts, cousin. But we will have many long nights on the road north to ponder and talk deeply of these things," Maddy promised with a smile. She turned back to her uncle. "Please continue, for we are eager to hear all."

"If you look clearly," Richard proceeded with candor, "you can see that Mary Magdalene is the true patron saint of our church of Glastonbury. Our hospice that cares for the wounded, sick, and dying is named Mary Magdalene Hospital. The front gate of the abbey is located on Magdalene Street—in fact, the gate itself is called the Magdalene Gate. The women's almshouses outside our gates are named for her. While the shrine in the Lady Chapel is dedicated to Mother Mary, the great painting that graces the wall there depicts Mary Magdalene as well, and the sculpture at the shrine is of Mary Magdalene.

"You hardly have to scratch the surface here, and you find our Blessed Mary, our Lady of Light. John, would you carry on with the history?"

John accepted with brief nod. "One hundred years after Joseph of Arimathea came, Pope Eleutherius in Rome sent two missionaries, Fagan and Deruvian, who settled in Ynis Witrin to continue the hermit tradition that had existed there since the time of Joseph of Arimathea.

"It wasn't until 433 that Patrick came from Ireland to Ynis Witrin, and with his coming, relations between the monks and Avalon began to erode. He preached a zealous gospel, with which it is said he had 'driven the snakes from Ireland' after a forty-day fast upon a hilltop. 'Tis known by the Irish Celts that there never were any snakes in Ireland!"

Stunned for a moment, the group burst into laughter, which lightened for a moment the concentrated weight of their concerns. As the humorous moment faded, Ben offered pensively, "Some say those snakes were symbolic—the Celts with their worship of the Goddess and their druid religion."

John smiled. "Abbot Bere believed this was Patrick's personal mission—to rid Ireland and Britain and Scotland of its pagan religion. 'Twas a sad development in our history, according to Abbot Bere. He was of the conviction that the druidic religion, with their practice of human sacrifice, was entangled in the minds of Christians with the magic of Avalon—although Avalon's magic was of a much higher and benevolent order, based upon a wisdom far more ancient than that of the pagan druids."

He shook his head in disbelief. "We human beings are strange creatures, indeed! Why can our different religions not live in peace together? Abbot Bere believed, as do we, that Patrick's teachings had a powerful effect upon the events that occurred during the reign of Arthur and Gwenivere, occurring some generations later. Things might have turned out differently if the schism between pagan and Christian had not taken root and grown."

John heaved a deep sigh. "Tis our belief that the mystic rivers of religion can come together in a universal understanding of God and Goddess, and even the plethora of primeval gods, spirits, faeries—all the denizens of the invisible worlds have a place in God's great creation. This is essential to the stream of knowledge that has been preserved, underground so to speak, by the Company of Avalon at Glastonbury Abbey over the centuries past. This is what Glastonbury Abbey stands for."

Geleis, who had listened with silent absorption, now leaned forward on his seat to follow their words closely, before he queried, "Please, say more about the Company of Avalon."

Richard rubbed his hands together as he roused himself to explain.

"Legend has it that the Company of Avalon was actually born among the Benedictines at the time of Arthur's death, when the Lady of the Lake entrusted his bones to the monks of Ynis Witrin. But we will come back to that. As to how the schism occurred, it is true that in the time of Patrick the druidic religion of ancient Ireland and Scotland was not far removed from their past and their bloody practice of human sacrifice. This may have been what spurred Patrick to his zealous path. But, we must ask—are our times any better?"

Richard's question was rhetorical, the answer obvious to all.

"Why is it that the baiting of bears is so popular in London today? Why do people flock to watch the burning of heretics, the hangings, the disembowelments? No, we have not come so far from the druids of old. The bloodshed and brutality of King Henry's quest for an heir and his desire to reform the church has been terrible to endure. Even the Holy See condones or turns its face from acts of wanton violence and inquisitions. As a Christian monk who strives to live by the teachings of Jesus and St. Benedict's Rule, I find this abhorrent."

Richard paused, lifting his cup to drink. He looked around at young couples, catching the eye of each one by one.

"In all times and within all religious traditions, there have been human beings who served either light or dark, even if only through ignorance and superstition, though meaning to do good."

Just then Angus and William appeared bearing trays with ale and platters of cold meats and flatbread. When Ben raised his brows questioningly to John, the bursar smiled.

"Angus and William are privy to all these revelations and much more. They are with us in the Company of Avalon and a pivotal part of our plans. Join us, if you will," he invited with a wave of his hand.

Angus shook his head, "Thank ye but no, Father John. I am up to my ears in the kitchen with our supper, which will be late. Tis the reason I brought these victuals, to tide you over, so to speak."

"And you, William?" Richard inquired.

"No Abba, I'll not stay. I've work to do as well, as you know." The two men smiled as they turned to go, then quickly disappeared into the manor. With the radical views of John and Richard brought to light, a lively conversation ensued, with Ben's questions penetrating back to John's remarks about Saint Patrick.

"According to William of Malmsbury, who wrote in his history, *Gesta Regis Anglorum*," John explained, "when Patrick came to Ynis Witrin in 433, he discovered twelve wise hermits, disciples of Jesus, living there in an unbroken succession since the time of Fagan and Deruvian. The hermits were mystics by nature, and they remembered the teachings—the legends and apocrypha—of Joseph of Arimathea. They had kept the histories and records and passed them on to coming generations. Patrick's teachings sowed seeds of dissidence between the monks."

Richard concluded, "There were those of the Marian faith and there were those who rejected Mary Magdalene. And it was this split , promoted as dogma by scholars and church pontificators, that relegated our Lady of Light to the status of a wealthy prostitute. Avalon was a constant thorn in the side of Christians who sought to repress the truth of Mary, the wife of Jesus. By the end of Arthur's time, which began some decades after Patrick's death in 472, Avalon had already begun to recede further into the mists, its powers on the wane.

"Eventually Avalon disappeared," John continued, "at least from the common view and perspective, though we cannot know what magic was involved or how this occurred. Even as Avalon disappeared into the Otherworld, the monastery of Ynis Witrin not only grew but flourished. But within that monastery were two streams: the exoteric and the esoteric. And while the veneration of Mother Mary took the public place, love for Mary Magdalene continued in the hearts of the Company of Avalon within the monastery while the memory of Avalon and the saga of Arthur Pendragon, Gwenivere, Lancelot and the Knights of the Round Table burned bright in the hearts of the people."

Richard pressed on. "When my thoughts wander over our extraordinary history, I sometimes ponder the fact that our Benedictine Order was founded in Italy at the same time that Arthur was ruling on British soil and perhaps around the time when he died, as legend says, at the hand of his own son, Mordred.

"It puts much into perspective when we consider that it was less than one hundred years later that St. Augustine, the first Archbishop of Canterbury, relayed his experience of Ynis Witrin, around the year 597. In a well-known letter, he wrote, 'There is on the confines of western Britain a certain royal island, called in the ancient speech Glastonia, marked out by broad boundaries, girt round with waters rich in fish and with still-flowing rivers, fitted for many uses of human indigence, and dedicated to the most sacred of deities.' "

Richard looked around at his small audience, who gazed back with keen eyes, their faces bright with inspiration. It was rare indeed to hear the abbot speaking with such candor, and they soaked up every word.

"Could it be that Saint Augustine of Canterbury perceived the true spirit of Glastonbury Abbey, dedicated to our Lady of Light, Mary Magdalene? It is an interesting choice of words, although he then writes of the essential tenets of Christendom. But, we cannot know how big his vision may have been—maybe big enough to include the pagan goddess, who cannot be separated in spirit from Mother Mary and Blessed Mary Magdalene of the Roman Catholic Church."

This was a heretical statement; it was apostasy, and yet it thrilled and exalted the hearts of the young people as it reverberated with the inner knowing of their hearts. A flame had been passed on to them, and it glowed, a vital fire within. Growing tired, Richard gestured to Colin to continue his train of thought.

"Four hundred years after Saint Augustine of Canterbury," Colin began, "Saint Benedict's Rule was brought to this monastery by Abbot Dunstan, a great man of God. As a student, Dunstan was educated by the Irish monks who came as pilgrims to Glastonbury to worship at the tomb of Saint Patrick. These Irish monks were men of wisdom, from whom Dunstan learned much of Celtic Christianity.

"In 934 Dunstan was ordained as a Benedictine monk by his uncle, the Bishop of Winchester, and nine years later Dunstan became Abbot of Glastonbury. He was a bonnie musician and composer, played the harp, was known to craft fine works in silver and gold. He had a brilliant intellect as well. Aye, it was Abbot Dunstan who gathered the many antiquarian texts and treatises, the *histoires*, tracts, and volumes that established our esoteric library, which we cherish today.

"Legend says that Dunstan was of the Company of Avalon. But it was Abbot Dunstan who began the draining of the waters to make farmland in the Somerset Levels. A dyke was built on the river Brue, and over the centuries, more dams and sea walls were made by the abbots and monks of Glastonbury, and the last vestiges of the lake around the Tor disappeared."

A pregnant silence fell upon them and Colin stood, stretched his back and walked the edge of the bower, pulling down a stem thick with pale pink roses and inhaling the fragrance of the blossoms.

"There have always been hardships in preserving the treasures of Glastonbury, to be sure," he mused. "A fire in 1184, and then, less than two hundred years ago, the monastery was damaged by a terrible earthquake that shook its foundations.

But we have always rebuilt the church on this holy site, and each time it came to a greater glory, infused with the power of its history and the sacred ground upon which it stands."

Seeing that the abbot had grown tired, John Thorne summed up. "Our abbey has grown and flourished, but always it has been the keeper of the ancient tradition—the threads that weave together the Old Powers of Avalon and the underground currents of Christendom with its Marion spirit. And now, the Abbot of Glastonbury is forced to send our relics away into exile. In truth, we have far too many precious relics and volumes to send them all to a safe harbor. Many will certainly perish in the dissolution that will inevitably come."

John's words sank deep into their hearts as his frankly iconoclastic philosophical side emerged in eloquent speech.

"Thomas Cranmer—archbishop of the new Church of England—and Chancellor Cromwell are Protestant zealots who wish to rid this world of not only the Roman Catholic Church, but any and all sparks of spiritual fire that might linger from ancient days to burn as embers in the hearts of the people! They seek to extinguish all flames of the soul that might ignite a revolutionary spirit—the spirit of truth.

"Cromwell and Cranmer's drive for reform is far-reaching and bespeaks a coming disaster of oppression. Surely, our Mother Church has faults and dark shadows, but the reformed church may prove to be even worse, which history will tell or not."

There were murmurs and nods of agreement among the companions, and a lull, steeped in both wonder and dread, crept in like the fog that enclosed the walls of Sharpham

Manor. They listened to the fire and the light patter of rain, each one pondering deeply until, bringing the gathering to a close, Richard spoke to his young guests.

"And so we begin with safeguarding the bones of the king and queen, and the volumes of our precious library. It has been a long day, and you have much to digest. And yet there is more—much more—to learn, which you will discover in the days ahead, when Roger arrives. Our sacristan will tell you about the other relics that you will remove and safeguard on Arrain. Now, let us part for a few hours before Angus calls us to table. Let us savor the fine supper he has labored over for us tonight."

John Thorne put down the vellum book held in his hands to pace the room restlessly. It was early afternoon, but already the aromas of supper, a work in progress plied by the capable hands of Father Angus, drifted in from the kitchen.

John reported with a dry intonation. "Yesterday I received word from Jack Horner that the king washed the feet of seven paupers on Royal Maundy before Easter, then gave out alms in silver coins to many more. A pious monarch, indeed."

The abbot nodded absently, watching the arrival of the two young couples and Geleis through the window. They had been out for a walk with William and now scurried down the worn footpath toward the front door of Sharpham Park Manor.

"The royals have fulfilled that sacred task for many centuries," Richard rejoined slowly, "to show their kinship with Lord Jesus, who washed the feet of his disciples on the holy Thursday before his crucifixion. It's good that King Henry observes such a tradition—who knows, perhaps he is changing for the better."

John scoffed. "Hmph! If I thought you really believed that I might be worried, but I know you are far from naïve, Richard."

The abbot moved away from the window. "There was a time, many decades ago, when I was naïve, but now, my idealism has been sorely tempered by the inexorable realities of experience."

Richard faced John, and the two men stood unmoving, looking at each other in wordless communication. The moment was interrupted by a series of knocks on hard wood. In three strides John opened the door to reveal Roger James. The slender sacristan was, as always, dressed in a clean black linen robe. Unlike the two elders, John Thorne and Abbot Whiting, Roger's hair was freshly shorn and tonsured, and he flashed a grim smile as he entered. Behind him walked Colin and Maddy, Anne, Ben, and Geleis.

"Ah! Here is Roger, along with our young accomplices," John observed as the young people arrived in the parlour. "'Tis a fine spring day! Let us go out through the conservatory door into the garden and walk together, while we still have the afternoon light. Father Angus will have ale and mulled wine, and then supper, awaiting us when we return."

The garden was ablaze with a colorful profusion of spring flowers, and as they strolled, passing under canopies of weeping willow, Maddy commented on the beauty of day. The afternoon air was filled with bird song and the drone of bees that zoomed past on pathways that intersected the lilting flight of butterflies. A peaceful quietude fell upon them as they walked amongst apple and pear trees, now laden with fruit that would ripen in the days ahead. Passing high banks of thorny blackberry canes, they reached a hidden glade where orchard and demense gave way to thick forest. There the monks had built a small stone pavilion with benches upon which they could sit and speak together. The idyllic scene belied the gravity of their mission, and they valiantly sought to bring faith to their sobriety, to lighten heavy hearts as they planned the task at hand.

Roger James began. "We will need to open the stone sarcophagus in the transept. It is heavy, hard work, and we will be helped by monks who are privy to our Company— Father Ambrose and Rowland, Simon, Jerome, and Isaac will be on vigil in the church, keeping watch to protect our work from prying eyes, while William and Angus help us move the bones from the shrine into the boxes you have prepared and into the wagon. Will we do the work after midnight, during the hours of the early morning when all are sleeping. The queen's bones are already encased in a smaller box of wood, and can be more easily moved that the king's, which are much larger and very heavy."

Colin slid his feet across the slick grass. "Based on the plan we devised here at Sharpham Manor after Christmastide, we have brought eight boxes, four for each wagon, well-crafted of strong cedarwood, so the relics do not draw the questions that a coffin in the back of our wagon would attract. We will cover the relics with bedding and household goods."

"An excellent idea," Roger agreed, "because the king's men will be patrolling the roads, especially when you reach the border of Scotland. They are known to stop and harass even innocent families traveling together, which is how you will appear."

Geleis had been listening thoughtfully. Now he injected, "We may need three cedar boxes to carry the king's bones alone, the queen's bones will take a fourth, that leaves four more boxes. What else will we be carrying?"

John responded. "In addition to the bones, we also have several other boxes of relics, which Roger will explain to you. Most certainly we will fill the two wagons, leaving little room for your personal effects."

With a quick glance toward his companions, Ben shrugged. "We have traveled as light as possible for exactly that reason."

At a signal from the abbot, Roger continued. "With the help of Angus and William, I have already gathered certain precious manuscripts, tracts, ancient volumes, that we will send with you. These must be kept dry, and we have wrapped them in heavy, well-oiled cloth and packed them with cedar and oils of lemon, clove and black fir, known to help preserve parchments, cloth, and vellum. The boxes themselves are also lined with oiled cloth—in fact we have taken every precaution, for these original books and texts are priceless and irreplaceable. The monks of our abbey have copied them, and these copies will remain at Glastonbury, but the originals will go with you."

Richard stirred, leaning forward. "These are exactly the relics that we believe the king most wants in his possession—first and foremost, the bones of King Arthur and his queen. There are other precious bone relics, but these we will have to leave at this time. We must assume that the king is not so eager to take the bones of Saint Dunstan and Saint Patrick, or Saint Indracht, whose remains lie in our crypts."

John postulated with a tone of conviction. "No, he does not stand to profit from the bones of those saints, as precious as they are to any person of faith. It is King Arthur he craves to bulwark the legitimacy of his new church in the eyes of pagan Britain, which runs deep in this land."

Taking a breath, he continued. "Did you know tis said that when Henry married Anne Boleyn, they dressed in as Arthur and Gwenivere? Hubris, to be sure, with a canny eye to the symbolic value that such a theatrical moment, played to great advantage, can have in swaying popular opinion and churning the emotions of the court and its public. But what do Cromwell and Cranmer want with the more secret relics? Do they want them to legitimize their new church?"

Ben leaned forward, his interest piqued. "What 'more secret relics' do you speak of?"

"We are coming exactly to that," John replied. Turning toward Richard, he posed another question. "How do you propose to engage your seneschal Jack Horner while we are accomplishing this arduous task in the middle of the night?"

"Tomorrow he leaves early on an urgent mission to London," the abbot responded with resignation. "He will attempt to deliver a message on my behalf to Thomas Cranmer and Commissioner Richard Layton. Because it is such an important task, I believe his avidity and avariciousness will be assuaged by this assignment. Certainly it is intended to soothe his mind and will of the grandiosity that plagues him so and drives him to dark deeds. He will travel with several monks, most of whom are not initiated into the secrets of Glastonbury, except for one of our most trusted senior monks, Father Ambrose, who will lead the expedition."

He explained further, turning toward Ben and Anne. "As you may know, Ambrose is my ecclesiastical benefice, who will be abbot after me, when I am gone."

John roused from his seat to interject. "Our scheme to preserve the relics and keep them out of the clutches of the king, Cranmer, and Cromwell has been passed by word of mouth, from ear to ear, one monk to another, amongst those sworn to the Company of Avalon—the holders of Glastonbury's hidden and not-so-hidden treasures."

Fully intrigued, Anne inquired, "Company of Avalon? You mentioned that last night. Will you tell us more of that?"

"We are coming to it," John replied. "The abbot has resolved that you should know all—or almost all—of Glastonbury's secrets." His face was enigmatic as he nodded to Roger to resume the lead.

"No one knows where the bones of our most revered saint, Joseph of Arimathea, may be. But we have more valuable relics, brought by Saint Joseph himself. Until last week these were safeguarded, disguised in small, hand-painted cases and kept under glass inlaid in the mosaic floor of the Lady Chapel, along with other relics. Now they are carefully packed in a wood casket, small enough that you and Maddy can carry it in your hands." He looked from Anne to her cousin. "It is locked, and I will give the key to you, Colin, on the morning when you depart, long before dawn."

Listening to his sacristan speak, Richard combed the snowy beard on his chin with slender fingers as Roger continued.

"It is this casket that contains the most precious of our treasures. One of them is a small Egyptian amphorae of blue glass embossed with gold. This was the vessel that contained the spikenard ointment Mary Magdalene used to anoint the feet of Jesus, when she declared him scion of the House of David, and therefore the rightful king of the Jews."

Roger paused, and not a word was spoken as they pondered the reality of what had been revealed. The afternoon light filtered through the stone columns and carved screens of the pavilion. Birds twittered in nearby branches, and the low limbs of the tall oaks swayed gently in the breeze.

The sacristan began again. "Along with the amphorae is another vessel—a shallow, round cup or chalice of gold carefully crafted with small handles of beaten gold, copper, and silver chased with a motif of three intertwining currents. Some have suggested this is the legendary grail, the cup from which Jesus drank at the Last Supper."

Geleis leaned forward with a question. "The description sounds Celtic. Can it be the legendary grail?" As Roger answered, his face became suffused with the light of a rare enthusiasm.

"The little chalice certainly is not a relic of Christendom. It is of Avalon. One cannot say that it is the cup from which Jesus drank, but it is a symbol of the ineffable grail that carries the secret of Ceridwen's cauldron, which is filled with a self-generating elixir of life.

"The stewardship of this golden chalice is a sacred obligation—as the Cymry of Arthur's time would say, a *geis*—that the monks of Ynis Witrin took on at the time of Avalon's dissolution. As the story goes, it is said that when Arthur died, he was brought to Avalon to be buried. Buried he was by a priestess known as Morgan le Fay, who was the last Lady of the Lake before Avalon disappeared from this earth.

"As Arthur's time ended, so within a generation did Avalon. Morgan le Fay and the priestesses dispersed, going into exile in unknown directions. Some of the people of Avalon merged with the Old Church of the Christians or blended with the villagers to live out their lives near the Tor.

"There is much that was lost during that era of great change. It was a harsh time, when the Saxons and Jutes and Angles returned with force, taking over Briton and eventually turning it into England. Later the Normans would come and invade our land, but Avalon was long gone by that time."

Roger stopped, stood and looked out at the sun that hovered low in the sky, while Richard addressed the unanswered questions that hovered between them.

"Many of us are the descendants of mixed races. We have Norman or German or Norse or Trojan ancestors, and perhaps we also carry the pure old Briton and Celtic bloodlines. Some of us even carry traces of the blood of the Old Ones, who created and preserved Avalon—the ancient race of humans who originally worshipped there upon the Tor, at the Red Spring, and its surroundings."

Richard paused, putting a blue-veined hand to his forehead.

"Uncle, you are tired." Maddy stood up. "We are eager to receive all that you have to tell us, but let us return to the manor so that you may rest. We can continue after supper. Yes?"

She held out a supplicating hand, which he took without complaint as he rose to his feet.

"No need to abstain, sir, now that Lent is well past!"

Father Angus chided the abbot, his tone affectionate as he heaped Richard's bowl with a thick stew of beef, carrots, and turnips. Candles flared brightly in the two candelabras on the table, causing the room dance with light and shadow augmented by the flames of wall sconces. The window was open, allowing the fine, sweet air of a late spring night to waft gently, lifting the linen drapes now and then. There were ten at the table, allied in their purpose and of good cheer as an excellent red wine was poured.

Father Angus set down the copper stewpot and carved thick slices from the loaf of hot bread. "'Tis fresh from my oven. Aye, and I have as well a lovely crock of whortleberry jam, made with honey by my mother and brought when she visited last from Ireland. I've saved it for a special occasion, and I deem this is it." He placed it gently before the abbot's plate, along with a bowl of fresh churned butter.

"Thank you, Angus," the abbot smiled. "You are kind, but you cosset me too much. A simple monk has few needs."

He looked around at the young people gathered at the table. "Here. I offer this *confiture* to you. Please, enjoy!"

Angus looked in supplication at John Thorne, who dropped his spoon into his bowl of stew and scolded.

"For God's sake, Richard. Will ye leave behind austerities for one minute? Will ye no enjoy a bite of jam and bread with yer stew?" The eruption of his heavy Scots brogue worked well to emphasize his point, along with the consternation on his face. Even Maddy had to cover her mouth with one hand to hide a smile.

Gazing in surprise at the loving faces that surrounded him, Richard put down his spoon with a sigh.

"Alright. If you insist. I suppose it's true these old bones have lost their taste for sweetness. A little honeyed whortleberry cannot do me any harm and most likely will do me good." He chuckled, to the relief of his companions.

They ate with gusto in silence for some time, foregoing ceremony to refill their bowls or pull hunks of bread from the loaves to slather on butter and jam. When they had finished and Angus and William had cleared away empty bowls and platters, Colin returned to the topic that consumed their thoughts.

"What is the news from London? I heard in Exeter that King Henry has had the Great English Bible printed last month and distributed to churches across the land. Now everyone who can read has no need of the priests and monks to tell the stories and teachings of Jesus and the saints. What do you think of this, Uncle John?"

John stirred on the bench where he sat. "Aye, well, tis based upon the work of William Tyndale, who was burned at the stake by Sir Thomas More on charges of heresy and treason. A strange turn of events, indeed, as at the stake tis reported that Tyndale said, 'Lord, open the King of England's eyes.' And now, three years later, his prayer has been answered. Tyndale's death was another tragedy, in our opinion, but we are known to be liberal in our leanings here at Glastonbury."

Geleis inquired, "What is your view on the English Bible, Abbot Whiting?"

"Well, I have never objected to religious reform, which is why I signed the Act of Supremacy five years ago, declaring King Henry the supreme head of the new Church of England. I believe every man has the right to worship as his heart is moved to worship. But I do object to the means by which this reform has been forced upon the people—the murder and mayhem perpetrated by the king and his men. In fact I abhor the burning of heretics, as would any true man of God, in my view. And, be assured that, despite all we have discussed, I remain a faithful servant of the Church in Rome. I suppose I am a hopeless idealist who still believes that the Roman Catholic faith can exist side by side with a reform faith."

Coughing, Richard pushed his chair away from the table, pulled a handkerchief from his pocket and wiped his mouth. Noticing that the air had grown chill, William withdrew for a moment, returning with a wool shawl that he placed gently around the abbot's thin shoulders. Roger James stood and moved to the open window, drawing the drape across to impede the breeze but allow an influx of fresh air.

"Tis said by many that Parliament will pass King Henry's Six Articles very soon, probably next month," Roger relayed. "These are the king's way of assuring that the established doctrines of the Roman Catholic Church remain the basis of faith in the Church of England, including celibacy for monks and clergy, but it is most interesting that this will force Cranmer to send his own wife away, if he wants to continue as Archbishop of Canterbury."

Murmurs of agreement and surprise echoed around the table as Maddy asked, "Uncle, are you strong enough to tell us more about Blessed Mary's amphorae, and about the chalice, which you said is not of Christendom?"

Pulling the wool shawl closer around his shoulders, Richard's face was impassive. One gnarled, long-fingered hand drifted up to caress the golden filigree cross that hung around his neck and rested upon his breast.

"As you well know, Maddy, what we are telling you is considered heresy by our Holy Father in Rome." Turning to the other young woman, he said, "Anne, now we will answer your question from this afternoon, and you five must swear to keep faith with the secrets, which we, as the Company of Avalon, entrust to you. There have always been a number of the laity amongst our company, who knew and followed the inner faith of Glastonbury. You will be the new guardians of that secret faith. I will begin, then Roger will tell you the rest."

Colin chuckled. "Yes, we have begun to speak of ourselves as the Secret Keepers."

"Certainly apropos," Richard agreed, returning the smile. "Now, as to the amphorae and the chalice and the other relics—the two vials brought by Joseph of Arimathea. In fact we cannot prove how these sacred objects came into our possession, and yet the tradition, passed *viva voce*, with the living voice, from one initiate to another, carries the ring of truth: that Joseph truly did bring the amphorae with him, along with the two vials or cruets, fifteen-hundred years ago when he sailed up the coastline of Briton to the Severn Sea to make his way to Ynis Witrin.

"As far as memory reaches, these two vials were protected and preserved by the monks of the Church of Our Lady Blessed Mary of Glastonbury. But as to Blessed Mary's amphorae and the chalice, the symbolic holy grail, not all of the monks of Glastonbury's great church have been privy to its inner secret these many centuries. Only to those who were ripe or receptive have had the words spoken. Roger, would you explain?"

Roger's black robes rustled as he moved about the table to stand near the window. Pulling back the shade, he looked out into the warm spring night, then at William, who stood wordlessly and walked to the front door.

Richard watched as William walked outside. "He will return straightaway, and then we may continue." When the younger monk had returned and taken his seat, Roger began.

"The abbots of Glastonbury have had good reason to keep the amphorae and the grail vessel in secret. First of all, there is the danger of theft, coming from many potential quarters. The cathedral at Wells, as one example, has always been jealous of the sanctity of our Lady's Church at Glastonbury. There are others—both secret societies and wealthy noblemen—who would steal such treasures, which would bring a fortune from many who seek to possess sacred and arcane artifacts.

"But more dangerous is the hidden wisdom that these objects represent. As you have learned, from its earliest inception, Glastonbury Abbey has been dedicated to Mary Magdalene, though many who worship here consider Mary, the Mother of Jesus, to be our patron saint. For those entrusted with the deeper mystery, it is understood that when Joseph of Arimathea came to settle in Briton, he and his companions brought with them a personal and intimate knowledge of the inner circle of disciples around our Lord Jesus. They knew, as all the Apostles did, of the true relationship between Jesus and Mary of Magdala."

Roger paused, straightened his shoulders and drew a deep breath before he continued.

"In fact, for some people Mary Magdalene represents the feminine pole of the Christos, or Christ principle. After the crucifixion, there was a terrible jealousy among the disciples. There were those who wanted no part of a woman leader among them, and perhaps especially one whom their master loved above all others, who he turned to as an equal, and kissed upon the mouth in their presence."

Maddy coughed lightly then intercepted his narrative. "Before my novitiate in Bruges, I learned these secrets from Uncle Richard. Since my return, I have spoken of this with Colin, who was initiated by you, Uncle John. But this was not strange to me or to Anne. As girls, we wondered and speculated, when we read the gospels. It always seemed that there was more to the story of Mary Magdalene than we were told—it seemed natural, as if this truth was intuitively evident and could be read between the lines, so to speak. But of course the truth was suppressed."

Roger picked up the thread of Maddy's thoughts. "Yes, the truth was suppressed for many reasons. As we know, Saint Peter was the disciple who established the church in Rome, and according to legend, he was not enamored of the wife of Jesus. Others of the disciples, such as Philip and Thomas, were close to her. There are many legends and a powerful oral tradition that endures to this day that tells a different story than that of the Apostle Peter.

"As the Apostle John tells us in the gospel, Joseph of Arimathea was a man of power, a successful merchant who had traveled across the seas of the ancient world, coming as far north as Briton, where he bought tin to trade in the Mediterranean. Legend tells that Joseph was the uncle of Mary, mother of Jesus—blood kin to the master himself—and that he had lived in exile in Egypt with the family of Jesus those twelve years after Herod ordered the male babies to be killed at the time of Jesus' birth.

"During those years of exile, Joseph brought his great-nephew, Jesus, on a trip to the isle of Briton, on the business of trading for tin. It was only natural that he was drawn back here after the Lord's crucifixion. At that time, Joseph was a member of the Sanhedrin—the political group that feared the power that would be unleashed if Jesus fulfilled ancient prophecy as a direct descendant of King David. Such a kingship would have focused both spiritual and political power in Jesus, taking the same away from the Sanhedrin.

"Naturally, the household of Joseph of Arimathea was close to Mary Magdalene, and it was to Joseph that the wife of Jesus went, begging for him to ask Pontius Pilate for the body of her husband. Joseph was allowed to take the body, which he did with Nicodemus, and they placed the Lord in the burial place that had been prepared for Joseph himself. Three days later, walking through the garden toward the tomb, it was Mary Magdalene to whom Jesus appeared first in his transfigured form. Even the most unschooled among us must wonder—why did Jesus appear first to Mary Magdalene? And why, when she attempted to tell them, did the disciples of Jesus doubt her word?

"After the ascension of Jesus into heaven, there was a time of great confusion and desolation. Even as the disciples were exalted by the Resurrection and transfiguration of Jesus—the actual proof of their master's divinity—they were lost for a time after he departed and they saw him no more. Finally, as he had instructed, they gathered their courage to disperse in many directions, where they would continue his work of teaching and healing.

"With enemies in many quarters, both within the Sanhedrin and within the disciples themselves, it was not safe for Mary Magdalene to remain in Judea, and she left with her child, making her way by boat with Joseph of Arimathea, the Apostle Philip, and some kinswomen to the shores of southern France, known then as Gaul. Traveling inland across estuary and salt marshes, they made their way into the mountains.

"It was there that Mary lived out the rest of her days in exile. She lived for many years in a cave high in a mountain escarpment, mostly in contemplation and solitude. It is said that during these years her soul joined completely with the Christos, and she began to minister to the people of the region. Many miracles were attributed to her. To this day there are churches in the south of France that harbor the legends of Mary Magdalene—as well as John the Baptist, who some say was the teacher of Jesus and Mary. There, in the south of France, her relics are cherished and she is worshipped in hidden shrines.

"The child of Jesus and Mary, who was called Sarah, carried in her veins the precious blood of the House of David, from which the King of the Jews would be born. Because of this, the child was also a refugee. Her life was in danger from political intrigue and the machinations of those who wielded power. She was sequestered away, protected by Joseph of Arimathea and others, like the Merovingian family, who were kings in the region of Languedoc in the south of France.

"Joseph of Arimathea joined with the apostle Philip, who bore the honor of being the only disciple that Jesus sought out, saying to him in Galilee, 'Follow me.' Philip was always unconventional and kept apart in some way from the others. It was Philip who encouraged Joseph of Arimathea to take a group to the place Joseph had known an dloved in his merchant travels of many years before—the wild shores of the place called Briton. Who knows? Perhaps Philip and Joseph already knew something of the holy place that existed at the Tor, on the Glass Isle.

"Some say that Sarah came with Joseph to seek a safe harbor in Briton, far from Judea and the turmoil that seethed in the wake of the crucifixion of Jesus. There are tales in the highlands of Scotland that Mary Magdalene came there, and legends of a son born to Mary and Jesus, named Martin—the brother of Sarah.

"At any rate, Joseph and his party of disciples established a Christian community at the foot of the Tor, where they built a small wattle and stone church. Joseph passed on the true story of Jesus and Mary Magdalene, and his little church was consecrated to Blessed Mary, the Lady of Light. Over generations, as time passed, most people found safety in the belief that the church was consecrated to Mary the Mother of Jesus.

"As the years passed and the Holy See gained power and authority, the gospels of Matthew, Mark, Luke and John were established as the authority and Word of God, the exoteric facade of Glastonbury Abbey was established and Our Lady Mary, the Mother of God, became the worshipped saint. In truth, in the esoteric underpinnings of our faith, it has always been Mary Magdalene who was worshipped by the Company of Avalon among us."

When Roger stopped speaking, the gravity of Glastonbury's secret descended upon them like a caul, somehow light and heavy at the same time. John stood and moved toward the sideboard, where he poured a cup of spirits for himself. Turning back with raised brows, he looked around at the others and poured cups that were passed around. The silence was companionable yet teeming with life and energy, and their thoughts ran helter skelter through the complex labyrinth of all they had learned during the past two days.

Raising his cup, John proposed a toast. "May this spirit succor our hearts and give us good rest." Tasting with a small sip, he then continued.

"The amphorae is a remnant of the living truth of Mary Magdalene. The chalice invokes the powers of ancient Avalon. The two artifacts together affirm and embody the shared knowledge, when the monks lived in harmony with the residents of Avalon and shared a love of Mary Magdalene and Ceridwen, Goddess of the chalice.

"After Arthur's death, when the priestesses and the Lady of the Lake went into exile and Avalon disappeared into the mists, their knowledge and wisdom passed underground as a river will sometimes do—much like the truth about Mary Magdalene went underground. The abbots and monks of the Old Church took on the obligation to protect and preserve the truth, along with the chalice, which was buried deep within Avalon's sacred red spring. The spring was considered the gateway to Annwyn and the Otherworld of the ancient Celts—it was at one time the most sacred place upon Avalon. Even today the underground rivers of the hidden faith erupt in the holy springs of Avalon."

Visibly tiring, Richard roused himself with a last word. "It grows late, and I must retire. In the morning we may speak again. But now, let us say goodnight. William and Angus, perhaps you will stay with our friends and answer their questions about the two sacred springs—one red and one white—that are so important to Avalon and to the abbey."

John and Roger assisted Richard, and together they mounted the stairs to the upper chambers of the manor while the five youngest conspirators looked at each other in awe. William was the first to speak.

"Surely you must have some questions. Even with this fine whiskey, it may be hard to sleep this night, with such exalted and deep legends and apocrypha flying about."

Ben was the first to speak. "Of course, the sacred springs of Glastonbury are well-known to many. These have been spoken of many times in the classrooms of Cambridge and Oxford, where students are eager to study the old mythologies of Briton. Would you speak of these?"

"With joy," William replied, a grin transforming his features. "There are two holy springs that have ushered from the Tor since the misty reaches of time—the waters of one is red and the waters of the other is white. The Red Spring has been called "the Blood Spring" from ancient times, because it is said that it has three qualities in common with blood: the waters are red, they are warm, and they coagulate like blood. The waters are so warm that even roses will bloom near the spring in winter, and at Christmas the Holy Thorn of Joseph blossoms nearby.

"Some say that the waters are red because the druids made blood sacrifices there—their sacrificial victims were drowned in a small chamber of massive stone that surrounds the spring, making a well. But this is not what has been passed down among the Company of Avalon. No, this water is red because it is like a fertile woman, Mary Magdalene, who bleeds and bears the child of Jesus. It is red like wine, the holy bloodline of Jesus, son of the House of King David. It has a red hue because it is full of passion and creation, like the cauldron of Ceridwen. It is red like the cloak worn by

Mary Magdalene as she has been imagined by artists across the years."

Angus stirred from his place beside the fire. "The White Spring flows not so far away from the Red Spring. It is white due to a mineral. Its pure waters are sweet and cool. Its pagan goddess is Brighid, but for me it symbolizes the transfiguration of Jesus after the Resurrection—the transparent purity of the Christ. Both springs are gateways to the spiritual worlds. Both springs issue forth from deep within the Tor, their waters flowing unimpeded and bounteous. In truth, I have spent many hours in prayer and contemplation at their waters.

"The White Spring is found down a footpath through a comb filled with overarching trees, mosses of all kinds that glow in many shades of green, from emerald to forest. It is easy to imagine the faeries at play there upon leaf and verdure and bracken, shining within the drops and the little hidden mounds and the crystalline depths of the lime pools were the waters collect. "

Anne's face was bright and animated as she listened. Turning to Maddy, she begged, "Will we have time to go to the springs? I must see them before we leave."

It was Colin who responded. "There is plenty of time in the days ahead to visit the springs. Our work must be accomplished at clandestine times when there are no supplicants or pilgrims about the church."

As he spoke, his grin was wry and humorous, and in that moment he reminded them of John Thorne. "As Abba said," Colin continued, this time more seriously, "we will work after midnight. But, there should be ample time, after we return from Sharpham Park to the abbey, to explore the springs. Maddy can take you there."

He smiled at his wife, who sat beside him, and squeezed her hand. "She has been there many times."

CHAPTER EIGHT

Glastonbury
July 1539

"All of England is suffering the avarice of King Henry," John Thorne protested, shaking his head in recrimination as he bent over the books he had brought upstairs to the abbot's chambers two hours earlier. Along with Roger James, he had been with the abbot all morning, reviewing the financial records and current needs of the abbey, severely affected by financial pressures due to rising inflation and Cromwell's constant demands on the abbeys. Frustrated that the quality of food served to the monks and pilgrims, and given as alms to the poor, had gone down, John's temper flared as he groused.

"Last year before Christmas we were serving pea soup, fish and fritters, beef and lamb stew and loaves with cinnamon and raisins. This summer we cannot replenish our stores of spice. We have only a weak vegetable soup with a few shreds of meat and plain oat bread for the pilgrims who stay in our guest house. Alms for the poor are more scant."

Roger commiserated with the abbey bursar. "The expense to replace broken glass in the chapel windows was high enough," he added. "Then there is the mending and laundering of the monks' robes and vestments, the provisions needed to prepare the sacramental bread. I have an order for eleven hundred pounds of wax for candlemaking, and several hogsheads of wine and oil. Some of the water conduits need repair and new paving stones are required in the Lady Chapel."

"The still master has asked for more money to produce the cordials and liqueurs we use in the hospital, which has numerous other needs as well." John put down the sheaf of papers he studied with a frown. "Christmastide will come soon enough, and the abbey is beholden to provide gifts for so many—especially the students we support at Oxford and Cambridge, who must receive gifts from the Abbot of Glastonbury."

"Yes, and well they should," Richard asserted, "to encourage their scholarship. But please, do not give the usual gift to me. I know, I know—the abbot usually receives a whole pig at Christmastide, but I ask you to overlook that tradition, at least for this year."

Roger acquiesced with a slight bow and a meaningful glance at John. The morning had passed, and a light lunch had been served to the three, which went largely untouched by the abbot. Outside, the early afternoon sun shone upon summer greensward and garden, but inside a pall of heartbreak hovered in the air as Roger continued.

"Even here at Glastonbury, which is arguably the richest religious house in the west country, we suffer from the king's greed, augmented by Cromwell's cravings. How much more will you be forced to give him? He is blackmailing you, Richard."

The abbot's response was pensive, but his demeanor remained markedly calm.

"Yes. He is. He has been for the past four years. In fact, a few days ago I received a letter from Jack Horner and Father Ambrose, sent from London, that Cromwell has his eyes fixed on Reading, Colchester, and Glastonbury—he intends to have the wealth of the abbeys of the western lands and now suggests that our 'overflowing coffers' should flux in his direction."

Richard glanced at the younger man. "Send him our finest altar plate, will you Roger? The new one, the large platter of silver and gold inset with sapphires. Tell him it is called, 'The Sapphire of Glastonbury.' Maybe he will think it's one of our ancient treasures he so craves. Perhaps that will stave him off for a time."

Roger's usually sanguine face was set in a deep scowl. He leaned back in his chair and listened as John gave vent to his fury.

"It was not enough that you gave Cromwell one gift after another for himself and his friends, with the threat that if you refused his demands it would only hasten disso-lution. Four years ago, you ceded Cromwell the advowson of Monkton Church in Somerset. My records show that on September 9, 1535, you gave him Sir Thomas More's corrody, along with 10 £ for unpaid debts, and at another time you sent the rents from your farm at Northwode Park as well as the mastership of game within the park, and the advowson of yet another church."

Richard leaned an elbow on the table to rest his temple against one palm and closed his eyes. The room swarmed with sunlight that glistened on the abbot's white hair, recently trimmed by Father William. John did not miss the fact that his friend was in pain, but the knowledge of it only fueled his outrage.

"Cromwell has harassed you ceaselessly with more and more demands and restrictions and rules, threatening dissolution with one hand then assuring you it will not happen with the other. The man is insane with power." John's voice was low and grave as he stood to prowl across the room then resume his seat at the table.

"He is evil. And the King of England rides in his pocket! Cromwell's henchmen deny the rumours of an impending dissolution here. Cromwell himself reassured you last year that Glastonbury would not be dissolved. They have been unable to prove any wrongdoing against us. But Cromwell cannot be trusted, and we know that he fully intends to move against us. Thank God the relics will soon be gone and hidden in a safe place."

Richard opened his eyes and shifted in his chair, moving to brush a string of lint from his black robe. "Yes, at the strike of two on the coming morn, they will open the stone altar and remove the bones in the transept. They will be gone long before sunrise. In fact, we must finish our business here, as Maddy is coming soon. I have asked her to visit me—today is the last time I will see her in this life."

His eyes, kindly and penetrating, fell upon John and lingered, taking in the woe that marked the lines on his friend's face.

"Go easy, John Thorne, for these young people will grieve our passing. Do not let your war with the king and Cromwell and all the evil in this world make it harder for them or for us."

He held out a hand in supplication, his face softly grieved.

"It is our cross to bear, John, that we are given this bitter cup to drink, and in it—nay, through it—we surrender to God's will. We do not know why it is God's will, only that it is. Acceptance, surrender...this is the only way to find peace in such madness, my friend."

John closed the books and reached over to take the proffered hand. "I bow to your wisdom, Richard. You call me to the high road of faith and compassion. That is why you are my abbot."

"Well said, indeed," Roger interjected with a grim smile, rising from his seat. "And on that faithful instruction, in which we renew our commitment to our highest purpose, it is time to take my leave. With your permission, Abba."

"Let us not hasten the end but play out our roles as best we can to the last moments of our last days." Richard raised a hand in blessing to the sacristan and bursar of Glastonbury, who bowed their heads then walked out together, closing the door softly behind them.

The abbot sat back in his chair, watching dust motes swim in a swath of sun that spanned from window to floor. Reaching for his rosary, he took the amethyst beads, worn smooth by prayer, in his fingers as he reflected upon the time that would come soon enough.

As he pondered his coming fate, it seemed to him that death kept watch from the corners of the room, where the heavy oak wainscoting of the walls, carved in ornate patterns of acorns and leaves, made a statement of gloomy beauty. How would he greet death? With dignity and equanimity? With regret, fear, or terror?

No, he did not fear death. He welcomed the release of death, embraced death with a strange inner joy. Nor did he regret. Deep within his heart, he had worked the fertile ground of acceptance and surrender these past years. Strengthened by the power of a stalwart faith, he knew that his path was clear.

Martyrdom called to him, a beacon that sparkled in the dawn of a distant horizon. Between him and that beacon stretched a chasm of darkness and certain pain, and yet, he would not relent and give Glastonbury to Cromwell and the king. Such an act would condone all the evil they had wrought in their war for riches, treasure, property, wealth and absolute power.

Years back in the fight for religious supremacy, Richard Whiting had compromised and bargained; for the sake of his monks and the abbey, he and his monks had signed the papers giving spiritual authority to Henry. Now, that time was over. No more bargaining, no more compromise. He would not go down in God's great book of the spirit, nor in the annals of history, as a traitor to his own conscience, a deserter to his own heart. They could not hurt him enough to make him an accomplice to their darkness.

The abbot sat in the crucible of his contemplation for over an hour, and when a knock came at the door, the sunbeam had moved, falling further across the floor, its radiance mellowed by the progress of late afternoon.

"Come in," he called. The door opened and Maddy walked in, her face pale, its beauty marred by a flurry of emotions. She moved quickly to his side and knelt at his knee, taking one pale hand, fragile and webbed with thin blue veins, into her own firm hand that pulsed warm and sure with life.

"Uncle," she whispered, her voice choked with sorrow.

"There, there," he patted her hand. "Do not cry for me—though I know you will, Maddy. Please, take a seat and let us talk together awhile. I thank you for coming."

They sat for a few moments, watching the ray of light grow dim as the sun sank deeper into the west. Outside the windows the distant Tor collected purple shadows, and Maddy gazed at it, falling into a reverie.

"Do you think that our lives, in some way, are parallel to theirs? The king and queen and her champion, I mean."

The abbot pursed his lips. "I know well what you mean, Maddy. Yes, I do sense that our lives are intertwined, connected in some mysterious way. Hearing the tales from Arrain, how Margaret's Welsh grandmother recounted a story of Gwenivere and Lancelot coming to Scotland—this is most amazing, and yet it does not truly surprise me."

A tear slid down Maddy's cheek. She did not move to wipe it away but sat still, her chest rising and falling with her breath, hands resting in her lap, eyes vigilant upon the Tor. After some moments, despite her attempt at composure, she burst out a great dry sob.

"How will I live without you, Abba? You have been my spiritual strength, my guide and refuge, all my life! It is you who led my heart to the love of Blessed Mary..." Her voice cracked on the last words and her shoulders began to shake with sobs.

"Maddy," Richard whispered, and though his voice trembled at first, the timbre of his words grew in strength with his resolve. "Blessed Mary will give you the strength to live without me, and very well indeed. I insist upon it!" His blue eyes crinkled slightly at their edges, compelled by an inner joy that passed across his face as a fleeting smile.

"I have grown old over these years. I have reached the venerable age of eighty this past year. By God's Grace, my life has been rich beyond measure, a panorama of wealth both outward and inward. It is simple, in one way—my time has come.

"My dear, let me speak bluntly, as you are not a girl anymore but a women grown and married. Listen to me now. You are strong and you will accept what has to come." His voice was calm, yet it carried a serious gravity as he squeezed her hand with gentle pressure. She fastened her eyes upon the abbot.

"The king's men will come, probably Layton again, with others. They will accuse me of treason, of hording treasures and wealth, of lying and maybe worse. They will find a way to declare me guilty, and they will kill me. Most probably, I will be hung, as we have seen them do with other 'heretics' against the king. They will probably hack my body into quarters to make their point."

A freshet of tears rolled down Maddy's cheeks, but she did not sob or cry out again but listened, helpless in the throes of their ordeal.

"John has trusted sources who say Commissioner Layton will come in the fall. I expect him in September..."

Maddy's words rushed out, colliding with his train of thought. "I will come back from Scotland, after the relics are hidden. Colin and I can make it back by September, to stand beside you. We want to go through this with you, to know that you have loved ones at your side..."

Reaching out a hand, he gave a firm gentle shake to her shoulder. "No. Absolutely not, I will not have you witness to this debacle. It will cause me more pain to know that you suffer this atrocity by watching the gruesome event. It is harsh enough that you suffer it with me as you do, knowing that you must bear it over the years to come."

He sighed. "Believe me, my dear. It is better for me this way. I will ask the same of your father and mother, blessed be James and Elizabeth Whiting, and the rest of our family. John and Roger will be at my side to bear witness, with Ambrose, Rowland, William and Angus and the monks of Glastonbury. And besides, if you attend my death, you will draw attention to yourself. You may become suspected by Layton and Cromwell's men.

"I command you, if I must, to go to Arrain and stay there until this has passed. I will instruct Angus and William to keep you appraised of all that passes here. They will send letters, and let you know when it is safe to return to Glastonbury. Ambrose will keep order here after I am gone. He will help my monks when the dissolution comes—and it is coming, Maddy. Although I still pray the abbey will go on, somehow, in some way, we must prepare ourselves for the worst."

"I cannot bear the thought," she protested, "of the horrible things that may happen to you, even as you describe them with such acceptance!"

"Maddy, I ask you again not to cry overmuch for me. I am prepared to leave this world. Cromwell, the king, their minions, cannot take what is most precious from me. They can end my life, but they cannot have my heart and soul. And though my body is weak, my spirit is strong. Know that, when the final hour comes, all the great saints who have sustained my life will be with me. Deep inside, I will be with Mother Mary, the star of the sea, and with Blessed Mary, the woman clothed with the sun."

Maddy absorbed the truth behind his words with a great sigh that heaved her chest.

"At one time I thought this madness would pass, but now I see that the reformation is here to stay. This is the coming future—the new Church of England will endure, just as Martin Luther will be victorious in Germany. King Henry will take this great cathedral and transform it according to his will. This is the truth we must face. I am grateful beyond words that you and Colin, and Geleis, Ben, and Anne, are taking the treasures away, until they find their proper home, someday, somewhere. Maybe even here, at Glastonbury Abbey."

He paused to inhale a deep breath. "But there is one more thing, Maddy. You may need to move the artifacts again. John will speak of this also with Colin. When Cromwell and King Henry realize that there are no bones in Arthur's crypt, they will be enraged, and their search may lead them to you, as our kinsmen.

"Tomorrow John will give Colin a bag of gold—enough to help you with all that you will need to accomplish the safeguarding of the relics, including to establish yourselves somewhere in the mainland of Scotland—or even abroad, in France, if necessary."

She nodded in solemn acceptance. As he took her hand again and raised her up to enfold her in a tender embrace, she laid her head upon his shoulder for a moment.

"You are my true child of the spirit, you and Colin," he whispered. "Remember, in the midst of grief and loss, there is always a way to praise and give thanks to God. And now, let us join the others in good cheer." They pulled apart and walked hand in hand to the door.

"We will dine in the kitchen refectory with all the monks tonight and the visiting pilgrims. I will say goodnight and goodbye to you all after supper and retire to my quarters. The best way to draw no attention to our task is to be perfectly ordinary.

"Tomorrow, you will be gone, and I will return to Sharpham Manor with John, Roger, and our usual companions, dear Angus and William. I ask you to pray for me, as I will pray for you."

A thin surly mist seeped across the land, hanging low to the ground in the warm velvet night as the conspirators moved through the darkness. The massive stone walls of the cathedral reared up before them as they approached the door, grateful that all was quiet and trusting in the knowledge that the Company of Avalon amongst the monks would keep vigil in the chapels and the great church until sunrise. The tower bell rang two times as Roger James, Angus and William stood before the black marble shrine, thick candles burning brightly in their hands, Colin, Geleis, and Ben looking on. Angus had cleaned the shrine that day, which he did every Thursday, removing the flowers and offerings that lavished the smooth length of the black marble sarcophagus that shone now in the glow of their candle flames.

It took the better part of ten minutes for the six strong men to slowly and carefully slide the black marble lid away and balance its heavy weight between the stone floor and one end of the sarcophagus. The men huddled over the lip of the shrine to peer into the depths of the dismantled shrine. In the flickering light a heavy wooden casket gleamed dim within the massive sarcophagus. On its top was a metal plate inscribed in Latin. "Here lies King Arthur and his queen on the Isle of Avalon."

At the sight of the epithet, a jolt of power pierced their hearts, and they gaped upon the coffin in wonder. Breaking the silence with a sweep of his hand over the hard oak surface, William whispered in awe.

"This is the original oaken coffin, interred in this shrine by the blessed hands of King Edward I and his Queen, Eleanor of Castile, in 1278."

There was no time to linger over the power of the relics, or to take in the otherworldly reverberations of their task. The reality of the work at hand catapulted them into action. Angus and William leaned into the sarcophagus to levy the lid open using a long iron crowbar, but it did not budge. For five minutes the men struggled to open the coffin from the top of the sarcophagus, still the lid remained in place.

William muttered, wiping sweat from his forehead. "We thought this might be impossible from above—this coffin was hoisted down into the shrine using pulleys, block and tackle, but we cannot do that now. We would need a team of men and hours that we don't have, not to mention the attention it would draw. It was worth a try, but fortunately we have an alternative plan."

Going swiftly to one end of the shrine, Angus and William worked with hammers and chisels to loosen the stone plate from its place. Anticipating the need to remove the coffin from its marble mausoleum, they had accomplished much of the work of prying away the old mortar on late nights and predawn mornings over the past month. Now the end plate came away easily, and the able hands of Geleis and Ben assisted in lifting it away.

"Alright, let's get the coffin out—we have to work fast now," Angus urged.

Roger James kept watch at the transept door while three men worked from above with long iron bars to levy and slowly inch the coffin toward the open end where Geleis and Ben waited to get a grip and pull. The powerful aromas of crumbling stone, musty grime, dust, decomposing flowers and greenery filled their senses. Underneath that redolence was a distant but potent smell that could only be the slow decay of ancient bones.

While the men worked feverishly, Maddy and Anne loaded their bags into one of the two wagons, which Rowland and Jerome had brought around to the guest house at the front gate on Magdalene Street. These were already packed with boxes of relics marked "kitchen goods" and "pots and pans" and "linens"—the effects of two couples moving their household goods. The horses waited quietly in their harnesses, as if they understood the need for concealment.

Maddy patted the soft pelt and nose of one of the huge beasts. She spoke quietly to Anne, who stood at her side. "I will take a moment at the Lady Chapel."

Anne looked at her inquisitively.

"No, I wish to go alone." Maddy answered the question in Anne's eyes before it could take form on her lips. "I will meet you here at the wagons in less than a half hour. The men will not be finished until after three bells have rung."

"Alright," Anne replied with some reluctance, "but I urge you to hurry, cousin."

Maddy squeezed her cousin's hand in reassurance. "Don't worry. I will not be late."

Hurrying toward the Lady Chapel, she glanced up at her uncle's chamber in the abbot's lodge and saw a light burning there. She could discern the shape of her uncle, standing at the window watching over the cathedral, the kitchens and gardens and grounds. She knew that his heart was with the men who struggled to move the heavy coffin in the transept, and with the loaded wagons that waited in front of the guest house at the abbey gate.

Holding up her long skirts, Maddy padded across paving stones toward the Lady Chapel. She had already made her prayers at King Arthur's shrine the day before, and she thought of it now, dismantled and in the midst of a transition that would change life as she had known it.

Walking in the hushed atmosphere of the Lady Chapel, she saw that two of the Company of Avalon, an older monk named Simon, whom she had known from childhood, held a vigil there with Rowland. Candles burned upon the shrine of Blessed Mary, and while Simon was deep in prayer, kneeling on the stone floor near the altar with hands clasped on his lap, Rowland greeted her at the door with a nod of his head. His smile was warm but his eyes were wary and alert.

She moved into the chapel, relishing once again the sculpted beauty of the sanctuary—the quaint figures of saints rendered into stone, the decorative interlacing of chevrons and floral designs depicting five-petaled roses, lilies, and oak leaves with acorns, thistle and ivy. She traced the patterns with one hand, letting images and memories of all the years of her young life flow through her. Though she hoped and prayed that this chapel, which many vowed was the most beautiful religious shrine in Somerset, if not the entirety of England, would survive the dissolution, the dread in her heart was unassuaged.

She glanced at the entrance to the crypt, where so many saints and monks were buried, but moved on with determination toward the shrine of Blessed Mary. Looking up at the painting of Mary holding the baby Jesus, with Mary Madgalene watching in the distance, she gazed in solemn contemplation for some moments, then she knelt at the foot of the shrine and crossed herself, her eyes fastened upon the sculpture of Blessed Mary, beloved of Jesus.

Her lips moved in silent supplication as she whispered, "Lady of Light, by Thy powerful intercession, together with Mary, Mother of God, and by the power of Saint Joseph of Arimathea, and of all the saints who have graced this Holy Church, open the way for the journey upon which we embark today. May our labors be fitting service in the name of Jesus Christ. Amen."

Cold stones dug into the bones of her knees as Maddy crossed herself again and rose to her feet, satisfied that she had been heard. Without a backward glance, she hurried out the door and moved through the warm misty night toward the wagons that waited on Magdalene Street at the front gate of the abbey.

Intense effort mingled with fear broke out in grimy beads of sweat on their foreheads as the men struggled to free the coffin from its stone confines. Straining every muscle in their backs and arms, they wrestled and shoved the coffin slowly over the gritty floor of the marble sarcophagus and out through the open end until, finally, held by Geleis and Ben, it landed with a muffled thud upon the stone floor.

"Quickly, let us open it," Colin urged as they set about the lid, which, to their surprise, was hinged on one side. Plying careful strength to chisels and crowbars on the other side, the lid yielded slowly with a loud creak of rusted iron hinges, as if the royal bones themselves protested this intrusion into their solitude. Puffs of fine dirt and decay rose in the air, sparkling in the candlelight. Inside the skeletal remains, bones and a skull, lay in thick dust and a pall of decayed linen, while on one end a small casket inscribed, "The Queen," was nestled into the corners of the coffin.

Poised for a timeless moment, their breath was the only

sound in the wide stone chamber that surrounded the high altar where the sarcophagus brooded, a megalithic barge of memories, prayers, hope and glory long past. The receptors of their senses, already piqued, sharpened as their awareness swelled to encompass church and abbey grounds, expanded across the humid summer night, moved past Glastonbury and on to the Tor that seemed to burn in the recesses of the night with hidden flames of gold and cerulean.

Lurching into action, their work was feverish. In one way, their concentration was so great that time seemed to stop, while they were simultaneously aware of the urgent need for haste, as if they could feel the earth turning on her axis, bringing the light of day closer and closer.

Angus and William first lifted out the box with the bones of the queen, which was handed to Geleis and Ben who carried the box directly to the waiting wagons. Turning back to the most vital part of their job still left to be done, Angus and William gingerly moved one bone at a time, handling each one with reverence as it was passed to Colin or Roger, who gently placed them in two cedar boxes, padded with raw wool and lined with linen.

Cold but dry and powdery, they removed ribs, long heavy thigh bones, backbones, foot and finger bones, collarbone and pelvis, and finally, the skull—the man had been huge, indeed. Roger crossed himself as he received the skull from Angus and placed it, carefully packing it with wads of wool to insure it would not break in the friction of rubbing against the other bones as they made their way along rough roads toward Scotland. The others followed the gesture, genuflecting and muttering prayers.

The wooden lid fit perfectly as William hammered it shut. Geleis and Ben had returned from the wagon, and with Colin and Roger, they lifted the two boxes.

"They are heavier than they look," Colin remarked. "We will be back in a few minutes to help you put the shrine back in place."

William nodded. Angus was already cleaning the area. Fifteen minutes later the six men had returned the lid to the sarcophagus with its coffin in place, empty of all but dust, tiny fragments of decayed bone, and the accumulated dirt of centuries. From the outside, the shrine appeared untouched, and Angus added a bundle of roses from the garden on top, as if a petitioner had come with prayers late in the night, seeking the refuge of the great king.

The light from John Thorne's lantern shone on the wet cobblestones of Magdalene Street as he stood beside Roger James to watch Geleis and Colin tighten the ropes over the heavy, waxed linen canvas that covered the loaded wagon beds. The four horses grew excited, stamped and neighed, impatient to be off. The sound of their hooves glancing off the cobblestones echoed into the night. John looked around uneasily, greatly relieved to see that the street was dark and uninhabited. In another hour there would be lights burning in the windows of the abbey and the houses up and down Magdalene Street.

The tower bell rang three times as Geleis and Maddy climbed up to settle on the bench of the larger of the two wagons. Ben held the reins of the second wagon, with Anne at his side. Testing the ropes a last time and certain all was secure, Colin turned to his uncle, who took him into an embrace both strong and fierce.

"No more words," John's soft voice betrayed the depths of his feelings. "God willing, we will meet again...somehow, someday, in this world or in the next." He placed a heavy pouch in Colin's hands. "This is to add to what I gave you yesterday. You will need more. Hide it in your vest. Now, Maddy and the others are waiting."

With a hand raised in benediction, John said, "God go with you."

Colin jumped up to take a seat beside Maddy, and with a click and soft whistle from Geleis, the lead wagon rolled away from the front gate of the abbey, followed by the second wagon with Ben at the reins. They trundled down the lane, leaving John Thorne and Roger James standing beside Angus and William in the gathering mist. Forcing herself not to turn for one last look at the monks and the abbey, Maddy watched the slumbering houses go past. It was the predawn hour when most people snored, plunged into deeper sleep, burrowed in their down pillows if they were lucky enough to have one, while the fog crept in from river and meandering estuary streams to fill the Somerset levels with a cloak of white. Within moments, the wagons were on the edge of the town heading into the fog, going north toward Wells.

CHAPTER NINE

Glastonbury
August 1539

"It's Friday, Jack. You know very well that I will be dispensing alms to the poor in the church all afternoon." Richard's words were terse as he responded to Jack Horner, who had returned unexpectedly that morning with Ambrose and the other monks who had been in London for the past few months. The abbot turned and opened his arms toward Ambrose, who had just walked up and stood waiting with a patient smile. "Ambrose, it is good to see you again."

"Abbot Whiting!" Ambrose bowed, one hand upon his heart, then taking the abbot's warm proffered hand in both of his own and leaning down to kiss it.

Their early morning arrival, accompanied by a number of the king's soldiers only hours after the wagons had departed, caused some stress for the abbot and his monks—relief at the close call mingled with a growing tide of fear and anxiety, knowing that the commissioner could arrive at any time to begin the process of dissolution.

"Yes sir, I am aware." Jack fidgeted, moving so that he stood directly between the abbot and his ecclesiastical benefice, Father Ambrose. Horner turned obsequious.

"Indeed, mendicants who arrive on our door are lucky, Abba Whiting, to receive charity from your own hands, which you never fail to dispense, every Wednesday and Friday. I told Bishop Cranmer so, and he was duly impressed. But even so, sir, there is an urgent need to attend to business. I am here to tell you that Beauvale Priory was shut down a week ago, on July 18."

Marveling at Horner's rabid ebulliance in conveying yet another piece of bad news, Richard's heart quailed at the memory of the brutal deaths of his friends, John Houghton and James Lawrence from Beauvale Priory in Wales, and the other Carthusian martyrs who refused to bend to the king's will in the matter of faith. Refusing to accept King Henry's supremacy over Rome and the Church, they had been imprisoned in the Tower in 1535 and then given a trial. Although the jury refused to find them guilty, stating "they did not act maliciously," Cromwell threatened the jury with violence until they relented and delivered a guilty verdict.

The execution had been ghastly, sending a clear message to all: Houghton and Lawrence were hung by the neck using a large rope in order to keep them alive, then they were taken down from the gallows to be drawn and quartered. It was Cromwell's way to insure that the prisoner was still alive when he was butchered.

"You predicted this would come soon," Ambrose added, attempting to ameliorate the tension.

Standing beside the abbot, John Thorne mused darkly.

"It is well that the new prior, Thomas Woodcock, has surrendered, or else he would be dead this day, exactly like his predecessors."

"Yes, well it is. Thank you, Jack and Ambrose," Richard managed a wan smile, "for representing me in London these past months, and for delivering my letter to Cromwell—in truth, my health could not have endured the stress of the House of Lords this season. Do you know how the chief minister took my request to be excused from participating?"

Jack vacillated, but Ambrose's response was forthright. "He was not happy, Father Whiting. His comments were sardonic, to say the least."

"Well, that comes as no surprise to any of us." John's voice was dolorous as he took charge of the conversation. "It had to be done, nonetheless, and in fact, Richard, you must rest before you give out alms this afternoon. Let us all leave and allow the abbot to retire until lunch is served."

The monks filed out of the abbot's quarters and down the hallway to the stairs, leaving Richard alone. Standing at his window, he saw Jack Horner walk alone toward his office near the gatehouse, while the other two monks moved away toward the garden. Seeing John and Ambrose arm in arm, the abbot's heart lifted as he muttered a prayer.

" Lord Jesus, give Ambrose the strength to do what is needed, to shepherd my monks when the time comes."

"Let us walk in the garden together, my friend."

Taking the younger man's arm in his own, John strolled with Ambrose through the cornucopia of the garden, beautiful in the flush of summer's bounty. The scent of wisteria wafted on the air, and the stone path curved through lily beds and thriving mounds of thyme and bee balm. The day before the sun had been shining; today the sky was filled with low-hanging clouds. The bright, misty air turned the colors of the garden vivid in a fine drizzle that came and went in sporadic fits of temperamental weather.

"Our task has been accomplished, Ambrose, and just in time. One more day and Horner would have been here with the king's soldiers at his heels, just when we were ready to load the wagons." John leaned close, his words circumspect. "They left only hours ago, at three bells, when the town was sleeping and dark."

John continued with a wry grimace. "Ambrose, do you remember when John Leland, the antiquarian of King Henry, came to Glastonbury in 1533? Leland wanted to see the grave of the king and queen, and spent many hours prowling about in our library and in the Lady Chapel, looking for the crypt of St. Joseph—which, of course, he did not find, since even we do not know where the bones of Joseph of Arimathea are interred. They must be somewhere in this great building, anonymous, unsung—probably the way Saint Joseph wants it to be. At any rate, Leland poked his nose into everything."

Ambrose listened, his hazel eyes calm. He waited for the senior monk to get to his point.

"As much as he searched and poked and prodded, nothing hidden was revealed. The abbot and I, and Roger, all felt at that time that John Leland did not have the heart for Glastonbury; he did not perceive, nor understand, the underlying spirit of our great abbey. Thanks be to our Lady, the Company of Avalon remained hidden from his view. We knew that he was the king's man. He was here to penetrate into our secrets—to understand what lies at the bottom of the sacred atmosphere of this ancient place that was founded by Joseph of Arimathea himself. Their jealousy eats at them like worms in a grave."

They walked toward an arbor of hawthorn trees, now heavy with clusters of yellow berries that would soon turn orange and then red in their own theatre of transformation.

"Let us sit here, among the holy thorn trees," John suggested. Taking a seat on a stone bench in the grove, they shared an intimate quietude for some moments.

"In London," Ambrose confided, intuiting John's unspoken questions, "I perceived a tremendous avidity toward Glastonbury, a pervasive curiosity and titillation, almost—a kind of gluttony. I saw the king only at a distance, but I was in the presence of Cromwell and Cranmer often, and in council with their secretaries and the bishops.

"There is a powerful buzz about Glastonbury, Reading, and Colchester Abbeys, but I must say, there is something quite different in the attitude toward our abbey. Strange emotions attend the words of those who speak of Glastonbury Abbey—awe, and as you say, a malevolent combination of vicious envy, mystic reverence, violence, and even fear."

Ambrose looked up at the hawthorn that hung nearby, its branches heavy with berries. Admiring their brilliant color, he pulled a laden limb down with his hand. The drizzle had receded to a light mist, but as Ambrose stretched the branch, they were showered with fat drops of water.

John chuckled with a delight he rarely exhibited. "I often wonder, what would Joseph of Arimathea say about this madness in which we find ourselves?"

"He was no stranger to persecution or to secrets," Ambrose released the branch with a smile, cheered by their shared remembrance of the abbey's founding saint. "All those years he spent in prison, before he came here to plant the Holy Thorn on Wirral Hill, and bring the truth of Jesus and Mary Magdalene to these shores. I believe he is helping us through this."

"As do I, Ambrose. These past few months I have gone almost daily, as often as my duties allow, to pray at Joseph's shrine in the Lady Chapel."

John asked, "What of your meetings with bishops and priests of the new church?"

"Mostly these were uneasy to the extreme. For the most part, I listened and said very little. Those bishops and cardinals I spoke with, former Catholics who have saved their own lives by converting to Henry's church, were secretly sympathetic, and in fact they are worried for Abbot Whiting, but they do not dare to support Glastonbury in the public eye. When I did see Cromwell, his comments were aimed at disparaging our abbot and hinting that Richard was hiding something of great value at Glastonbury. He stated numerous times that Glastonbury is fat with wealth..."

John snorted. "Perhaps once it was, before he drained us dry." His tone grew serious as he added, "In truth, we never had the wealth the king and Cromwell believe us to have."

Ambrose nodded slowly in agreement. "But it is not only gold and land and the beasts of our fields that Cromwell wants. His aggression is not only driven by money and power but also by religious zeal. He wants the mystic legacy of Glastonbury, he wants our secret, and he wants to destroy it. He cannot abide the truth that Blessed Mary of Magdalene was more than a harlot. I know it with every bone in my body. In his war against all the saints of the Catholic church, he wants to bury that knowledge forever. He will not be stopped until he has everything." Ambrose cast a piercing glance at John.

"And, like you and the abbot, I believe that Jack Horner feeds information to one of Cromwell's spies, although I was unable to ascertain exactly how or to whom. Jack is a slippery eel of a man. His hopes and schemes to rise to Abbot Whiting's right hand have been sorely disappointed over the years, and now he has his revenge. It was not always pleasant to share Horner's company these three months past, but it was a necessary to accomplish our mission to secure the artifacts. I am grateful to play a part in our aim. Blessed Mary be praised!"

John reached a hand to Ambrose's shoulder and squeezed gently. Their eyes met and lingered, and in that moment, both knew their time together would soon end.

"God bless you, Ambrose, and may Saint Joseph, Mother Mary, Blessed Mary, and Jesus Christ be with you through this to the end and beyond. When the dissolution comes, the monks of Glastonbury are going to need your steady strength, your wisdom, and your faith. You will help them carry on."

CHAPTER TEN

Journey to Arrain
September 1539

With stormy autumn weather and other setbacks—a broken wagon wheel that lost them several days, as a new one had to be built, which meant a two-day walk to a village—it had taken almost four weeks to make their way through Wales and Cumbria to the border near Carlisle. On the days that were sunny and bright, they delighted in the beauty of the landscape as they trundled along in wagons laden with their precious cargo. Often they were slowed down or forced to stop by pouring rains and muddy, rutted roads. Beyond the broken wheel and inclement weather, the young people enjoyed the adventure, cheerfully enduring the discomforts of sleeping on the ground under the wagons and a few times under spreading trees.

There were many nights when they received the hospitality of kind farmers and their families, taking shelter in crofts and barns or in spare rooms offered to the women by the farmers' wives they met. Several times they had encounters with displaced, wandering monks who had been evicted from their monasteries. Once they slept in a barn with three nuns who had no place to go. They told the story of how they had survived only by the beneficence of the farmers and villagers who took pity upon them. It was dangerous for women to travel without men to accompany them, but they had no other choice. Somehow, they had managed so far.

These meetings were poignant and heart-rending, for the "Company of Avalon," as they had begun to think of themselves, could not offer help as their hearts were drawn to do, and as they would have in other circumstances. The urgency of their task demanded a discretion that restrained their naturally generous dispositions, but Colin gave a few silver coins to these heart-broken men and women, and received their blessings in return.

Memorable among them were two Carthusian monks named James and Peter, from Beauvale Priory in Wales. Their abbot, John Houghton, had been executed years before, and since the terrible time they had been wandering. As they shared their story one night around a fire, their grief and shock made an impact upon the young couples.

"Do ye not receive the allotted money from the king?" Colin had inquired, his heart contracting with concern for their welfare.

Taking a stick to stir the fire, Peter had answered, "Yes, we go to Cardiff once a year to collect our £5, and it keeps us from starving. But we choose to wander as mendicants rather than go to a religious house now ruled by the king. At least we are alive and free."

His companion James elaborated further. "And we do not want to go to Glastonbury, where the same is likely to happen again at any time, as everyone knows Cromwell is bent on the destruction of that place, and of Abbot Whiting, as well." The companions glanced uneasily at one another but said nothing in response, changing the conversation to ask where they were headed next.

Even with the sorrows of these encounters, Maddy was convinced that the ease of the journey, so far, was due to the direct intervention of Blessed Mary, not to mention the magic bestowed upon their quest by Arthur, Gwenivere, and Lancelot—and Avalon, so she liked to imagine. Now she shivered inwardly as Geleis reined in the horses while a group of soldiers approached. The rain that began at dawn and continued all morning had stopped, mercifully, but everyone was drenched, including the king's patrol who rode forward, their dark red coats turned the color of old wine and their plumed hats dripping. Nonetheless, they came on with hands on the hilts of swords that clanged at their sides.

"Halt, there!" The captain commanded, six soldiers with lances held high backing him up. As their wagons rolled to a stop, Colin jumped down.

"Good day to you, captain!" He adopted his best English accent and a manner that was neither too friendly nor too antagonistic.

"Who are you, and what business brings you to the border of England and Scotland?" The captain frowned as he eyed the canvas covers on the two wagons.

"My name is Colin Hamilton Thorne. I am recently married, and my wife and I are moving our household from Exeter, where my wife's family lives, to my home on the Isle of Arrain, where I am laird at Castle Kildonan, under the auspices of the House of Stewart, Lords of Carrick and King James of Scotland."

The captain frowned, blinked, then gestured to two of his men, who jumped down from their horses and moved toward the wagons.

"And what exactly do you have in there? Stolen goods?" He laughed, and the other four men shifted on their horses, their faces stony and churlish. "Another thieving Scotsman, eh?"

"No," Colin laughed, "only some pots and pans and dresses, a few trinkets and remembrances that make my wife happy." He smiled and held his arms wide, gesturing generously toward the wagons.

Geleis and Ben jumped down to untie the ropes that secured the canvas on the wagons. Pulling the covers back, the guards looked over the top layer of boxes, opening one to find fry pans and linens. They lifted these and showed them to the captain, who had dismounted his horse and now walked over to see for himself.

Looking at Geleis and fingering his sword hilt, he turned back to Colin. "Who is your driver, and who are the other two?"

"This is Geleis Blackwater, my liegeman of Kildonan, helping me to move our household goods. These good people," he gestured, "are Ben Pritchard and his wife, Anne, cousin to my wife. Ben is a professor in Exeter. They have come to spend a year on the Isle of Arrain with us."

The captain looked from Anne to Maddy, his eyes lingering a breath too long as he pursed his lips and rubbed his chin. Two more boxes were opened—in one they found blankets and woolens. Geleis stood outwardly calm, but a single drop of sweat trickled down his temple as he stood close to the soldiers while their rummaging brought them closer and closer to the boxes of relics.

Beads of sweat popped out on Colin's furrowed brow as he shifted his weight from one foot to the other, attempting to appear relaxed. The captain shot a fierce glance at him just as the soldier who was rifling through the third box pulled out a lady's silk nightgown. He held it up for the amusement of the captain and his men.

"Looks like a fine gown for a strumpet, sir. But I'd rather see her without it than within it!" The other men sniggered as the soldier reached for the next box.

Maddy had been watching with mounting tension from her seat on the wagon, her armpits wet with nervous sweat. Her eyes bolted to Colin and back to the box, which the soldier now jiggled, trying to lift it from its snug spot. She knew she had to do something fast to attract their attention away. She jumped down from the wagon with a shout of outrage. "Sir! How dare you treat a lady's intimate garments in such a way—are you not Christians?"

She charged around the wagon, feigning outrage, to snatch the nightgown from the soldier's hand. He stood dumbfounded if not aghast, the garment in question now firmly held by Maddy. Seeing that the role she played was having the desired effect, she threw herself headlong into the theatre of it.

"Holy Jesu, surely you are damned for such behavior!" Maddy swore, scolding the man, her educated English accent underscoring her fury and her class advantage. "You insult a loyal subject of the king. I was born and raised in England, sir. My father is an Oxford scholar from a honorable family! Are the king's men no more than scurls, lowly thieves and brigands?" Shaking one finger in front of his face, she called on the leaders of the religious form for added clout as she shifted gears.

"What will Lord Cromwell say of this? Not to mention Bishop Cranmer, both of them being godly men. The Son of God sees everything you do," she chastised vehemently, banking on their religious dread, just in case their fear of political reprisal was not enough. "Have you no fear of the hereafter, of the Day of Judgment?"

The soldiers shrank back and glanced uneasily at their captain, who watched Maddy's performance with narrowed eyes, while his men's horses neighed and tossed their heads, becoming restless and jumpy. Catching the captain's eye, Colin arched his brows and shrugged humorously. Suddenly the captain burst into laughter.

"Good luck to you, man, with a harridan like you have there!" His sardonic chuckle was derisive. "She's pretty enough to bed, but with a mouth like that, your road will be hard enough as it is!" He gestured abruptly to his soldiers. "Leave it. We have to get to Carlisle before dark."

Looking at Colin, he advised, "There is likely to be more rain before the day is out. You would do well to make your way to Carlisle as soon as possible. Report to the king's constable as soon as you arrive and secure a safe passage for Arrain. Be aware, sir, that there are, as a matter of fact, Scottish brigands on this road."

Mounting, he urged his horse forward a few steps. "They may steal your household goods and accost your... women." His smile was tainted by the thinly-veiled sarcasm. "There is an inn there—you will find it quite amenable. For a coin they will stable your horses and wagons."

"I appreciate the warning, captain. We will be on our way, then." Colin helped Maddy up on the wagon and jumped up to take a seat beside her. The captain and his men wheeled on their horses and galloped off to the north without a backward glance.

With a snap of the reins and a whistle, Geleis pressed his horses onward, Ben and Anne following in their wagon. They plodded along in a tense silence, and when finally the patrol had disappeared around a bend in the road, Maddy heaved a sigh of relief.

"One more box and he would have discovered..." Her whisper died before she finished.

Colin began to chuckle softly, and a wide grin spread across Geleis' face. Anne burst out laughing, and even the most somber of them, Ben, smiled. Maddy looked around, her brows arched and her mouth quivering with suppressed mirth.

"Well, I'm happy to have entertained you all as well!"

Putting an arm around her shoulders and pulling her close, Colin kissed her cheek. "Twas a fine performance, lass, and fast thinking on your part. I think you saved us from disaster, Maddy."

"Aye, save us you did." Geleis' admiration showed in the sparkle of his eyes. "You were brilliant. That soldier had his hands on a box underneath the ones he had examined—had he pulled it out to open, that would have been a terrible thing indeed. They would have known then that we had a secret to expose."

"I always knew you were a fine actress, cousin," Anne called to Maddy. "We shall have to put on some plays, during the long nights on Arrain in the winter to come!"

"Indeed," Ben agreed. "I know just the thing. You can play Gwenivere and Colin can be Arthur."

Maddy shook her head. "Not Arthur—someone else can play that role. Colin should be Lancelot."

Ben widened his eyes in surprise. "Is that so?"

"Oh yes. Lancelot's love was true, from beginning to end. He was the queen's champion in all things." She smiled, putting her arm through Colin's as they jostled along.

A few moments later Geleis turned to Colin, leaning forward to glance across Maddy. "I dinna savor the idea of running into those soldiers again. Let us not stop in Carlisle—what do you say, Colin?"

"Nor do I trust the captain not to send us into trouble, telling us to go to the king's constable. The border around Carlisle is not a safe place for a Scotsman, but not because of Scottish brigands. I ken a farmer not more than an hour from here. We will ask if we can sleep in his barn. I would rather wait until we are well over the border and into the highlands before we trust to stay in an inn."

George Findley was the farmer's name. He had known Colin's father and grandfather, and he greeted them with warm affection. His wife, Elspeth, hustled the women into the kitchen to dry before the fire while the men unharnessed, brushed, fed and watered their horses, while George finished his chores with his own animals—he was busy with three cows to milk and a sheep pen full of ewes to feed. At dark, they were all invited to supper. When Geleis declined to join them inside for the meal, choosing instead to stay with the wagons, George looked at him curiously.

Colin explained. "We ran into the king's patrol today on the road—a captain with six soldiers. They advised that there are brigands about in these parts. Geleis just wants to take extra precautions. I will bring out a plentiful bowl, never fear!"

"Get on with ye," Geleis chided with a chuckle. "I am as happy as can be out here in the drizzle and howling wind! Reminds me of home."

An hour later, Colin appeared in the barn with a large bowl of mutton stew and wooden spoon in one hand and a lantern in the other. Across his back was slung a cloth bag filled with crisp red apples from Elspeth's orchard. Her harvest was so abundant this year she had already given the travelers a bushel of the red fruits to take on the road in the morning. Colin sat down beside Geleis on the clean, dry straw and handed over a steaming bowl. With a nod of appreciation, Geleis tucked in with relish.

"Tomorrow we should arrive in Dumfries." Colin watched as Geleis slurped down another spoonful.

"We should be in Scotland then, and we can stay in the inn there. I know the innkeeper from years of traveling past his place on my way to and from Arrain. He is a good man, like George here, and will not ply us with intrusive questions. From there we go due west to Givran. Just north of there we should find the merchant boat we want—big enough to take our wagons and horses across the firth. What do you think of landing on the shores at Kildonan?"

"It depends upon the weather, of course." Geleis chewed thoughtfully as he considered the question. "But even in good weather 'tis highly risky. Many a ship has floundered on the rocky shoals around Pladda at Kildonan. I think we should stay with our plan and land at Viking Bay, as you did last time."

Colin picked up a piece of straw and sucked on it. The horses neighed softly, happy to be out of the rain that drummed steadily outside the barn doors.

"Do ye have all the blankets and such that ye need, Geleis?"

"Yes, I am comfortable, cousin." He smiled and nudged Colin, "Dinna fash yourself. 'Tis as it should be—you sleeping with your wife tonight."

Colin's blush was hidden in the dim light of the lantern, but his laugh was light and joyous. "She is my heart and soul, *bràthair*."

"Hmm. I can see it. A fine woman, as bonnie as can be. And smart as a whip. I hope to find such a one someday. And I meant it when I said she saved us today. That soldier had his hand on the box with the king's bones."

"I saw it happening but, to be honest, I was flummoxed as to what to do. I was grateful when she leapt to action, though I was concerned for her. It could have gone badly. Hopefully that will be the last time we encounter a border patrol. Soon enough we shall be in the land of our blood. Then we only have to deal with the bloodthirsty Scots!"

Their laughter was easy but underneath their

camaraderie was the knowledge of the dangers they still faced. A trade boat big enough the carry the wagons and horses would need to have three masts and sails, and men at the oars. Questions would be asked, and Colin would have to negotiate the situation with a gold coin or two. Robbery was common on the Irish Sea, and many rogue ships sailed into the Firth of Clyde. Hopefully, their luck would hold for the next two weeks, as they made their way to Kildonan.

Bidding Geleis a good night's sleep, Colin left the barn and walked through the rainy courtyard, kicked the mud from his boots, and went into the kitchen door to the two-storied farmhouse. Maddy had already retired and waited for him in their tiny attic room. Stopping to say a polite goodnight to his hosts, who sat around the kitchen hearth in the glow of the fire with their three children, he moved toward the door to the stairs. For the first time on their journey, Colin and Maddy would sleep together, with four walls around them and a modicum of privacy, on a bed with a mattress of straw and linen sheets. Desire flooded warm through his loins, and he closed the kitchen door behind him, climbing the stone steps two at a time.

CHAPTER ELEVEN

Somerset
September 1539

It was a magnificent early autumn day. The sun shone in a blue sky, and the gentle breeze of early afternoon lifted and swirled falling leaves that shimmered yellow and red-orange in transparent sheets of sunlight. Abbot Whiting walked from his lodge along the stone path through a glorious display of flowers toward the cathedral, where he met John Thorne at the northern door to the transept. He stopped briefly to look at the hawthorn trees planted there, reaching out to touch the ruddy gold of its berries.

"This was a good idea, John," Richard commented as they walked, "in fact it is nigh past time to address the monks as a whole, prepare them as best I can."

John nodded. "Yes, time is of the essence now, especially since we heard that the king ends his summer progress this week, and Cromwell will certainly urge him to turn a dour eye toward Glastonbury. I will go with you, back to Sharpham Park, after you have spoken. I am finished with receiving the season's tithes at the Grange."

"Very good. Sharpham Manor has been a refuge for us this summer. I look forward to greeting this splendid autumn weather there, with the trees turning yellow and then red."

John smiled. "It makes my heart glad to see you in good spirits, Richard." The abbot said nothing, but returned the smile, his blue eyes crinkling with kindness. But John was not fooled; he could see the bittersweet shadow just below the surface.

They proceeded through the transept, where the abbot looked around in satisfaction at the nave on one side and the choir on the other, noticing the order and cleanliness of the shrines with their ornate vestments, the well-swept floors, the fresh flowers and rush mats, the tapers and oil lamps that burned throughout the vast space. Several parishioners and pilgrims were there, some on their knees praying in one or another of the alcove shrines, while others worked at cleaning or other small tasks given to them by the monks.

"I have always believed that order and cleanliness is vital to a true spiritual life," Richard reflected. "Through order, we bring beauty to our world, even when the beauty is already present, as it is here—in the sculptures and in the sacred geometry of these stone walls."

Stopping to gaze at a stone rendering of Mary with the baby Jesus in her arms standing in a niche, and another of Jesus in the agony of crucifixion, his eyes roved to the stone buttresses, vaulted ceilings, and the soaring heights of the cathedral. Richard closed his eyes for a moment, and it seemed to John that he lingered to absorb the atmosphere of the cathedral one last time. Keeping his thoughts to himself, John watched and wondered if his friend prayed, gave thanks, or wrestled with private grief.

Moving on, the two men crossed the transept, past the shrine of Arthur and his queen, then exited the south door and walked through the cloister garth to the refectory, where the monks of Glastonbury were gathered and waiting. Roger James had called them together to hear Abbot Whiting speak to them after lunch, before they returned to their duties. For the next hour the vigils within the church would be conducted by three of the laity, permitting the monks to gather as one body. Even Jack Horner would be present, and Richard knew that whatever he said would find its way to Cromwell's spies, who were known to be in and out of Glastonbury town and often seen skulking around Magdalene Street or found drinking at the George and Pilgrim's Inn.

They had even been seen at the parish church of Saint John the Baptist, asking questions of local people about Abbot Whiting, if they had ever heard him disparage the king and his church, or whether he had been at the Tribunal recently, against the king's orders. Since the abbot's judicial authority had been stripped away by Cromwell, and he was no longer allowed to preside over Glastonbury's Tribunal, cases were backlogged and people were angry and frustrated with the absence of their judicial system. The people of Glastonbury trusted Abbot Richard Whiting to be fair, just, and wise in his judgments. He was sorely missed, and Cromwell's spies were frustrated in their attempts to find damning testimony against the Abbot of Glastonbury.

Holding open the refectory door as the abbot entered, John's senses were inundated by a palpable blanket of sorrow that lay upon fifty monks sitting in disciplined rows. The silence was punctuated only by a sniff or muffled cough as Richard walked to the head of the room to the heavy oak podium where liturgies and prayers were read during meals.

"Fifteen hundred years ago," the abbot began, "Joseph of Arimathea sailed up the Bristol Channel and the River Brue, coming to Ynis Witrin with eleven disciples of Christ, sent on a mission to preach the gospel of Jesus by the Apostle Philip. Weary from their journey, they stopped upon yon hill to the southwest of where we sit today. There Joseph encamped to rest with his companions, to give thanks and say his prayers. And there he planted the Jerusalem thorn tree to signify that he had found his *cynefin*. As many of you know, that is old Welsh for the place where nature tells you, this is your sacred place to be. The descendants of that hawthorn live and flower to this day, outside our great abbey, and on Wearyall Hill.

"We are the keepers of the legacy of Joseph of Arimathea. This place has been our *cynefin*—our spiritual home—for many years. Our souls have been nourished and protected within the sanctuary of these hallowed walls and grounds. We have lived well, had every opportunity to grow in spirit, in gratitude, in harmony, in charity, and in faith.

"Our sacristan has called you here today that I might speak openly of what we all fear. Indeed, this comes as no surprise; events of the past years have lead inexorably to this very day. We have done all we could to mitigate the damage, to divert the punitive eye of Chancellor Cromwell and the dissolution of this great monastery and church. Five years ago, we all agreed to sign the paper sent by the king, renouncing obedience to the Holy Father in Rome. Soon after, we also signed the paper recognizing the king's royal supremacy.

"We signed with our spiritual names—Arthur, Philip, Gildas, Aidan, Dunstan, and Abaramathea, to name only a few. We did this, despite our most profound reservations and heartbreak, despite our unswerving loyalty to the Catholic faith. We did this to declare the spiritual glory of Glastonbury Abbey, to preserve this place as the most sacred ground in England. We did this to insure that our abbey's charitable works could continue—almsgiving, our hospital, hospice and house for widows, scholarly pursuits, and many righteous causes in service to God, for the good of humankind. We did this in hopes that peace might be found, and that this sanctuary of God might survive the changes wrought in the temporal world."

The abbot paused and looked around at the monks, all dressed in the long black robes of the Benedictine order. Only one person among them was dressed in the garb of a layman—James Renynger, the music master and organist, who Richard had hired five years before and who had become an integral part of the spiritual community of the monastery. James had a deep love for the abbot, who had been kind and generous to him, and who loved to hear the choirmaster play the organ. Now, tears streamed down his face.

Many of the monks were as old as Richard Whiting; others were of a middle age, in their prime. Some were young, under thirty years, like William and Angus. All kept their eyes fastened upon the tall, thin form of Richard Whiting. In the front row sat the sacristan, Roger James, and the bursar, John Thorne. Beside them were Ambrose, Rowland and Geoffrey. Further down the row sat Jack Horner, his head tortoise-like as he looked up at the abbot, a scowl upon his features. He shuffled his feet under the bench and looked around at the men who, unable to stifle their tears, began to openly weep.

"Yes, we have done all we could to stem the tide. But the flood is upon us, my friends and brothers. We must turn a realistic eye upon what is to come. Cromwell will move against us soon—probably in the weeks ahead. I will not sign any more papers renouncing my faith or surrender this church to the king's reform. It is inevitable that Glastonbury Abbey will soon be in the hands of Cromwell."

Broken sobs rent the air, and many of the monks buried their faces in their hands, attempting to contain their grief. One of them, a novice named Frederick, called out.

"What will happen to us, Abbot Whiting?" Father Ambrose glanced sternly at the young man, but his distraught face wrenched the senior monk's heart with pity, and Ambrose turned back with a heavy sigh to listen to his abbot's reply.

"You have some options. I have heard that many monks have received a pension from the king upon the dissolution of their friary or monastery. This is may be determined by whether or not you convert to the king's church, which is an option that you have. Or, you can leave the country, go to France, take refuge in the Holy Church there. You are also free to relinquish your vows, enter into the life of a lay parishioner. You can go back to your families, those of you who have them, or take to the road as a mendicant beggar and seek God on a path of greater renunciation.

"Whatever you do, I pray that you do not give up your faith. Realize that God is universal. A true faith will see you through all of life's adversity and endures despite religions, sects, and creeds. Have courage, be of good spirit, as much as you can. Remember that Jesus and his disciples endured hardships much worse than ours. Take our Lord Jesus and Mother Mary with you in your heart, and remember your time at Glastonbury Abbey. You have my personal blessing for whatever choice you make."

He paused, as if considering his next words. "You all know that it is most likely I will be executed here at Glastonbury, as other abbots have been. Should that happen, pray for me. Forgive me for my trespasses against you, whatever they might be. And do not grieve... I have wrestled with my own devils. I have made peace with my life and death, and I feel the call of my Creator.

"Today I will retire again to Sharpham Manor and stay there for the next weeks to pray in solitude. Father Ambrose will carry on for me here. Now, it is time for your afternoon prayers, and to resume singing in the choir of our great cathedral. The sound of your voices raised in songs of praise lifts my heart more than you will ever know."

He genuflected slowly then raised his hands, palms open in benediction, to the assembly. Many of the monks crossed themselves as he gave his blessing.

"I bless you all, in the name of Jesus Christ and Mother Mary, Blessed Mary, and Joseph of Arimathea. May their wisdom guide us in the days and months ahead."

The anguish in the room vibrated against stone walls as their abbot stepped down. John rose to lend a hand to steady Richard, who reached trembling fingers to his forehead as he walked out. Several monks rushed to touch the hem of his robe, while others called out, their voices broken but bold.

"We are with you, Abba!"

"Mother Mary blesses you, Father."

Within moments he was gone and the bells began to toll, calling them to None.

Two weeks later, at ten o'clock on the morning of September 19, Dr. Richard Layton appeared at the Magdalene Gate, asking for Abbot Richard Whiting. Four years before, when Commissioner Layton had come to Glastonbury Abbey in August 1535 at the king's command, he had combed through the abbot's personal effects and the abbey records, searched the library, hovered over the king's shrine—and found nothing. Nor was he able to incite rumours amongst the monks or the abbot within the township. Since then, Layton had become known for his knack for digging up mud and muck—he had "uncovered" foul gossip and innuendo, which he gleaned at other abbeys and presented as fact, including stories of concubines and sodomy, excesses of wealth, gluttony, and power. This evidence, whether true or false, provided Cromwell with the justification he sought, heaping ample fuel on the fires of dissolution.

But Glastonbury Abbey had been a tough case for Cromwell. Its abbot was known to be a man of simplicity and honor, and the previous commissioners had been unable to find any problem with the abbey, its financial records, or any of the monks. Now Layton was accompanied by two other commissioners, Pollard and Moyle, and two scores of armed soldiers. He intended to redeem himself in Cromwell's eyes, and to meet the Chancellor's demands for a guilty verdict for Abbot Whiting, opening the door to claiming the abbey's largess for the Crown — lands, money, jewels, and relics of great value.

The three commissioners were shown straightaway into the gatehouse, where they waited a short time until Father Ambrose arrived to ask, with a courteous bow, "How can I help you, good sirs?" With him was Father Rowland.

"We are here on orders of the king to question Abbot Richard Whiting. Where is he?" Layton slapped his gloves against his palm imperiously and pressed his lips together while Moyle and Pollard glowered.

Ambrose inclined his head, as if to calm the man's ire. "Abbot Whiting is at his manor in Sharpham Park, sir." The commissioners blanched, insulted that Ambrose was answering only the question he had been asked and no more.

"Hhmmph. How far is it?"

"Less than two miles," Father Ambrose replied evenly.

"And which road do we take?" Pollard inquired pointedly, with a sarcastic sneer.

Rowland quickly outlined the route they would take and within moments they were gone, their horses trotting down Magdalene Street toward High Street and beyond. Standing at the mullioned window of the gate-house, Rowland looked out at the faces of the soldiers left behind to stand guard on Magdalene Street. He turned to Ambrose, whose face betrayed the depth of his sorrow, and whispered, "Now it begins."

That morning, well before dawn, Richard had had a dream. In it Blessed Mary had come to him and told him to pray, for on the coming day the king's commissioners would arrive. Richard had shared the dream when he broke his fast with John and Roger, then asked them to sit in meditation with him. They had been in the chapel for hours. Roger had read a liturgy, and then began to read from the Psalms. After awhile, they fell into a deep silence, rosaries in hand. At the sound of horses and men, John and Roger glanced at each other, their faces shadowed.

Richard whispered, "William and Angus will see to it." Holding his rosary between trembling fingertips, he pressed one amethyst bead after another, and with each one, his lips moved in silent prayer, his eyes closed.

John's eyes roved over the chapel, with its Glastonbury Abbey coat of arms and mullioned eastern window of stained glass in red, yellow and blue. It might very well be the last time he would see this place. His heart thudded with anxiety as he listened to the sound of strident voices escalating in pitch until Richard opened his eyes and turned to his companions.

"Let us go and attend to this."

By the time they reached the parlour, William and Angus had reluctantly ushered in the three commissioners who stood stiffly, looking over the velvet couch and brass candlesticks on the polished oak table. They turned as Richard came in. Dr. Layton took command of the exchange.

"Abbot Whiting. It has been some years since we last conversed. I see your health has not benefited from time. And John Thorne, as well." He glanced at Roger. "And you are...the sacristan, Roger James." He raised his brows, magisterial and preemptive.

"We have some questions to ask you. We have received information that you are plotting treason against the king; that you have conspired against his sovereign church; that you are not only hoarding treasures at Glastonbury, but have stolen for yourself, from the wealth of the abbey, that which rightfully belongs to your king. What do you say to this, sir?" He addressed Richard directly.

Taking a seat beside the fire, Richard coughed and smoothed his robe. "Autumn has come, and I fear it has already grown too cold for my bones. May I sit whilst you interrogate me, sir?"

Layton said nothing but squared his shoulders and frowned. The other two shifted their weight, hands on the brass buckles of their wide leather belts. They had no need to wear swords, for the contingent of soldiers outside the manor gate provided any coercion that might be needed. Angus moved quietly in the shadows to throw another log on the fire.

Growing impatient, Layton smacked his lips in consternation. "Well sir. Answer the question."

The tension was thick as Richard replied. "I have not plotted treason against the king, sir. I am merely a man of faith, and I do not choose to convert to King Henry's new church, although I remain his loyal subject."

Layton sniggered lightly. "Then you will not have a problem with surrendering your church and everything in it."

The abbot did not flinch. His eyes remained steady upon the commissioner as he spoke. "I will not surrender Glastonbury Abbey. It really is as simple as that. As to treasure, Glastonbury has sent money and many precious objects to Cromwell as gestures of good will over the past years. Surely you must be aware of that?"

"Gestures of good will mean nothing when you have the richest ecclesiastical house in England," Moyle interjected with a snarl, "and you are keeping your wealth to yourself—vast lands and farms, growing fat on beef and pigs and salmon, heaping your granaries high with tithing and collecting coins in your coffers, amassing gold and silver plate while the Crown suffers the insult, not to mention the indignation of knowing that there are many secret treasures within Glastonbury's precincts. We aim to find them."

Layton moved a step closer to Richard, hovering over him. "Now, Richard Whiting," he snapped, "get up and come with us. We will go to Glastonbury and see for ourselves exactly what you have hidden."

John stepped in, wedging himself between Layton and the abbot. "Can you not see that Doctor Whiting is not well?" he charged, emphasizing Richard's status.

Layton flushed and turned slowly to glare at John. "We will brook no interference from you. If you resist us, it will get worse. Of course, we prefer to be polite."

He narrowed his eyes as he ordered, "Move. Now!"

Roger turned to the young monks in attendance. "William, you and I will hitch the horses to the carriage and bring it around for the abbot. Angus, you and William close up the house and return to Glastonbury when you are finished here. I will drive the carriage." He walked out with William, leaving Angus staring at the commissioner with helpless fury in his eyes.

John leaned down to help Richard to his feet while Angus moved to fetch their cloaks and then hovered by the door as the group filed out into the chill autumn air. Within minutes Roger appeared, reins in hand, in the driver's seat of the carriage. Layton, Moyle, and Pollard mounted their horses and sat impatiently waiting with the soldiers as John helped Richard into the carriage.

They arrived in Glastonbury at dark, and Layton began his search in the abbot's chambers without delay, beginning at dawn the next day and continuing until dusk. The abbot sat in his chair with John Thorne at his side while Roger accompanied the commissioners as they rifled through every drawer and bookcase in the room, pulling copies of papal bulls and casting them on the floor, searching for evidence of treason and hidden treasures.

"What is this, sir?" Moyle charged angrily across the room to Richard, holding up a manuscript of arguments against Henry's divorce of Queen Catherine. Richard sighed. "You can read it for yourself and determine what it says. I stand behind it. It testifies to the tenets of our Catholic faith."

"It is proof of your crimes against the king," Layton called from the other side of the room, where he prowled through Richard's books. He held up a hand-printed copy of the life of Saint Thomas Becket and signaled to Moyle. Taking the manuscript in hand, Moyle strode to the door where three soldiers stood with sharp-tipped lances.

"Pack it in my saddlebags." The soldier bowed from the waist then hurried away, manuscript in hand.

The afternoon dragged by, with sporadic interrogations that grew more threatening while the commissioners grew more frustrated. Dusky shadows cloaked the chamber as, with night coming on, Pollard walked over to the abbot, leaned down and fixed him with a menacing eye.

"Where is the golden chalice? Where are the much-taunted vials of Arimathea?" The candle flame on the table beside the abbot wavered, almost extinguished by the forceful huff of the man's exhale.

Richard gazed back at Pollard and said nothing.

"Very well, perhaps the sacristan knows." He turned toward Roger. "Where are these relics kept, monk? You know very well where they are, you are the sacristan of this house. Your life depends upon your answer."

Roger denied with a shake of his head. "I know of no such artifacts, sir. They are nothing more than a legend."

John said nothing but watched as the interrogation proceeded.

Moyle continued to rifle through Richard's bookcases as Pollard and Layton hovered over Roger, who sat at

Richard's desk.

"You don't have to die, sacristan, like the other two. We can spare you. Tell us where to look, and we will ask Cromwell for leniency in your case. You could leave with the other monks when they disperse."

Roger did not move or speak but stared back into Pollard's eyes. The man threw his hands up in frustration and turned to Layton.

"They are impossible. Even pain of death does not loosen their lips. We will get nothing from them."

Layton dismissed Roger with a wave of his hand. "Since we cannot find any letter from Whiting that is material to our cause, and these two are clearly accomplices, let Lord Cromwell deal with them." Moyle stopped his rummaging to listen as Layton turned to Richard.

"Tomorrow after dawn you and your two accomplices will leave with a contingent of soldiers." Layton's clipped instruction conveyed his satisfaction. "Your friends will go with you. *Doctor* Whiting, you are bound for the Tower."

Roger bowed his head then glanced up at Layton. "There will be no need to bind us, on the morrow. We will come with you without a struggle. Just allow us to attend to the abbot."

"Very well. No need to bind a frail and sickly old man. At any rate, the abbot will live or die on the way." Layton's green eyes were icy and bulging, his words dripping with scorn. "It doesn't really matter, for he is a criminal."

Standing at the door, one soldier sniggered to the other. "Maybe he will take a knife to his own throat, like the coward, Wolsey!"

John Thorne bristled with a response, but Richard laid a hand upon his arm and whispered, "Be prudent, John. Do not provoke them."

Within minutes the commissioners hustled out of the chambers, leaving a bevy of soldiers at the door, where Layton paused. "Consider yourselves prisoners of the king. Say goodbye now to your chambers, Abbot Whiting. You will be escorted shortly to the chamber above the gate, where you will spend the night. There will be guards outside your door—do not try to talk with anyone."

Ten minutes later the three were escorted by armed guards to the Magdalene Gate, where they climbed the stone stairs to the upstairs chamber. Layton had set a soldier at the door, and, once they were locked in, John insisted that Richard take the single cot, while he and Roger sat in the chairs that appointed the meager room. It was a grueling, cold night, with no firewood to stoke the hearth. Pulling the chairs near the cot, they huddled close together and awaited the coming of daylight.

Shortly after dawn the next morning, Richard Layton arrived with a statement to be signed by the abbot, in which Abbot Whiting admitted that he refused to turn over Glastonbury Abbey to the king's new church. The bursar and sacristan listened solemnly as Richard read the document aloud.

"Well, my friends," a tender smile flickered upon the abbot's pallid face, "this is our moment of reckoning."

Layton snorted with disdain. "You are a fool, Whiting. You and your accomplices will hang for this. If you are hoping Chancellor Cromwell will stay his hand in your case, your hopes will be sorely disappointed. You are not so special, after all."

Richard said nothing, but his eyes lingered for a moment on John's. His hand trembled as he signed willingly. Snatching the document away, Layton left. The three men sat in silence, eating a little of the cheese and cold bread from the platter that had been placed upon the table. At nine o'clock an officer of the guard knocked then opened the door. Looking to his friends, Richard gave words to the obvious.

"It is time to go." Emerging from the door of the gatehouse into the chilly air, the daylight was glum and weak, as if the sun sorrowed at the magnitude of the moment behind layers of thick and foreboding clouds. They were escorted by the king's guards to Magdalene Street, where they were unceremoniously loaded at spear point into the abbot's carriage. The abbey monks had been ordered to stay away; only Ambrose and Rowland were allowed to witness their exodus, and they stood at the gate, faces lurid and drawn.

Over the next days they traveled at a brisk pace with an armed guard of ten mounted soldiers, while the three commissioners continued to ransack the abbot's papers and tear through his apartments. The dissolution was only just beginning. On September 22, as the envoy and carriage carrying the monks of Glastonbury approached London, the commissioners sent the following letter to Lord Thomas Cromwell.

Please it your lordship to be advertised that we came to Glastonbury on Friday last past, about ten o'clock in the forenoon. Because the abbot was then at Sharpham, his manor a mile and somewhat more from the abbey, without any delay we went into the same place and questioned him there. His answer was not to our purpose, and we advised him to call to his remembrance that which he had forgotten, and so declare the truth. That same day we came with him to the abbey and proceeded that night to search his study for letters and books.

We found in his study a written book of arguments against the divorce of his king's majesty and the lady dowager, and also diverse pardons, copies of papal bulls, and the counterfeit life of Thomas Becket in print; but we could not find any letter that was material to our cause. And so we proceeded again to examine him concerning the articles we received from your Lordship. As we take it, in his answers appears his cankered and traitorous heart and mind against the king's majesty and his succession.

By the same answers, signed with his hand, and sent to your lordship by this bearer, more plainly shall appear. And so, with as fair words as we could, his being but a very weak man and sickly, we have conveyed him hence into the Tower. We have in money £300 and above; but certainty of silver or gold plates and other stuff at Glastonbury, we do not know as yet, for we have not had the opportunity to search for the same. Shortly, we intend (God willing) to proceed to that task. Then we shall ascertain your lordship as soon as as we may.

This is also to advise your lordship that we have found a fair chalice of gold, and diverse other parcels of plate, which the abbot had secretly hid from commissioners as have been there in times past.

It may please your lordship to avail us of the king's pleasure by this bearer, to whom we shall deliver the custody and the keeping of the abbot's house—the abbey and abbot's chambers—with such stuff as we intend to leave there, to be convenient to the king's use. We assure your lordship it is the finest house of that sort that we have ever seen. We would that your lordship did know it as we do; then we doubt not that your lordship would judge it a house meet for the king's majesty and for no other man. This is to our great comfort, and we trust verily that there shall never again come any treason against the king within that house.

Furthermore, we advise your lordship that there is not one learned doctor within that house; there are bachelors of divinity, which are only meanly learned, as far as we can perceive. And thus our Lord preserve your good Lordship.

With the abbot and the two most senior monks on their way to London, Layton, Pollard, and Moyle were comfortably ensconced in the abbot's chambers. A fire burned merrily as Layton frowned over the freshly penned letter, a glass of fine French wine at his hand beside the bottle. Tossing back a gulp, he muttered as he signed the letter, then held it up and waved the thin vellum to dry.

"Glastonbury is known to be one of the largest and most revered Benedictine monasteries in this land." He commented with a sage glance at his colleagues.

"Cromwell has informed me that the king is avidly interested in the legend that this abbey is the home of the Holy Grail. King Arthur's bones are buried here—in fact the natives of Somerset and south Wales worship the ancient king here at his famous shrine. Cromwell believes we will discover a chalice or golden cup. Therefore, it would be to our advantage to find something that will serve as such a mythical item."

By the heat of a candle flame he melted wax upon the letter, then sealed it with his ring and handed it to Moyle, who took it to the door and handed it to the waiting courier. When the man had left, Moyle returned and Layton continued, "And, as with all our great Tudor monarchs, our king is particularly enamoured with King Arthur—rightfully so!"

He plucked a piece of venison from the platter on the table and popped it into his mouth. Chewing thoughtfully, he added. "Interrogate those two senior monks. What are their names?"

Moyle offered, "Ambrose, I believe. And Roland."

"What about the chamberlain, Jack Horner? He has provided information to the Crown before," Pollard offered.

"The abbot's chamberlain Jack Horner has not been seen since we arrived." Moyle responded with an offhand shrug.

Layton pursed his lips. "Yes. Well, find out what Ambrose and Roland know. I am sure there is a conspiracy going on here. Somewhere we will find the chalice of gold that Cromwell seeks. Tomorrow, we will open the sepulcher in the transept, exhume Arthur's bones and then transport them to Whitehall, where the king is presently residing. I deem he will be thrilled with the gift. Who knows what rewards we may gain from such a find? It is as it should be, that the House of Tudor will be in possession of the greatest artifact in the history of Britain and her kings."

CHAPTER TWELVE

Glastonbury
October 1539

In the days ahead, Layton's desire to send the bones of King Arthur as a gift to the king was delayed as chaos erupted at the abbey. When Ambrose was called before the commissioners, he was of no help to their task. He insisted that he had never been involved in the administration of the abbey and was nothing more than a simple monk, who sometimes called the role for Roger James. Several other monks, including Simon, Geoffrey, and Rowland, corroborated his story. In the process of their interrogations, Ambrose and Roland managed to send the commissioners on several wild goose chases that continued to delay the opening of the king's sarcophagus, and thus the commissioners intruded into every nook and corner, hell bent on locating a chalice or cup.

The commissioners ordered the careless deconstruction of shrines throughout the church, leaving them desecrated in their search for gold and silver. They took every plate they found, rifled through the library, pulled out valuable books and packed them away to be taken to London along with precious art. Priceless manuscripts and paintings were destroyed in the process. The gardens were trampled into little more than a muddy pulp. The commissioners upended John Thorne's office and read through his financial records in minute detail. They instructed the soldiers to ransack the sacristy and, finally, they began to take the abbey apart, stone by stone. The monks looked on in stunned horror while, among their own ranks, bewilderment and grief took over. After the abbey dormitory was searched, five of the monks disappeared during the night.

Although the fabled chalice had not appeared, the commissioners were excited by their initial finds, and they wrote to Cromwell on September 28 that the riches of the abbey were so abundant that they had never seen such wealth. Indeed it was a prize fit for a king. They reported that there were four large parks adjoining the property, the farthest away only four miles from the abbey. Indeed, there was also a great mere pond of five miles' breadth only a mile and a half from the abbey; this was well stocked with fat fish—pike, bream, and perch—ready for the taking.

Finally, on October first, Layton turned his attention to the king's shrine. He personally oversaw the opening of the sepulcher, calling in several soldiers to help.

"Look at this, sir." Moyle pointed to the stone slab fitted into the end of the sepulcher, which fell easily into the hands of the two soldiers who were assisting the deconstruction of the shrine. "This stone looks as if it had been replaced recently."

Layton watched, the frown upon his face growing into consternation and then anger when the men exclaimed over the light weight of the coffin as they hauled it out of the crypt. They labored with iron bars to open the coffin lid, which had been nailed down. When it was finally open, a shocked silence spread among the bystanders—Layton, Moyle, Pollard, and five sweating guards who had labored to free the coffin.

"Bring Ambrose to me in my quarters. Immediately!" He charged out fuming and stormed across the muddy yard that was once a garden toward the abbot's lodge.

"What is the meaning of this?" He snapped at Ambrose, who stood with calm aplomb, his hands clasped behind his back.

"I do not know what you speak of, sir."

"Oh yes you do, monk. The king's crypt is empty," he charged, surging forward with hands in tight fists. "This is theft and sedition. Your abbot will pay dearly for this. If you don't divulge what you know, the monks of this abbey will also suffer for it, more than they already do, I can assure you. I have a mind to advise Cromwell to put you to the rack."

Ambrose did not move or flinch but kept his eyes locked on the commissioner, and it seemed the monk weighed the character of the one before him. Layton's face turned red and blotched as he snorted and huffed, throwing himself angrily into his seat at the abbot's desk. He called out to the soldiers on guard to bring Moyle and Pollard. Finally Ambrose stirred, mustering an attitude of abject humility.

"My apologies, sir. I do not know anything about the king's crypt or missing bones. You see, King Arthur has never been of interest to me. I am a simple monk. I spend my days in prayer to our Lord Jesus Christ and his holy mother, Mary."

A soldier knocked on the door and escorted Rowland and Geoffrey into the room. They stood beside Ambrose and awaited the commissioner's next move. Regaining his composure, Layton stood up.

"I remember quite well when I was here in 1534 that Roger James was responsible for the king's shrine. Who among you were assistants to James?"

Roland answered. "Two young monks named William and Angus assisted Roger James. They left days ago, along with three other monks who decided they would not stay for the impending dissolution. At this point I have no idea of their whereabouts."

This admission brought on a spate of furious queries levied at Ambrose and Roland as to where the monks might have gone. Taking the lead, Roland answered, keeping his voice firm and yet resigned as he faced the angry commissioners. Frustrated, Layton dismissed the monks and turned his attention to dispatch two soldiers to London with a terse message for Thomas Cromwell, scrawled upon a scrap piece of vellum torn from a book:

Please be advised that Whiting, Thorne, and James have stolen the bones of King Arthur. The king's shrine in the transept is empty. No one knows where they have been taken. They are guilty of robbery.

Layton smiled to himself as he thought over this new development. This would work quite well: he had received a letter recently from Cromwell, who was frustrated that more gold and money had not been located. He had written that he was certain Whiting was guilty of stealing from his own abbey. Now it was confirmed. Layton would surely find other instances of theft, as well. He redoubled his efforts, sparing no destruction in the process.

On October 2 the commissioners wrote again to Cromwell. Once the king's bones had been discovered missing, Layton was even more anxious than before to secure for King Henry the bounteous lands, orchards and gardens, the oxen, cattle and sheep herds, as well as the riches of the abbey itself.

Without any further ado, the commissioners issued the edict dismissing all servants of the church, including James Renynger the organist, and evicted the monks from their abbey. Cromwell was too savvy to turn the monks loose upon the English countryside to foment discontent and revolution; instead of leaving them penniless, he offered each one £5 a year. It was not much, but it was enough to keep them from starvation.

A few days later an agitated crowd was gathered at The Crown in Glastonbury when Pollard and Moyle showed up again—as they had one week before—to take statements from residents of the town about the abbot's public or private opinions, which might condemn him further to the charge of treason against the king. A scene erupted when Jack Horner showed up and was confronted by two monks who, objecting to the statements being made, also accused

Horner of spying and subterfuge. James Renynger was among the locals who intervened, spiriting the monks away to his own home and giving them shelter.

By October 10, the news arrived from London that King Henry had agreed to marry Anne of Cleves. Dr. Layton's work was finished, and he was soon to pack the rest of his "evidence" and largess garnered for the king for the return trip to London. When he arrived in London on October 15, he carried in his possession gold, silver, and jewels, gilded altar plates, rare books, tapestries, paintings and statuary, all of which was personally delivered by Richard Layton to Cromwell.

Within days, everyone in London had heard how the Lord Privy Seal's manuscript, "Remembrance," listed Cromwell's final assessment of the case in hand outlining the guilt of the abbot and the riches taken from Glastonbury Abbey. In the manuscript, the "plate of Glaston" was described as 11,000 ounces of pure gold. It also declared a confiscated surfeit of £1100, as well as outstanding debts owed to the abbey as over £2000.

Rumours flew about, dashing into the seasoned stone corners of London's elite circles, of an addendum that had been read and passed on, whispered from one to another of the officials and courtiers and magistrates. Cromwell had shown his hand clearly in a personal addendum written upon the Lord Privy Seal's document—an item which read: "The Abbot of Glaston to be tried at Glaston and also executed there with his accomplices."

The decision for death had already been made.

CHAPTER THIRTEEN

Scotland
October 1539

The conspirators had arrived at Kildonan on the first day of October, grateful that their wagons held up throughout the long and often rough and arduous circumstances of the trip—especially the loading and unloading on and off the merchant ship, which had been a dangerous and risky undertaking. The boats were sturdy and big enough, but loading heavy wagons with two horses each was nerve-wracking enough without the added tension of a precious and secret cargo.

When at last they rolled and clattered into the grassy yard of Kildonan early one morning, Margaret Hamilton Thorne was standing outside near the chicken coop assessing the state of her flock with Kenna.

"Thanks be to Mother Mary, you are back!" She smiled broadly, holding her arms open wide. Maddy was the first to reach her, then Colin, who hugged her firmly.

"Mòrai! You cannot imagine how glad we are to be here!" Colin laughed as he gathered her slender form into an embrace. She reached a hand to his cheek as she extricated herself and turned to embrace Geleis with a warm smile. "And *you* have been sorely missed, Geleis!"

Her smile of pleasure deepening, she drew the young women to her side. "Maddy and Anne, it is with all my heart that I welcome you as part of our family here at Kildonan. It is fine indeed to have you with us, and Jennet is as pleased as I. She is out collecting herbs today with Broderick. They will return for supper. We are anxious to hear everything."

Gathered at Margaret's sumptuous table at promptly six o'clock, the new arrivals sat with Broderick, Jennet and Margaret, who were eager to know all that had transpired in the past months. Margaret listened carefully, her face grave, as she asked about a trial. Kenna served their bowls with fish stew, moving silently about to bring in platters of boiled beef and turnips.

"Any trial will be a sham, Mòrai, nothing more than a spectacle. They will most assuredly die." Colin's voice grew heavy with the weight of grief as he finished his report. "We can only pray that the end is merciful and swift."

Margaret genuflected, her face betraying her inmost feelings. Their earlier mood had been high spirited; now they grew silent as each reflected, plunged into their own inner worlds. Their hearts were sore, and Maddy sought to assuage their pain as she settled upon a couch after supper with Jennet and Anne.

"Ben has been looking through our library—he has found some compelling books. Ben, would you share what you have told me about William of Malmesbury?"

Ben's smile was broad as he accepted a cup of whiskey and walked to the fire, where he leaned against the mantle. "Well, with Margaret's permission, I will bring the book from the library and read to you from it."

Within ten minutes he was back with several ancient volumes in hand, all hand-copied vellum. Geleis tended the fire while Colin had pulled up a low seat near Margaret's chair. As Ben explained, the Oxford scholar in him emerged.

"William was born around 1090 of Norman and English blood in Somerset. His father recognized scholarly propensities in him at a young age, and so he was sent to Malmesbury Abbey to be educated. There he studied logic, medicine, ethics and history, eventually becoming the librarian of his abbey. In the year 1125 he visited Glastonbury Abbey and stayed for several weeks at the monastery, exploring the shrines, plumbing the treasure trove in the library, and talking with the monks. He was compelled to compile chronicles of ancient times and the history of England, and in that cause he journeyed around England.

"His peers asked him to be the Abbot of Malmesbury, but he graciously declined the request—he died in his middle years with some renown and a great deal of respect as a scholar and man of God. From his sojourn at Glastonbury came *De Antiquitate Glastoniensis Ecclesiae*, which he dedicated to Henry de Blois, who was abbot at the time.

"In this book Williams speaks of the Old Church, calling it in Latin the *vetusta ecclesia*, built of wattle and daub—as legend had it, by Joseph of Arimathea and his group of disciples. Of course it was repaired many times and even rebuilt over the centuries, incorporating whatever remained of the old structure each time. We know it today as the Lady Chapel. Then the Lady Chapel was reconstructed as well, after the fire in 1184 that destroyed what was left of the Old Church, as well as the vestments, relics, and books of the abbey."

Holding the volume in his hand, Ben continued, "In the opening chapter of *De Antiquitate Glastoniensis Ecclesiae,* William writes that Saint Philip, preaching in France, converted many people, baptizing them as he was taught by his own teacher, John the Baptist. He chose twelve disciples to go with Joseph of Arimathea to Britain.

"Writing of the sanctity of Glastonbury Abbey, William had more to say on precious documents, still in existence at the time, which he read with his own eyes. These detailed the founding of the church in the first century after the death of Christ, stating that there were 'documents of no small credit' which testified that the abbey at Glastonbury was erected by the disciples of Christ."

Anne's face shone with pride as Ben opened the book and read, gingerly turning the cracked and yellowed pages.

The church of which we speak is commonly called by the Saxons the Old Church on account of its antiquity. It was first formed of wattles, and from the beginning breathed and was redolent of a mysterious divine sanctity which spread throughout the country. The actual building was insignificant but it was so holy. Waves of common people thronging

*thither flooded every path; rich men laid aside their
state to gather there, and men of learning and piety
assembled there in great numbers...The resting place
of so many saints is deservedly called a heavenly
sanctuary on earth.*

Ben looked up, his face flushed with excitement.
Maddy queried, "Did you find something about the discovery of the bones of King Arthur?"

Ben grinned as he answered. "William of Malmesbury
writes with wonderment about the incredible numbers of
saints and holy men who were buried at Glastonbury Abbey
over the centuries. In particular he commented on the two
sculpted, pyramid-shaped stone tombs outside the church
walls. These stone pyramids were extremely weathered but
still in place when William of Malmesbury was writing in
the twelfth century.

"The monuments may have been markers or actual
graves or 'coped tombs' and were engraved with names of
abbots and holy men who were buried or entombed in or
around the abbey. Between these two is the place where an
unknown Welsh bard confided to King Henry II that the
body of Arthur lay. 'Dig there and you will find him,' the
bard assured the king. In fact, it was Henry who sponsored
the project to locate the king's bones.

"Another chronicler, a monk named Gerald of Wales,
was writing in the same time period. He wrote before the
year 1192, and this is what he had to say."

Pulling another book from the pile, he read.

Now the body of King Arthur...was found in our own days at Glastonbury, deep down in the earth and encoffined in a hollow oak between two stone pyramids...in the grave was a cross of lead, placed under a stone not above it, but fixed on the other side...I have felt the letters engrave thereon, which do not project or stand out, but are turned inwards towards the stone. They run as follows: 'Here lies buried the renowed King Arthur, with Guinevere his second wife, in the Isle of Avalon'...two parts of the tomb, to wit, the head, were allotted to the bones of the man, while the remaining third towards the foot contained the bones of the woman in a place set apart; and there was found a yellow tress of woman's hair still retraining its colour and freshness; but when a certain monk snatched it and lifted it with greedy hand, it straightway all of it fell into dust... the bones of Arthur...were so huge...his shank-bone when placed against that of the tallest man in the place...reached a good three inches above his knee... the eye-socket was a good palm in width...there were ten wounds or more, all of which were scarred over, save one larger than the rest, which had made a great hole.

Ben looked around at his audience, his brows arched in speculation. "Most compelling, is it not? It comes as no surprise, then, that our king, Henry VIII, wants these relics to augment his claims to divine right. I suppose he would put them in Westminster Cathedral, to convince his subjects of a more direct connection between the Tudors and the ancient King of Britain."

Margaret tapped her cane on the stone floor, drawing their attention as she spoke. "'Tis a sad day, indeed, when Glastonbury Abbey has had to send its great relics into exile, but this reading may bolster our grieving hearts. Surely the abbey will survive this terrible travail to rise again."

Colin's face was sad, his eyes betraying his mood. "The Company of Avalon may seem to be broken, and certainly it is dispersed for this time. But we will carry on. We are the Company of Avalon now..."

He reached a hand out to each one. "Ben, Anne, Geleis... And now you, Jennet, and Broderick, Mòrai and Magdalyne." His eye fell last upon his wife, who smiled with appreciation for her husband's gift for lifting the spirits of others. In this moment, he reminded her of Abba, her Uncle Richard, as Colin concluded.

"It is our sacred task to keep the relics of Glastonbury safe. And this, my friends, we will do—until they may be received back again within those hallowed walls."

Ben broke a stretch of silence to reflect the sentiment they all shared. "What a relief it is to be in a place where we know our cargo is safe, to know that our mission will soon be accomplished."

"Aye," Geleis nodded, "and we should leave as soon as we can be ready for the two-week trip north into the island's wild places. We will need to get the relics to the hiding place. Seamus tells me that he has it ready."

Colin agreed. "We canna take the risk that the king's men could trace the bones here, if—and most probably when, knowing the zealous lust of Cromwell—they discover that the bones are gone. The vials of Jesus' sweat and blood, brought by Joseph of Arimathea, are well known to all, but the existence of a chalice is often dispatched to the realm of myth."

Margaret listened thoughtfully before she voiced her concern. "When Cromwell's commissioners realize these relics are not to be found at Glastonbury, they will search for them. Tis possible this could have already happened. Should they trace the obvious link between our families and Glastonbury Abbey—and they will—then they may very well arrive at our door asking questions. It will not go well if the relics are still here. Indeed, we must be free to invite them to search Kildonan."

Her wise counsel carried the weight of truth and common sense, which prevailed among them all to close the evening with a clear agreement to plan upon the morrow the necessities for a trek into the mountains as soon as possible. Seeing the eyes of the weary travelers begin to droop, Lady Hamilton sent them off to bed.

Four days later the men left with the stonemason and his son, Seamus and Carey Carrick, from the village. Their family had been loyal lieges of the Hamilton clan for many generations, and Seamus had gone on the first exploration to Goatfell with Colin and the men, months earlier. While Colin and Maddy had been busy with Geleis, Ben, and Anne at Glastonbury, the stonemasons had built a thick cairn to hold the boxes. Seamus had designed a stronghold that would be impervious to the rain, sleet, and snow that landed on Goatfell every winter. Nothing would penetrate inside the cairn, which sat deep inside a cliff overhang in the remote reaches of the mountain. The question remained, how far could the wagons go into the wilds of the mountain itself, and how far would they have to carry the heavy bones of King Arthur? They took tools, wheelbarrows, block and tackle and enough food for two weeks. In addition, they would hunt, as the mountains of Arrain were rich with game.

With their sturdy horses pulling the wagons, they left excited and ready for the adventure. Seeing their menfolk off with embraces and watching them disappear over the hill, Maddy and Anne turned back to their task of settling into the rhythms of their new life. While the wagons trundled north, Anne helped Jennet in the drying shed as she supervised Kenna and several of the women in the drying of herbs, vegetables and fruits of the autumn harvest.

Maddy assisted Mòrai in her rounds to the elderly and infirm within the village. The local folk looked forward to these visits, when Lady Hamilton came once a season to see that their needs were well-met. These excursions Margaret made usually with Father Gordon, the priest at the small chapel that served the hard-working souls of Kildonan, but with Maddy's arrival, the ritual visits would change. Lady Hamilton would visit the villagers with the laird's new wife.

Maddy held Mòrai's hand as they walked arm in arm, picking their way along through white sand and rocks. A strong wind blew in from the churning surf, bending the tall sea grasses as they made their way down a path that cut deep through shallow dunes toward the cottage of old Shona—mother of Seamus and grandmother of Carey. Thinking of the men just beginning their journey to Goatfell, Maddy glanced out at the sea and the gathering mountains of silver-lined clouds, hoping it would not rain before they made camp that night. She turned her thoughts to the importance of meeting Shona Carrick, who she had heard was acknowledged by all as the headwoman of the village.

The door of the low, turf-roofed stone cottage opened with a loud creak to reveal an ancient woman with red cheeks and bright black eyes. Her craggy face broke open in a bright smile of welcome as she stood holding onto the wooden door with one hand and propped herself up with a cane in the other.

"Why, Lady Hamilton! Ye are most welcome in my humble home."

Shona Carrick hobbled across the floor behind Margaret, gesturing with her cane toward two wooden chairs at the table. She wore woolen mittens, frayed ends open to show that the tips of her rough fingers were reddened from wind and water. Her long woolen skirt was stained and soiled from months of wear, and about her bodice was a heavy, blue-grey woolen shawl tied across a thick woven tunic of dark brown lamb's wool.

"Shona, have ye met Magdalene Thorne, the wife of my grandson Colin? I am pleased to say that I have a new granddaughter! She will be Lady Hamilton at Kildonan after me. Maddy will accompany me on my rounds, from this time on."

Shona looked Maddy over with enthusiasm, then

250

quipped in her lively way, "Ye're welcome, lass...though likely I will need to call ye Lady Hamilton soon enough."

Margaret chuckled as she cast a gleaming eye about the cottage. Its roof was slanted, so that the low ceiling on one end required one to stoop to climb upon the low bed that rested against one wall. An oiled woolen curtain was stretched tight upon the wooden frame of the only window, which faced south and the sea, shielding the room from winter's cold. A peat fire glowered and spit upon the tiny hearth, and above it hung an iron pot. They talked a while, mostly in the Gaelic dialect of the isle, about sheep and fishing and babies that would be born in the village in the months ahead. Though Maddy was happy to discover that she followed most of it, she was relieved when it veered back toward English.

"Are ye hungry?" Shona asked eagerly. "I've a stew of fish and turnips, tis tasty to eat, spiced with salt and sheep fat. Will ye not join me in a bowl?"

Margaret smiled, reaching a hand out to touch the older woman, her elder by perhaps ten years. "No, Shona, but I thank ye. Ye've always been generous to a fault, what with feeding everyone who comes by this cottage, keeping Seamus busy with hunting and fishing!" She chuckled. "But we came today to see how *you* fare, with winter comin' on. Is there anything ye might be needin' that I could provide?"

Shona's grin displayed missing teeth, with the remaining ones blackened. "No, ma'am. There is nothing I need, but I'll warrant that ye might be the one in need. We folk of Kildonan—all of us—are with ye." She glanced knowingly at Maddy, whose face turned quizzical at the oblique reference in Gaelic. A penetrating look passed between Margaret and Shona while Maddy looked on with interest, covering her mouth with one hand and waiting until, after a time, Margaret rose to leave.

Back out in the cold fresh air, they trudged carefully along the sand path, Maddy holding Mòrai's arm to steady her progress. After a few moments, she pursued her question, leaning close to Margaret's ear to be heard above the wail of the wind.

"Mòrai, what did she mean, that the folk of Kildonan are with you?"

Hitting a rough patch on the path where they had to navigate through a stretch of small boulders, Margaret clutched the younger woman's hand tightly.

"She means that the villagers stand behind us in the safeguarding of the artifacts."

Maddy's eyes grew wide. "They *know*? Surely that is dangerous, Mòrai! Who told them?"

Margaret stopped and turned to face Maddy. She placed a soft, warm hand upon the young woman's cheek, growing chill from wind-lashed drops of rain that had begun to fall.

"My dear," Margaret began, her brogue growing thick, "dinna fash yerself. Of course they ken everything. Just because they are poor does na mean they dinna understand exactly what is goin' on." She paused and gazed at Maddy, then pointed toward the path with her cane.

"Dinna worry. Ye'll come to understand our ways in time."

Her smile was warm as she patted Maddy's face, then grasped her cane firmly in hand and continued on toward the next cottage.

News traveled surprisingly fast to Kildonan, with all the trade ships sailing the Firth of Clyde and the Irish Sea, not to mention the patrols of the Royal Navy that watched over the salt waters held in common between England and Scotland, which were invariably a source of contention and conflict between the two countries. Merchant ships were welcomed not only because they brought goods to the island but because they delivered letters and messages from the mainland. Near the end of October, Maddy was excited to hear from Colin that a ship was soon to dock at Viking Bay.

The ship had sailed from Aberdaron in Wales, bringing with it goods from France and Spain and more exotic places to the south and east—wine, wheat, oranges and lemons, raisins, dried figs, saffron, cumin, cinnamon and bolts of silk. The ship would be in port for two more days making trades for salt cured beef, venison, fish, bags of oats, and—most importantly—the highland whiskey of Arrain.

It was always a lively and sometimes dangerous scene when such a ship docked at the pier of Viking Bay, or further north at Brodick Castle. Business deals were honored or dishonored, sometimes giving rise to disagreement that could turn into brawls or fights to the death. Men drank at the tavern inn, and the local girls who tended them tucked coins into their bodices for favors rendered in the back rooms. From Mòrai's point of view, it was no place for a lady of Maddy's standing. However, after some pleading and negotiating, Colin hitched the horses to the wagon and drove Maddy over the mountain along the coast and down into the hamlet where the ship was harbored in Viking Bay, not far from the Holy Isle.

He stopped the wagon and helped her down. A silver mist was falling, making a sheen of tiny water beads on their thick woolen cloaks. Colin sniffed the sea air, noticing that the water lapped placid at the shore. The ship, with its sails carefully folded and tied to three tall masts, floated easily at the long rock pier. They hurried to the ship and approached the first mate, who was busy shouting orders and overseeing the loading and unloading of goods as sailors and local merchants trotted to and fro carrying heavy boxes and casks of whiskey.

When they asked for mail, the ship's mate pointed to an old sailor who sat on the timber pier. The man had a ruff of gray whiskers all along his jaw and rheumy blue eyes—his job was to dispense the mail to those anxious to receive expected letters or small packages. A reputable merchant ship such as this was trusted to deliver such things for a fee, and most of the time they provided a much needed and honored service. With growing excitement, they hurried to his side.

"Hello kind sir, and welcome to Arrain! Any mail for Kildonan, or for Colin or Magdalyne Thorne?" Colin queried.

The sailor glanced through the letters stacked on a low table beside him, then through the tied parcels that filled a low wooden box at his feet. "Nothing, sir." He looked at them oddly, mouth open to reveal a row of blackened teeth, then pointed.

"Ye may have something to do with those two fellows. They said they were coming to Kildonan."

Squinting against the bright afternoon light that shone down in shafts through clouds and mist, Colin saw two familiar faces walking along the strand, dressed as clerks or ordinary laymen.

"Angus! William!" Colin called out, breaking into a run with Maddy close behind. The monks fell into Colin's welcoming embrace, greeting his wife, the abbot's niece, with warm reserve and huge smiles.

"Mistress Thorne," Angus began.

"Please, Angus," she turned to William, "and William, I beg you to call me Maddy. Surely we are of the same age, and we have been through too much together for such formality. But tell us, how did this happen? What is the news?"

The monks fell silent and tears welled in Angus' blue eyes. "Our worse fears have come to pass, mistress. The dissolution is underway at Glastonbury. Abbot Whiting, Father John, and Father Roger are in the Tower in London, awaiting trial. Before they were arrested, they told us to come to you, to deliver the news. The abbot said you would be anxiously awaiting word. He said to ask you," Angus choked back tears, "if it might be possible for us to take refuge at Kildonan."

William finished with a soft gulp, eyes pleading as they came to rest on Colin. "We understand there is a chapel and a priest there. And we can help guard the artifacts, we are able-bodied and can work hard."

Colin placed an affectionate hand on the monk's shoulder. "You are both welcome here, Angus. Let us go to the wagons—you can tell us everything on the ride back to Kildonan. Mòrai, my grandmother, that is, awaits us, eager for news, and she will be glad to welcome you."

William continued the story as they walked along toward the wagon, with Angus wiping his eyes and frequently blowing his nose into a linen handkerchief. Soon they trundled south over the mountain, the clatter of the wagon wheels background to the story that unfolded. When they crested the hill, the monks fell silent, drinking in the view of Kildonan and the vast spread of sea and sky.

"And here we are—welcome to Kildonan. I know some people who will be happy to see you! Of course, you will need to tell the story over again at supper. Come to meet my grandmother, Lady Hamilton." Colin emitted a desultory chuckle. "Then, as soon as you have cleaned up a bit, we will sit down to table for hot food—after which, I will pour you some good Arrain whisky." The monks remembered the taste of Arrain whisky and murmured with happy anticipation, their faces still awestruck by the beauty and novelty of their surroundings.

The sharp eyes of Geleis had seen their approach long before anyone else, and he met them at the outer gate to the road, his face bright with joy as he embraced the two monks. Proceeding to the castle yard, Geleis took the horses and the wagon to the stable while Colin led them to the house. The shining misty day had passed into late afternoon, with storm clouds gathering over a sea that sparkled with the last rays of the sun.

Margaret was sitting beside the fire in the large parlour. Hearing Colin's voice, she called out, "Did you receive any word of Glastonbury?" A question formed on her face as she looked at Angus and William. "And who are these fine young men?"

Colin stepped forward. "Indeed, we did receive word of Glastonbury! William, Angus, this is my grandmother, Lady Margaret Hamilton Thorne. Mòrai, this is Father William and Father Angus, two monks of Glastonbury who are very close to Abba Whiting and Uncle John. We told you about them. They are of the Company of Avalon; they have been trusted members of our conspiracy these past months, and in addition, they are the apprentices of Roger, the sacristan. One of their prime duties was the care of the king's shrine."

Margaret absorbed this information with interest, leaning forward in her chair to greet them with out-stretched hands. They were duly impressed by the Hamilton matriarch, leaning over to take the proffered hands, gnarled with age but warm and soft, with reverence into their own. Father William bowed, Angus following.

"We are honored, Lady Hamilton." She gazed into each of their eyes, and they looked back with candor.

"And we are grateful, with all our hearts, for the refuge of this fine castle keep," Angus continued. "Would that we had met under other auspices, for we have sad news to share of Glastonbury Abbey."

"I imagine you do," Margaret pursed her lips, taking in their woolen trousers and long cloaks. "Tomorrow you will meet our priest, Father Gordon. I am sure he will welcome you was gladly as we do. He can help you get back into your proper garb as monks—that is, if you wish. But we will talk of that later. Now, let us get you properly settled in. We will meet here for dinner at six sharp."

Gathered at supper around Margaret's sumptuous table, they spoke of the events at Glastonbury Abbey, beginning with the arrival of Layton, Moyle, and Pollard, and their sorrow to leave Richard Whiting, Roger James, and John Thorne. They spoke of how they had reluctantly followed the abbot's instructions to the letter, leaving soon after he was taken from Sharpham Manor, but they lingered in town until the dissolution was well underway, taking refuge with the abbey organist James Reynenger and his family, who lived in Glastonbury. With the help of James, they had removed their monk's robes and donned the clothes of a layperson, stashing their robes in the packs they slung over their shoulders.

Their story unfurled, a powerful wave that carried everyone through supper, as the monks relayed all they had seen and heard. Around the table all eyes were fastened upon them, their attention rapt upon the words of the monks, unshed tears gleaming in their eyes by the light of the candelabras. Kenna came and went, clearing away dishes and bowls while they sat and listened, hungry for every detail.

"Abbot Whiting spoke to all the monks a few days before Layton arrived," Angus explained. "He begged us not to grieve, even though we each will grieve in our own way. But most of all, he wanted us to carry on with good spirits—he begged us not to let this destroy our faith."

He looked to William, who then relayed the abbot's speech almost word for word. Angus wiped his eyes, as did many of those listening, as the poignant memory was brought to life. After the platters were taken away and the table cleared, they rose from their chairs to settle around the fire while Geleis served the promised whiskey.

A well-embellished tale unfolded of how they had escaped Glastonbury with the help of James Renynger, the organist at the abbey who had been a close friend over the past few years. They described how Pollard and Moyle had arrived at The Crown in Glastonbury, hoping to elicit statements that would condemn Abbot Whiting for treason against the king. Jack Horner had been there, telling lies, and Angus and William had started up a ruckus, calling him a spy and a traitor. James Renynger had hustled the young monks away, taking them to his own home for protection against the king's men.

From there William and Angus had struck out on foot going north. They had been lucky all along the way, getting rides from sympathetic farmers going to market with their harvest. At times they received help from other displaced monks and friars, who had lost their abbeys and friaries to dissolution.

"The stories we heard from these mendicants were long and sad, often tragic," William sighed. "We will tell more of these another time, should you wish to hear."

Finally, they reached Scotland and eventually arrived at Ayr, where they had played upon the sympathies of the captain of the ship that would sail across the firth to Arrain. They attributed their good luck to the grace of Blessed Mary. Angus' eyes filled with tears.

"We wait now, with you, to hear what will be the fate of our dearest abbot and his companions, our beloved friends." He crossed himself. "May God be with them."

CHAPTER FOURTEEN

London
November 1539

It was an autumn day in London—wet, gray, and drizzling. Thomas Cromwell walked through the iron grill at the gate to the Tower, Sir Richard Rich beside him dressed in a dark plum-colored brocade waist-length cloak over woolen hose, jaunty ostrich feathers dancing in his velvet hat, a rich silver chain of office draped about his shoulders. Cromwell wore his characteristic black robe, but his gold chain of office was far more impressive and ornate. They strode across paving stones toward a massive oak door surrounded by a bevy of guards in the king's livery. One of the guards opened the door and stood aside as the two officials clambered briskly up the stone steps.

Thomas Cromwell's silver buckled shoes resounded upon the stone steps of the Tower as they climbed. Strands of straight brown hair straggled out beneath the velvet drape of his hat. His face was a cold mask, his sharp hazel eyes hooded and small in a dim, pasty face. He had read and digested the written report from commissioners Layton,

Pollard, and Moyle, who were on their way to London and would arrive within the week. A cold fury had settled into his gut at the second reading of their epistles, including the short note advising him that the king's bones were gone.

The nerve of the man!

There was no time to waste. He had considered putting Whiting and his two accomplices to the rack—that had worked well to get the truth, or at least a confession, from many others. But there was too much grumbling going around these days at the tortures he had sanctioned, he had too much to risk at the moment, with the king already grousing over Cromwell's choice of a new wife—Anne of Cleves. And the woman had not even arrived in England yet!

No, he had come to the conclusion that a horrific public death was enough. He didn't have time for a secret racking, which would draw the whole process out longer. He could feel Henry's wrath searching for a place to land, and his instincts told him that he needed to offer the king a distraction, a gift, something to assuage his merciless mood. Cromwell's gut clenched: he would tear that church apart until they found the damned bones, the relics. They had to be there somewhere.

The sooner Richard Whiting was dead, the better.

England had to come to understand—this is what happens when you do not obey your king. The dissolution was an unpleasant business, altogether, and had become more and more onerous as time went on. There was no other solution for it, and it would be over soon; Glastonbury Abbey was one of the last to fall.

As they arrived on the landing at the third floor, Cromwell frowned as he gestured tersely to the guard, who unlocked the door and pushed it open for the king's chancellor to enter.

"Wait here for me, Richard." Cromwell dictated, his voice curt as they entered the antechamber to the prisoner's cell on the third floor of the Tower. Rich had asked to accompany Cromwell on this interview, and now he looked at Cromwell with consternation stamped on his face.

"What?"

"I have decided to speak with Whiting and his accomplices alone," Cromwell snapped. Rich bristled, the muscle in his jaw working.

"Then I will leave you, sir."

"Suit yourself," Cromwell muttered with a shrug then gestured to the guard that stood against the wall with lance in hand and the keys jangling from his waist. "Open it," he ordered as the sound of Sir Rich's boot heels on stone as he hurried away reverberated in up the Tower stairs.

Stepping through the door, Cromwell's eyes swept over the room, a large bare rectangle of grey stone that contained three narrow beds, a table and some chairs. He raised his eyebrows at the stack of firewood beside the small hearth: who had approved such luxury for these villains? He would look into it later. His eyes lingered on the three men—Richard Whiting, who sat in a chair beside the fire, Roger James, who read a book at the wooden desk, and John Thorne, who was standing beside one of two windows, gazing out over the river. It was dark and dank, and the fire burned courageously against the dim light and chill that exuded from the walls, rising up from the Thames to permeate the dreary stones of the Tower. Whiting had a woolen shawl about his shoulders, and he appeared to have aged many years since Cromwell had last seen him, two years before.

"Well, gentlemen. I see that your comforts have been well arranged," Cromwell observed with a drawl as he entered the room. He eyed the fireplace, the sparse beds of straw mattresses and woolen blankets. On the table were bronze candlesticks with tallow tapers, a jug of water and three cups. A crust of stale bread lay upon a platter.

Richard looked up, his eyes penetrating and clear despite his frail condition. "Master Cromwell," he said evenly. John Thorne turned from his stance at the window and moved to the abbot's side.

"What are you reading?" Cromwell enquired, looking at Roger James and ignoring John Thorne.

"I am reading King Henry's English translation of the Bible, which is the only book we have in this prison cell." Roger's reply was composed and even.

"Hmm. Well, that is encouraging. Perhaps there is some hope for you, after all."

Roger's rejoinder was wry though not bitter. "I doubt that very seriously, sir."

Cromwell shrugged. "Well. Let us not waste time. As you know, the king is not eager to execute priests. But," he sighed, "those who stand in the way of his church and the true faith, as it has been revealed to our pious and wise monarch, must be dealt with, and with a firm hand. Treason is a crime punishable by death. As is robbery."

Pulling up a chair to sit in front of Richard, the king's chancellor pursed his lips and sucked in his pockmarked cheeks to cast a gloomy, meagre eye upon the abbot. A pause ensued as the two men faced each other, eye-to-eye, then Cromwell spoke casually.

"You have aged, Richard. Lying and stealing do not become you."

Richard said nothing but kept his gaze upon the chancellor.

"Where did you put them?

The three monks did not flinch or blink. Roger answered with a question in return. "Pardon, sir. What is it that you refer to, exactly?"

"You know, *exactly*," Cromwell emphasized Roger's term with sarcasm, "what I am talking about.

John Thorne burst out laughing. "You must be joking, chancellor. Your commissioners are surely on their way back to London as we speak, their coffers—and their pockets—full of all they have ransacked and pillaged from the abbey. And you accuse us of stealing?"

Cromwell frowned. "This is not going to go well for you, John Thorne. You and the sacristan are going to hang, along with your friend, Richard Whiting." He turned a dour eye back to Richard. "We know you have taken Arthur's bones. Where are they?"

Richard raised his brows and rubbed his white beard, which had grown long and thick. John stepped up. "We know nothing of missing bones. We had no time to abscond with the bones, surely you know this. Your spy, Jack Horner, and his friends have watched us for the past two years. They can tell you."

Cromwell jutted out his chin, stood and paced to the window, turned and challenged. "I suppose you also know nothing of the other relics you have guarded for the past years as abbot, like a dragon over its treasure. Where are the relics of Joseph of Arimathea? The vials, the cup?"

Again Roger laughed. "Superstition and legend, sir, just as the skeptics and scholars have said. It was all a hoax to get money from the people. Nothing more."

When silence ensued, Cromwell turned back to the window and mused, "In fact, there should have been a great deal more than we have found, including gold and silver. You, Richard Whiting, are without question guilty of stealing from your own abbey—you have been using the abbey's wealth for your own purposes for years. Perhaps you have even sold off the relics."

Walking back, he leaned over Richard's chair, menacing him with a snarl that spurred John Thorne to action, but the abbot held out his hand and whispered, "No, John."

Glancing at Thorne, Cromwell laughed. "Do you really think you can protect him? That is humorous. Nothing can protect you now." He leaned in, his face only a few inches from Richard's as he spoke between crooked and rotten teeth, spittle gathering in the corners of his lips. "How would you like a turn on the rack, Richard? John Thorne?"

Richard looked down at his folded hands. The two other monks did not speak or move but watched Cromwell closely. "The rack is a most convincing experience. It brings the truth out of everyone." Cromwell watched the abbot with beady, calculating eyes.

"Yes, I think we can arrange that for tomorrow. What say you, Abbot Whiting?"

Richard looked up, blue eyes, gleaming. "There is nothing you can do to me that will change anything, Master Cromwell. I have made peace with my God, and I am ready to suffer and to die."

"Oh come now! Everyone wants to live, sir. No one wants to be tortured." Cromwell smiled sardonically. Richard met the chancellor's eyes with a steady blue gaze. Seeing the certainty there and assessing the impossible John Thorne, Cromwell changed tact, turning toward Roger James.

"Only one thing will prevent your execution. Tell us where the relics are. The vials, the cup, King Arthur's bones. Then, I will show the mercy of my hand."

Straightening his back, Cromwell's gaze lingered on Roger.

"You are a young man. You don't have to die with these old men. Don't fool yourself. When you are dead, I will destroy Glastonbury Abbey, dig up every grave, tear out every stone until these articles, which belong to King Henry, are found. Have no doubt, I *will* find them. Think about it...what is your name? Oh, yes, Roger James."

He stalked to the door, barked an order to the guard, and strode out. The door slammed behind them, and the Benedictines could hear the sound of a key rattling in the lock on the other side of the heavy oak door. They looked at one another in silence. Richard took out his rosary, John returned to the window, and Roger moved back to his chair at the desk, the Bible open before him.

CHAPTER FIFTEEN

Tower and Tor
November 1539

John's soft rampage bounced off cold stone as a miserable afternoon light bled through the two windows of their room in the Tower.

"This is an unbelievable travesty of justice—but then the Tudors have always held themselves above the law, especially Henry VIII. Richard, as a member in the House of Lords, you should have been arraigned and tried before Parliament! At least you would have the satisfaction of a trial before a jury of your peers. But no. When we heard that they postponed the farce of a trial, set for the first day of November, we believed it might be only for a few days. Already it has been over a week."

John dropped into a chair, his head in his hands. Anger kept him from the dregs of bitterness and utter despair, and no one understood this better than Richard, who listened patiently, even respectfully, to his diatribe.

"Aye," Roger continued his train of thought, "unbelievably, due to the arrival of Anne of Cleves—the poor soul who will be Henry's fourth wife."

John looked up. "Of course, our chivalrous king will be full of anticipation at meeting his new bride."

The clang and jiggle of a key in the lock captured their attention. They watched as the door swung open and Richard Pollard walked in with two guards at his heels.

"Lord Cromwell has asked me to inform you that you will be taken to Glastonbury tomorrow. I myself will escort you. Be ready to leave at dawn." He stared at the three men, then turned on his heel and walked out.

John pressed his lips together, muttering. "Thanks be to Blessed Mary, tis almost over."

"It will be a great relief, will it not?" Richard eked out a wan smile. "We have waited a long time for this, my friends. The end will not be pleasant, but we are fortified by our faith. Come, let us kneel together and pray."

The next morning dawn's pale light suffused the mists that rose from the wide and slow-moving Thames in a hovering blanket of white. It was cold, and their breath left their mouths in vapours that plumed the air as they wrapped their heavy wool cloaks tight about them. The three monks climbed into the carriage, Richard Pollard looking on, surrounded by armed guards. He gave the order to roll, and as the carriage wheels clattered across the cobblestone streets of London, Richard began to tremble from the cold.

John leaned out the window and shouted over the din of the carriage wheels at the nearest guard who accompanied them on horseback alongside Pollard.

"We are freezing, sir. Please, can we stop for a moment to get a blanket for the abbot. He is not well."

When the guard ignored him, John raised his voice in an appeal to the commissioner.

"Mr. Pollard, sir, I insist that you stop and attend to the abbot's needs. This is the abbot's carriage from Glastonbury, there should be a fur rug in the luggage box on the back."

Reluctantly, Pollard called to the driver to halt their progress, opened the box and lifted out the fur blanket, handing it to John, then ordered the driver to carry on. With a weak smile and shadowed eyes, John covered Richard with the fur, tucking it in carefully around the older man, who received the ministrations of his friend in silence. When it was done, John's face crumpled and one tear coursed down the craggy terrain of his cheek. The wily and wise man who was their anchor, who never cried but bore every hardship, pain, and threat of death with humour, wit, and courage, now broke down and wept. Richard reached out, took one of John's hands in his own and, putting an arm around his shoulders, pulled his friend to his chest.

Muffled sobs filled the air as John wept, leaning his face against Richard's chest. Roger watched for a moment, then looked away, his face contorted with pity and grief. He had always been inspired by the love the two elder Benedictines had for one another, as he was nurtured by the kindness they showed him. They had mentored him, guided his spiritual life, and loved him unconditionally for over twenty years. His heart swelled and burst with myriads of feeling: gratitude, profound brotherly love, the unbearable sorrow of the situation, and the irreconcilable truth of its injustice. Underlying all was his faith. Somehow, by the grace of God, he would face what was coming.

Two days later, as they drew near to Glastonbury, to their surprise Pollard gave the order to stop in Wells, where only a year before Bishop John Clerk had surrendered the abbey and cathedral to Cromwell. Exhausted and disheveled from the rigors of traveling at a bone-jarring pace, they were taken at spear point from the carriage into the bishop's palace, where the abbot was shoved alongside other felons being tried for rape, burglary, and petty crimes. It soon became clear that Pollard was charging Richard Whiting with robbery, not treason against the Crown, and that his accomplices were named as John Thorne and Roger James.

The trial that ensued was a shocking blur for the monks. Two notable men of Somerset were brought forward to testify against the abbot—Thomas Horner, a kinsman of Jack Horner, and Nicholas FitzJames, who a few years earlier had written to Cromwell on behalf of Richard Whiting, begging for leniency and reprieve from the barrage of harassment that was levied against the Abbot of Glastonbury. Now as he hurried away from his mendacious testimony, his face was etched with misery as he met Richard's eye, and the abbot knew that he had been threatened with death or torture. Two abbey tenants, one of whom was George Welton, were brought forward with grievances against the abbot, who had at some time or another ruled against their cause.

After the witnesses called to defame the abbot's character, Pollard rose from his seat, adjusting his wig and the black judiciary robes he had donned for the occasion, having been empowered directly by Cromwell and the king to lead the prosecution.

"This man," Pollard pointed at Richard Whiting, "Richard Whiting, and his accomplices," he glared at John Thorne and Roger James, "have been stealing from Glastonbury Abbey for years! They have robbed the church of its wealth, rightfully belonging to their king, and furthermore, they have stolen relics and concealed treasures of antiquity renowned of the church for centuries—a fact that was disclosed by the king's commissioners Layton, Moyle and myself in October upon our arrival at the abbey to secure the church on the king's behalf. These three men are traitors, guilty of theft and treason. The king demands the death of Whiting, Thorne, and James!"

As Pollard's astounding charge of robbery was levied to the judge and court speech, the accusation buzzed in whispers between the gathered audience of the hall and made its way through the spectators to the larger crowd that stood waiting outside. There was no defense or cross-examination. The trial ended almost as soon as it was begun. The three Benedictines sat quietly, staring straight ahead, saying very little, though they occasionally spoke a word or two to one another. Richard was not given the opportunity to speak for himself; instead he was condemned to death and, along with John and Roger, dragged from the palace through the milling, anxious crowd that waited on the street and quickly pushed into the carriage.

They were taken straightway to Glastonbury, only eleven miles away. An hour later the carriage rolled to a stop at the abbey gatehouse on Magdalene Street. As they were shoved inside, they caught only glimpses of the cathedral, its grounds, abbey, and the abbot's lodge—even so, Roger and John were shocked to see the condition of the church, which swarmed with soldiers, gangs of workers, and random men intent about nefarious deeds. The flower garden existed no more but was a muddy field. The hawthorn trees had been cut down along with many others, and workers hacked at the walls while teams of horses hauled away immense stones that had stood in place in the church walls for centuries.

Pollard deposited them in the gatehouse and turned to leave without a word, his face hidden in shadow. When he was gone, John walked to the window and looked out. His eyes roved in shock and wonder at the Lady Chapel, its smashed stained glass windows and the roof under demolition.

"Did you see the horror of it?" John turned to Richard.

Richard's reply came in a monosyllable, "Yes." Since they had left the Tower, the abbot had become more inward. He had spoken only when absolutely necessary since the trial.

John looked at Roger with a snort, attempting a bit of levity. "I just saw a man carrying away a desk I once made, when I was crafting furniture for my office." His choked laugh was bleak, the humour falling flat. "They are even demolishing the roof. I suppose they will sell the lead from it."

Roger was solemn and deeply reflective.

"Yes, you are a fine woodworker, John, among your many other talents."

His face conveyed deep affection and respect as he gazed at John. When Roger spoke next, his voice was hoarse and cracked with emotion.

"There is no more speculation left in me as to what they will do next. This is our last night in this life. We three will die together on the morrow. I wish to say something to you both."

Richard raised his head and looked toward Roger, and he saw that the abbot's blue eyes were ablaze with an inner fire. John sat down beside him, hands lying limp in his lap.

"You have been my elder brothers of the spirit all these years. I am grateful for our time together, for all that I have learned from you in our many years together. You have never led me astray. You have always strengthened my faith. Though we made our confessions to each other in the Tower, I wish to confess one last time."

Richard nodded once. "Of course, my friend."

The youngest of the three swallowed hard. "I am guilty of the sins of anger and hatred, and I wish to purge myself of these before I die. I ask for your blessing, and I ask you to forgive me for any way that I have sinned against you, John, or against you, Richard."

Making the sign of the cross, Richard stirred to respond. "In the name of Blessed Mary and Jesus Christ, you are absolved, my son. Let us all three die with the certainty that we are forgiven, that we are held in the arms of Mary, and let our last words be of forgiveness, when we are taken to the gallows."

John bowed his head and whispered. "So be it."

There was no more to say. Only Richard slept a little that night. The other two stayed awake in a vigil of prayer.

Two hours after daybreak on November 15 the guard opened the gatehouse door and ushered the monks into the street where Pollard awaited them.

"This is your last chance to confess to your crimes. Who were your other accomplices? And where have they taken the king's bones, the chalice and gold that belongs to King Henry?"

Richard raised luminous eyes and gazed at Pollard. "I have nothing to say."

Pollard snapped, "You have condemned yourself." He stalked out the door to his horse that stood tethered outside the gatehouse.

They were trundled into the carriage by the soldiers and driven near the edge of town, where the Tor rose majestically, a proud and mysterious presence. Three oak hurdles hitched to sturdy horses awaited them at the foot of the Tor.

A crowd had gathered, and as the carriage rolled to a stop Richard saw the familiar faces of many people he had known and served as their spiritual guide over the years. There were a large number of Benedictine monks who stood out in their black robes as they huddled nearby. At the front of their tense knot stood Ambrose and Rowland, their faces blanched with sorrow, inwardly chafing at the instruction they had received from Richard—to do absolutely nothing at the time of the execution. They could not interfere, step forward, speak aloud, or seek to ameliorate the suffering of their beloved friends. Through the carriage window the abbot looked into their eyes, one and then the other, and raised his hand in blessing. Seeing the abbot give his blessing, a woman began to sob loudly; her husband pulled her close and scolded her to be quiet. It was dangerous to draw the attention of the commissioner and the guard, who shifted their feet nervously, moving into position to hold back the growing crowd.

As the guards pressed in toward the carriage door, John and Roger moved quickly to help Richard out and down the carriage steps. His eyes were steady, and yet his hands trembled. When the soldiers came forward to take the abbot to the hurdles, John interceded, as he had so many times, on the abbot's behalf.

"Please, let us help him. We will go without a struggle to the hurdles, only let us help our abbot."

For the first time in a long life, John pleaded. Though his face had grown gaunt and deeply lined, John's silver hair shone in the dull light of an overcast, chilly morning. His brown eyes were blood shot from lack of sleep, and yet, like Richard's, they were radiant as embers in the ashes of a dying fire. Several of the monks surged against the outstretched arms of the guards and a loud murmur of unrest resounded through the brooding crowd.

Richard Pollard gave an almost imperceptible nod, his mouth turned down and eyes cleaved to the ground. The soldiers stepped away. With Roger on one side and John on the other, they held the abbot's hands and supported him with arms around his waist as they led him forward and then gently eased him down upon the length of the oak hurdle. Wasting no time, the soldiers shoved them away.

The guards lashed the abbot's arms to the wooden frame and checked to make sure the hurdle was securely attached to the livery of the horse that would pull it. Looking from one soldier to the other, Richard whispered, "God bless you."

Just as quickly, John and Roger were tied to hurdles on either side, and with a command from Pollard, who sat astride his horse, the captain gave the order and the horses started their slow progress through the streets of Glastonbury. Richard Pollard rode behind them.

They proceeded, soon beginning the slow ascent at the foot of the Tor toward the tower of St. Michael that rose on its summit. The hangman's gibbet was in stark silhouette, constructed on the north side of the Tor, facing the abbey. No one in the crowd missed the intentional cruelty—the last thing Richard Whiting would see in this life would be the destruction of his beloved abbey. And anyone in Glastonbury town, including the displaced monks, who looked up toward the Tor would see the gruesome deaths of their abbot, bursar, and sacristan.

"God bless Abbot Whiting! God bless John Thorne and Roger James!" Anonymous voices began to call out from the hidden recesses of the milling crowd that now walked along with the hurdles.

"Silence! Stop your caterwauling! Be quiet!" The captain of the king's guard yelled, pulling out his sword and brandishing it, jerking the reins to surge his horse into the crowd. Try as he might, neither he nor his soldiers could not stop the anxious crowd that milled, ten times their own number, some of them armed with cudgels and knives stuck in their belts. Finally, satisfied that they were not starting a riot, the captain stopped trying to command them to silence, and they walked along the torturous way with frequent outbursts of support and the loud drifting of wails.

It was an agonizing uphill road that the holy men of Glastonbury were dragged along, strapped and tied to their hurdles. The road, no longer cobblestone but dirt, was pitted and rutted, causing the hurdles to bounce and lurch along, so that their bodies were continuously bumped and slammed against the hard wooden surface. The sun was hidden behind thick, purple-black clouds, and, as if nature objected, there were no birdcalls or whoosh of the wind. The only sounds were the wracked sobs and snuffles of weeping townspeople and the displaced monks who watched helplessly as the king's guard—a phalanx of twenty-five armed and uniformed men—rode along beside the hurdles.

"We are with you, Richard Whiting!"

"Blessed be John Thorne and Roger James, Blessed be Richard Whiting!"

"Saint Mary, Holy Mother of God, Jesus Christ be with you all! Blessed Mary be with you, Abbot Whiting!"

Pollard and the captain of the guard eyed each other uneasily, but the commissioner gave a small shake of his head, indicating to leave it—let the local people have their grief. This execution would be hard enough on the people of England; a rebellion in Somerset of the West Country would not please the king or further his cause at this point. Pollard wanted the execution to go off without further problems; he longed to be done with this most unpleasant part of the dissolution of Glastonbury Abbey, which Commissioner Layton had assigned to him, not wanting to endure it himself. Pollard was anxious to be on about his audit of the abbey's riches, knowing that he was personally sure to reap a handsome reward from Lord Cromwell—perhaps a parcel of land, or at least a bag of gold.

Their progress slowed as the horses plodded up the flanks of the Tor toward Saint Michael's tower. The crowd that walked up the hill beside the hurdles could not avoid the sight of the platform with three gallows that had been erected there. The abbot and his companions were unable to see these until they arrived at the top of the Tor and were released from their fetters to stand. When they reached St. Michael's tower, the guards untied the two younger men, forcing them up from the hurdles and prodding them, disoriented and stumbling, to the platform where they were marched up the stairs to stand beneath the ropes that hung down.

Despite his best efforts, and no matter how he was commanded and prodded, the abbot could not rise up, his infirmity was so great. He clutched at his chest as the guards pulled and pushed him forcefully toward the gallows, where John and Roger watched in agony as Richard Whiting gathered the last filaments of his strength to stagger up the stairs. His mouth hung slack and his breath came harsh and ragged in his lungs as he worked to straighten his back and stand swaying beneath the rope. His eyes gazed out over the meadows and marshes of Glastonbury and the Somerset levels, then fastened upon the sight of the great cathedral in the near distance.

Ambrose and Rowland stood at the front of the crowd that jostled for position in front of the gallows platform.

Tears streamed down their anguished faces, and they gripped the hands of the monks who stood beside them. Only a handful of monks had made it up to the summit—the rest could not bear to go further and had stopped half-way up the Tor, overcome by grief. Richard Pollard stood on the platform and, as was the custom, asked the three condemned men the usual question, as the executioner moved toward Roger James to place the rope about his neck.

"You are an accomplice to the crimes of Abbot Richard Whiting. Do you have any last words?"

"Forgive me," Roger choked out the words as the noose was tightened at his throat, "for my sins, and may God have mercy upon me."

The hangman moved next to John Thorne, lowering the noose over his cropped hair and struggling a moment with the knot before it tightened properly about his neck.

Pollard's words were strained, his back rigid. "And you, John Thorne. Do you have any last words?"

"I ask for forgiveness for my sins," John Thorne uttered, his words clear and grave, "and I ask for the mercy of God upon all our souls, and upon the soul of the king."

The executioner came last to Richard Whiting. The hangman, who had grown up in Glastonbury and loved the abbot, set about his work, glad for the hood upon his face that kept Pollard, the guards, and the anxious crowd from seeing the tears that streamed down his face. His instructions had been to hang John Thorne and Roger James until dead, but to hang Abbot Richard Whiting with a thick rope and only until he lost consciousness, in order that he would be drawn and quartered while still alive, then beheaded. The hangman had already made his decision: he would not do it. He would hang the abbot until he was dead, then claim it an innocent mistake if Pollard or the captain of the king's guard noticed that Whiting was already dead when he was drawn and quartered.

As the executioner lowered the noose over Richard Whiting's white hair and down around his neck, Pollard called out. "Abbot Richard Whiting. You have committed crimes against God and against your king. Do you have any last words?"

A chill wind had begun to blow, and it whipped the abbot's black robe about his frail form. Somehow the abbot had marshaled an uncanny strength, and he stood firm in the rising gale. Making a valiant effort to speak with a firm voice, his words trembled upon the air, spoken clearly despite his extremity. His eyes were fixed upon the horizon as he spoke.

"I ask for forgiveness from my Lord and God. I ask for forgiveness for my king, his commissioners, and for Thomas Cromwell. My God have mercy upon us all."

The hangman stepped back and lowered the lever. The hinged doors below their feet fell away and the three men dangled, their necks snapping instantly. Loud, keening wails rent the air.

The ghastly scene became more macabre as the bodies were taken down. The weeping and wailing of townspeople and monks alike grew to such cacophony that the captain began to yell again in a desperate attempt to bring order to the scene. A hard wind rose and buffeted the summit of the Tor, and a cold, thin rain began to fall, as if the old gods themselves protested. Long before the abbot's body was hewn into four pieces, but not before he had given the order to have the abbot's head on display at the Magdalene Gate, Richard Pollard strode away to mount his horse and trot downhill toward town.

By the time the grisly deed was finished, Pollard was in his rooms at the Crown, where he drank himself into a stupor, slept like a dead man, then awoke in the morning to write a letter to Thomas Cromwell that he sent with a messenger that morning.

Pleaseth it your Lordship to be advised that on November 15 the late abbot of Glastonbury went from Wells to Glastonbury, and there was drawn through the town upon a hurdle to the hill called the Tor, where he was put to execution. At that time he asked God and king for mercy for his great offences towards his highness. Before his execution, Whiting was examined and interrogated again by me, but he could accuse no man or himself of any offense against the king's highness, nor would he confess more gold or silver or any other thing beyond what he confessed to before your Lordship in the Tower.

I suppose it will be near Christmas before I shall have surveyed the lands at Glastonbury, and take the audit there...

In the intense crucible of that moment, with the glaring heat of passion distorting or clarifying all things, it would be easy, perhaps, to misunderstand those two small words—"from" and "for"—in Richard Whiting's last statement: "I ask forgiveness from my Lord and God. I ask forgiveness for my king, his commissioners, and for Thomas Cromwell. My God have mercy upon us all." Pollard was, if nothing else, adept at making falsehoods appear as truth, perhaps even to the extent that he himself believed the lies in the web he spun, even as he told them.

CHAPTER SIXTEEN

The Isle of Arrain
January 1542

Maddy woke up long before dawn, filled with awe at the dream. It was lucid and bright, detailed yet subtle. Pushing back the quilts and furs, she wrapped herself in a warm woolen shawl and slipped her feet into warm lambs' wool slippers, then made her way carefully to the fireplace, where a banked fire smoldered. Taking a slender length of wood and lighting it from the coals, she moved silently to the tallow candle beside her bed. A tender flame caught at the wick, shedding enough light to look down at Colin who slept deeply. She was mindful not to wake him; he had worked for many hours the day before, hauling in the nets with Geleis and the fishermen in the *currachs* off Pladda—one of the many reasons the villagers were so loyal to their laird.

It was the time of the long dark months on Arrain, and even the excitement of the dream would have to wait—she knew she would write it down when the dawn came. Until then she would mull it over, take it in for herself before she shared it, even with Colin. Carrying the candle in its brass candleholder, she padded down the stone steps and made her way into the kitchen, grateful for the warmth of her lambs' wool houseshoes—a gift from Anne, who had become quite accomplished with needle and yarn and with tanning and leathercraft since their arrival.

She bent down to pull out several sticks of kindling to start a fire in the old iron cookstove. The flame caught gently at first, then grew to leap and dance in the dark cave of the kitchen. Dipping a gourd of icy water from the bucket, she put on the kettle for hot water then sat down to ponder the meaning of the dream.

She had been stunned by the vivid images and living presence of the dream. In her heart, Maddy knew that it was a true visitation. But what would the others say? She had grown accustomed to having dreams of her uncle. For months after his death, she had dreamt often of him. Richard always appeared bright as the sun bursting through the clouds over the Irish Sea. Often John Thorne stood nearby, and she could sense the presence of the sacristan, Roger, as well as others. She had the feeling they were her guardian angels now.

The first time she had dreamt of Richard, he had smiled and beamed upon her and said, "You have done well, Maddy." Then he raised his hands in blessing. As she called his name, he turned and walked across a beach of white sand and into an infinite blue sea whose wavelets danced with the radiance of a million diamonds. She watched in wonder as he disappeared into a blaze of light that shone on the horizon.

After that, when she dreamed of Abba, he was counseling or supporting her in some way. She rarely remembered what he said: it was the mood that lingered and sank deep into her heart. Truly, she had come to cherish these dreams since the execution and destruction of Glastonbury Abbey, which had cast them all into a long time of grieving with sore hearts. But this dream was exact, compelling, unforgettable even in its complexity.

Pulling the thick shawl close around her shoulders, she added small sticks to the fire. When the water boiled, she made raspberry leaf tea, adding a handful of garden mint to the pot. Inwardly she gave thanks to Jennet, who made tinctures and cossets and liniments for their ailments, kept them stocked with dried herbs for tea and cooking, and tended to them when they were sick. Leaving the leaves to steep, she held her hands over the stove to warm them, then sat at the long oak table and rested her arms on its surface, polished smooth by years of use. She inhaled the fragrant curls of steam that wafted up from the teapot to her face. When it was ready, she poured a cup, her thoughts wandering back to the day when the news of the deaths had reached them.

It was mid-December, over two years ago. Grief had come and lodged itself in her heart, a constant visitor that became a part of her over time. She had cried so many tears in the first weeks after they arrived in Arrain with the relics that her eyes remained dry as she read the letter that arrived from Father Ambrose by boat. With a dull ache in her throat she had read his description of the execution, and his discreet explanation that the abbot's body parts had been stolen or somehow disposed of in the aftermath of the debacle. Even with the horror of it all, the letter had touched her heart like the balm of Gilead that her uncle had gone to such lengths to help her with the weight of grief. Ambrose had written:

Dear friends, the abbot asked me to write this message to you: Do not despair, he said, for he knew very well that this was coming, down to the exact details of his death. He wanted you to know and have faith that he was held in the loving hands of Blessed Mary through it all. He also requested that Rowland and I to come to Arrain—as he instructed William and Angus, and I trust, by God's grace, they are there already. Our abbot always knew what was best for us, and we intend to fulfill his request as soon as possible. First I must see to the monks who have been evicted and help them into their new lives, as God allows.

Ambrose and Rowland had arrived by boat in the fall of 1540, just before the Feast of All Soul's, which the natives of Arrain knew as Samhain. William and Angus wept when they saw their fellow monks, but their tears were soon replaced by bright smiles of joy as the clan of Kildonan greeted them with a big-hearted, clamorous welcome. Right away, the two new arrivals declared their decision to renounce their vows and enter the life of a layman. They would teach or work as clerks or serve in unforeseen ways, as God willed them.

Ambrose did not spare them in his detailed account of the execution and its surrounding tragedy, but he assuaged their sorrow when he spoke with reverence of the dignity and peace with which all three had gone to the gallows—an example, he said, that they would never forget. He relayed the brutal confrontation afterward, as the monks bore witness to the way Richard Pollard, by order of Cromwell, dealt with Abbot Whiting's body. His head was displayed on a spike at the Magdalene Gate of Glastonbury Abbey. The other four parts of his body were sent to Wells, Bath, Ilchester, and Bridgewater, sending a message of the horror and violence that would be visited upon any who opposed the king and his chancellor.

Ambrose wiped away tears that gathered in his wide hazel eyes. He was not the only one who wept, and they sat in silence for some moments, taking in the gruesome reality of what had occurred. Finally the senior monk continued.

"At the same time, the abbots of Colchester and Reading Abbeys—Thomas Marshall and Hugh Farington— were executed outside their abbey gates as traitors. At Glastonbury, the aftermath was terrible—gangs of workmen tore down the abbey walls, windows were smashed or taken down and sold. The well of St. Dunstan, under the Lady Chapel, was desecrated, left covered with filth and trash as the chapel was destroyed. The king's soldiers hauled away many things. Richard Pollard sold the vestments and anything that was left of the shrines; sculptures and paintings were sold off to local lords and gentry alike. Jack, the abbot's chamberlain, did quite well for his service as a spy: weeks after the executive, just before Christmastide, the king allotted Sharpham Manor to the Horner family. In London they sing a little ditty."

He turned to Rowland, who sang in his beautiful tenor voice, which before they had only heard resounding in hymns and liturgy in the choir of the church:

Little Jack Horner sat in a corner
Eating his Christmas pie;
He put in his thumb and pulled out a plum,
And said, "What a good boy am I."

Speechless, they listened, some wiping their eyes again. Ambrose's sharp laugh was dry and rife with irony. "The story of Glastonbury Abbey has spread over the west country and all of England, and beyond, to France, Spain, and the other countries of the continent. People know that something very strange happened there. As with the other religious houses, all of the abbey's vast lands were distributed to one noble or another—favors of the king. But none of the other abbeys in the dissolution have been utterly destroyed—not just ransacked and stripped of their wealth or religious artifacts but devastated, torn to the ground, taken apart stone by stone—in the way that our abbey has been. What remains a mystery to most people is why Cromwell and the king levied such a vengeance against Glastonbury Abbey and its abbot."

In the moment of silence that ensued, Rowland's words resounded with confidence as he interjected, "Only the Company of Avalon knows the real truth. But people are asking—to what avail did the king tear the abbey apart, destroy its walls and foundations? Were they looking for something? Was it the work of religious zealots? Or of men merely mad after power? And why was the abbot accused of stealing relics?"

Ambrose sighed heavily. "God works in mysterious ways. You must have heard that Cromwell was sent to the block in July this past summer—only eight months after Richard, John, and Roger. He displeased the king in his choice of Henry's next wife—Anne of Cleves, God bless the poor woman. At least she got away with her head intact."

Colin listened thoughtfully. "Yes, we heard the news of Cromwell's execution not long after it happened. It spread like wildfire, making its way even to our remote island within weeks."

With a shrug and a wry smile, William looked at Angus. "We tried not to be happy about it, as Father Gordon tells us regularly that to forgive is divine, but it is nigh impossible not to rejoice in small moments of triumph."

Angus finally spoke with a twist of his mouth. "I have made my confession and will make it again. I find no fault with happiness when justice is served."

"Even so, nothing can repay the damage that has been done, not only to our families," Colin glanced at Maddy, his words solemn, "but to England. Nothing can assuage the blow that has been ruthlessly dealt to the sacred ground of Glastonbury Abbey and the spiritual treasures guarded by our church."

William nodded thoughtfully, "In truth, there is no measure to the damage that has been done to future generations."

The companions fell into a thoughtful lull. The fire cracked and popped loudly, and behind that, they could hear the muffled sound of rain through the heavy wool and sealskin coverings over the leaded glass of the windows. Ambrose looked up at the vaulted stone ceiling of the main room of the castle where they had supped and were now gathered around a roaring fire.

"It is good to be here. There is peace in this place."

Following Ambrose's gaze, Colin's eyes traveled over the stone walls and fastened upon the fire. He pressed his lips together, then responded.

"Yes, it is a peaceful, but has not always been so. We have news as well. Six months after the execution, a regiment of the king's soldiers arrived, led by the Earl of Sussex, on their way—so they said—from Carlisle to Ireland. They sailed into the firth from the Irish Sea, heading directly to the shores of Kildonan. They anchored their boats in deep water then came ashore in *currachs*—the Earl and twenty soldiers, bearing guns and swords and every sort of weapon."

Colin glanced at Maddy, who picked up the story. "Our men were all away for a few days—on a hunting expedition in the valleys north of here. It was Jennet, Anne, Mòrai, me and the village liegemen and crofters who carry on the work of Kildonan, the blacksmith and stable master, the gardener, the workers who make repairs and such, the cook and kitchen servants and village children running around underfoot. When we saw the English flag, we knew there was trouble. As soon as the ship sank anchor, we sent Angus and William down into the village to hide among our loyal people there, with Father Gordon, our priest."

She glanced at Anne, who continued, filling in details. "I was on the beach that morning with Jennet, collecting seaweed with Kenna and some of the women of the village when we first saw that a boat was sailing north from Ailsa Craig, heading straight toward Kildonan. They had a good wind that day, and by noon they were here, as Maddy said, flying the English flag. The Earl of Sussex himself came ashore, asking for the laird. He was both threatening and terrifying, flanked by his armed men and stating he was here on the king's business related to the reform of the church. We explained that Colin was off hunting and would not return for a few days, but we bade him to come in to the castle and meet Lady Hamilton."

Jennet chuckled, "And quite a meeting it was! Mòrai would brook no insults from him. She took command of the situation as only she can—with bold finesse. The Earl of Sussex had more than met his match. Even so, he won the exchange about allowing his men to search the castle and grounds—of course she had to say yes."

Mòrai tapped her cane on the stone floor and squirmed in her chair. "Exaggerations! I simply did what was called for."

Undaunted, Maddy carried on, embellishing the description with her natural flare for storytelling. "We asked, of course, what he could possibly want with us or what he might think to find at our remote castle in the Scottish highlands. He was cold but cordial at first, saying that King Henry knew that Richard Whiting had stolen treasures from the abbey before it was confiscated by the Crown. King Henry, he said, 'means to have those relics.'

"Then he told us that it was known to him that the niece and nephew of Richard Whiting and John Thorne had been handfasted the year before the dissolution at Glastonbury Abbey. He said, 'Since I was on my way to Ireland and close to your family lands, I thought I would pay you a visit and see if you have any knowledge of your uncles' schemes—if you know about some relics from the church. You will not object if my men look around a bit, will you?' His voice was as oily and unctuous as melted fat spilled on a kitchen floor."

Seeing dismay appear on the faces of Ambrose and Rowland, who were shaken to the core by all they had endured, Ben interjected, cutting to the bone of the story.

"They did not stay the night. They went through all the rooms of the castle, into the kitchen and buttery, the stable and storage rooms. They even examined the smithy and brewery. Of course they found nothing."

Colin added, "They did notice the oil painting of Arthur, Gwenivere, and Lancelot on the third floor, which the earl found quite interesting. His soldiers brought it down to the main floor, where Mòrai was sitting with him, entertaining him with cakes and whiskey."

Mòrai smiled at the memory. "He wanted to take it with him, 'To give to the king,' so he said. Hhmmph! I doubt that very much."

She pointed toward Maddy with her cane, indicating she should continue in the telling of it, which she did with relish.

"It took some wheedling and negotiation, but Mòrai finally convinced him not to take the painting. She said that her great grandmother, Briallen, was from Wales, and it was a family heirloom, worthless really to anyone else in its faded and cracked condition, but a nice memory for 'an old lady.' It was her elegance and charm that won him over in the end, what with her speaking French to him, plying him with spirits, the Arrain whiskey flowing like the Thames."

Mòrai chuckled. "In fact I gave the earl a cask of our finest year, which had been aging for a very long time indeed. It was a prize whiskey and not so easy for me to let it go—but it was a small price to pay to appease him. Things could have been much worse. I wager it was a blessing that our men folk were not here when the ship arrived, and it was just we women to contend with the Earl of Sussex."

Ambrose inhaled sharply. "This most dramatic adventure continues!" He looked around at them, speaking the truth that none of them had been ready, as yet, to face.

"So, the king is on your trail—and on the trail of the relics. What will we do now?"

Stoking the fire and sipping her tea, Maddy's thoughts roved over the weeks and months after Ambrose and Rowland arrived. When Samhain had passed that year, the painful time that marked one year since the deaths of Richard Whiting, John Thorne, and Roger James came. They busied themselves with activities of preparing for winter—cutting wood, turning over their garden plot and barley fields and planting them with vetch seed, weaving, mending, and hunting, tending to the herbs and vegetables in the root cellar, then the curing and smoking of fish and meat of the hunt or of the animals that were culled from their herds.

Ambrose and Rowland were eager to explore Viking Bay, where their ship had docked on Arrain. They were charmed by the long, slow curve of the gentle shore, the thick forests that grew almost down to the beach of sand and rocks, where a delicate green algae grew upon the stones at the lapping water's edge.

They could see the tip end of the Holy Isle to the north of the bay—a barren hump of rock alive with mosses, bracken, and heather, with a few sturdy white beam trees growing near the shore along with stands of oaks, twisted and gnarled from the weather and wind coming off the firth. The isle was known to have a cave and a holy spring that had been considered sacred since ancient days, and these drew the attention of the men.

Two weeks after their arrival, Ambrose asked for the use of one of Kildonan's wagons to make the trip back down the mountain to Viking Bay. They were gone for five days, and upon their return, their spirits were high with enthusiasm for the potentials of a new life that had begun to take shape. At supper that night Ambrose spoke of their adventure, and his face glowed with joy just as Geleis came in, cold air wafting in about him.

"We spent two nights on the Holy Isle, where Saint Molaise once lived, and we found the cave and its sacred spring to be a powerful place of healing. Back on Arrain, we walked to the double falls, which the village folk call *Eas á Chrannaig,* not far from the strand in Viking Bay. Have you been to these waterfalls?"

Hiking up his kilt and throwing the plaid over his shoulder, Geleis answered. "Aye, tis known to be a place of great magic and a strange, unearthly benediction that permeates its atmosphere." The others nodded in agreement, knowing the place well.

"In the village," Rowland said, "we spent many hours with the innkeeper, a kindly old man named Angaidh with no living children of his own. Angaidh has grown old, and his hands are as stiff as his knees these days. He needs help in the inn and the tavern, and he offered to give us room and board in exchange for our work. We will go within the week and establish ourselves. There are only a handful of houses and some farmers who live around the bay. The inn and tavern exist for the ships that come to trade with farmers who live up in the moors and valleys. There are children who live in those parts. Surely they could use schooling. Perhaps we can teach them. It will be a simple life. We hope," he glanced at the younger monks, "William and Angus will come, and together we will build a chapel."

Ambrose's enthusiasm was contagious. "We have been struck by what Lady Hamilton calls the *càin* spirit of this place. Indeed, we have a vision. The little bay and its village, with its rock pier for trade boats, is not a place of violence and bloodshed, as the name 'Viking Bay' implies, as it was in the days when the Vikings came with their karves and knarrs to conquer and plunder the old tribes of this island. Nay, it is a place of deep peace and rest—a blessed place, where Saint Laisren came—Saint Molaise—and made his way to the Holy Isle.

"We sat many hours there, watching the salty wavelets flow toward shore in colors of blue and silver and brown. While we were there, two swans floated lazily, grazing among the rocky places of the shore for their dinner. They must have floated down from Brodick Caste to the north. Across the firth we could see massive white clouds in fantastic shapes—like castles, towers, and mansions—over the lands of Ayrshire."

He sighed with satisfaction. "When we have settled there, we will call that beautiful place Whiting Bay, to honor our beloved abbot. We believe the name will catch on."

Months and seasons passed, then another year. Ambrose and Rowland had moved in the springtime past to Whiting Bay—the new name that came easily to the inhabitants of the cove, though they had no knowledge of its true meaning. For them, it was enough that the waves washed in to gently lap the shore with a constant, ever-changing ribbon of white foam.

But it was Lamlash where the monks of Glastonbury settled some months later, a few miles north of Whiting Bay on the road toward Kildonan. It was more central to the needs of families with children and closer to their friends as well. They cherished the beautiful view of the Holy Isle from Lamlash—the rising hulk of the mountain covered with purple brown heather in vast sweeps of color. They soon began the building of a small school, and this drew Father Angus and Father William, and then Anne and Ben, who moved to Lamlash and were busy building their own house, near the school.

As their new lives took shape, the friends came to visit Kildonan as often as they could, and the conspirators spent many evenings regaling each other with various versions of the story of Arthur, Gwenivere, and Lancelot, reading from the chroniclers, Geoffrey of Monmouth and Chrétein de Troyes or listening to Anne and Ben recount the Welsh tales and complex mythologies.

At other times they spoke with great intensity of their task to preserve the relics and what would come next. Everyone agreed that since the Earl of Sussex had come out of his way to land at Kildonan, the relics were no longer safe on Arrain. They knew full well that the king's men would, sooner or later, return to their island looking for the artifacts—a logical reality that gave rise to seemingly endless discussions of various possibilities.

Time went by until two years had passed after the dire events of Glastonbury. As Christmastide drew near, on the night of the winter solstice the Company of Avalon gathered at Kildonan to celebrate—they would stay on as guests for the next week. When they were settled around the fire in the big room, Colin spoke about something that had been on his mind for weeks.

"We all ken the need to transport the relics to another hiding place. Once we hoped they would be returned to Glastonbury Abbey. Now, Scotland seems to be their new home. But where?"

Geleis suggested, "What about a place far north of here in the Hebrides, near the big standing stones called Calanais, on *Leòdhas?* The only place more remote that that is Orkney, but then we would be in the lands of the clan Sinclair."

"I have heard of a place, called the "Cave of Melody"— *Uamh-Binn*—known as Fingal's Cave in the islands north of here," Anne ventured.

Broderick shook his head. "I made the journey into the Hebrides once as a lad. What ye say is true, Anne, the Hebrides may be a good place to hide the relics, but *Uamh-Binn* tis a fierce place, beautiful beyond imagining. Tis full of magic and unseen powers, but nigh impossible to reach with heavy boxes, and flooded daily with the tides as well."

Rubbing his chin, Colin spoke thoughtfully. "Mòrai, doesn't our family's branch of the Hamilton clan have a home—a castle and estate—south of Glasgow? Perhaps there is a little known chapel or church somewhere near there where they relics could be housed in secret?"

They all turned to look at Margaret, who tapped the tip of her cane against the floor. "Tis possible," she admitted reluctantly, "but may not be the safest place. The English king can reach his arm to Glasgow very easily."

"I know of a more remote isle," Ben offered, "profoundly sacred and north of here—a small isle where Saint Columba built his monastery a thousand years ago. Broderick told me it is called *Chaluim Chille*. Could that be the place we seek? Most difficult to get to, I wager. And then, not as far north is Mull, sacred to the Old Ones who built the standing stones all over this land."

William and Angus glanced at each other, then Angus spoke up. "A pity it could not be our own Holy Isle, just near Whiting Bay, where Saint Molaise had his monastery just as many centuries ago. There is nothing there now, though the village folk still make their pilgrimages to the cave and the spring." The group fell silent, digesting this idea.

Pressing his lips together and shaking his head, Colin responded. "Too close, and too many people go there."

Tucking a stray lock into her braided chignon, Maddy wondered aloud. "If the king and queen were here, what would they say?"

Everyone looked at her, their faces pondering the question. Ambrose was the one who answered her question with the encouragement she needed.

"Why not ask them, Maddy? Abbot Whiting once mentioned to me that you had a special gift for dreams." He smiled warmly and glanced at Rowland.

"Go to the painting upstairs and ask," Colin suggested. "Maybe they will give you a dream. You have had so many dreams these past two years."

"Aye, give it a try, *piuthar*. It canna hurt anything at all and may verra well be the help we need. Even if tis just a hint." Jennet's urging was enhanced by the enthusiastic response from everyone.

Broderick chuckled, wagging his head with reluctance. "The mystic streak runs in this family, for sure, lass. Ye must tell us all, if sich a dream comes to ye. Call a meeting of the Company of Avalon. We shall get word to Lamlash for everyone to come."

The next week a winter storm hit the southern shores of Arrain with a vengeance, moving north overland toward Lamlash, Whiting Bay, Brodick Castle, and Goatfell Mountain. The castle Kildonan stood strong and steady as always, but their spirits were sorely diminished when Mòrai took to her bed with an ague.

During the autumn their concern had deepened to angst as they watched their grandmother grow weaker;

after the winter solstice and Christmastide her fragile condition had grown more pronounced. Now Maddy stood at her bedside with Jennet, who worked at a small brazier to prepare another strong brew of feverfew and anemone. They had nursed Margaret day and night for over a week, and with every dawn it seemed that she grew frailer.

"This *droch-shìde* has brought illness to many in the village. Broderick told me this morn before he left with Anne and Ben that there is another *stoirm* coming. I hope they reach Lamlash before dark."

She shook her head in dismay as she looked down at Margaret, who slept fitfully propped up on pillows to allow for more ease of breathing. Jennet had steeped the dried leaves of mullein, which she called *lus mor*, the great herb, blended with strong mint, thyme, and sage for Mòrai to breath—it had eased her discomfort long enough for sleep to take over. They were taking turns at her bedside, spelled by Colin or Geleis, to sit at her side and wipe her hot face with a wet cloth in an effort to bring the fever down. On her chest was a poultice of *lus mor* crushed and steeped then wrapped in loose-weave linen cloth. Jennet hoped to ease Mòrai's hacking cough and break up the congestion that seemed to suffocate her attempts to breathe.

Colin opened the door and poked his head in, looking toward the fire. "Do ye need more wood?" he queried, pausing. "Or anything else I might bring? Geleis and Broderick are here in the sitting room as well. We have a fire going and will wait here. Is there anything we can we do?"

Without turning, Jennet replied. "We can use more small sticks and chips for the brazier, another bucket of fresh water...oh, and bring another bottle of bourtree syrup—tis deep purple, ye must remember. Not the amber or brown tinctures, *bràthair*."

Without another word Colin closed the door quietly. Jennet breathed in slowly through her nose, lips pressed tight, rubbing her eyes with one hand.

"In the Summer Country around Glastonbury, the bourtree, the small berries that hang in dark purple clusters, are called elderberry." Maddy put her hands on Jennet's shoulders and squeezed, rubbing away some of the tension there.

"It is used by everyone as the best tonic against ague, chills, catarrh, fevers—in fact, tis good for whatever ails a person or for strengthening the body. Many wives make a fine wine of the elderberries and also a cordial is made of the flowers, as well as cakes and *tisane* and *comfiture*."

Jennet nodded, keeping her eyes on the flame of the brazier where it met the bottom of the pot. "Yes, I have made some of those with bourtree—tis truly a gift of the goddess."

With a smile, Maddy glanced at the grave young woman intent at her side. "Jennet, when you speak so, which goddess do you mean?"

"I mean Ceridwen, our ancient goddess. But you know very well, Maddy, that in my eyes—and in my heart—she is no different than Mary, the mother of God, or Saint Mary Magdalene."

Maddy smiled. "Speaking that way you remind me of my Uncle Richard. I miss him terribly, still. I often feel that Abba is with me." She admitted, "I have been asking for a dream of the king and queen, Jennet, as you and the others encouraged me to do, not two weeks ago."

"It will come." A fleeting smile passed over Jennet's face. The water in the long-handled copper pot she had held over the flame came to a boil, and she shifted on her seat, dropping in another handful of dried anemone flowers, then more of the feverfew.

"I will put in as much as the pot will take, and then simmer the brew gently for perhaps an hour to make the draught for Mòrai to take, if she can. I hope we can bring down her fever before nightfall."

Mòrai's eyelids flickered then opened, her eyes coming into focus and honing in on the two young women. She stirred under the linens and heavy seal fur blankets, struggling to sit upright. Maddy reached to help her, but Mòrai made a familiar sound of irritation and shook her head.

"Tsk, tsk. Dinna want ye to help me, Maddy. I can do it." Her hands shook as she pushed against the bed to lever herself up.

"Mòrai, I see you are as stubborn as ever!" Jennet scolded sweetly, a smile on her face. "*Seanmhàthair*, helping you is our great gift. Even so, we are glad to see you awake and feisty. Will ye drink some more teas I have made?"

"Must I? Listen, for I have something to say." Her eyes were sharp yet glazed and burning with fever in the dim afternoon light. Her soft, wrinkled cheeks glowed as if lit from within. "In January, only a few weeks' time, I will pass eighty years on this earth. I have been blessed with a good life, and I am ready to go."

Seeing their downcast faces, she reproved. "Stop your

sorrowing. I go to join many whom I love." She wheezed and paused to cough. "My beloved husband, Thomas Thorne, his brother John, and Richard Whiting, and my parents, grandparents, my sister Jennet—your namesake." She swallowed hard, and they could see the effort it took for her to speak at all.

"Is your throat terrible sore, Mòrai?" Jennet began, "Colin is coming with the bourtree syrup..."

Margaret rasped, gently pushing away the spoon in Jennet's solicitous hand. "For God's sake, no more! I've had enough herbs to drown a woman—although your bourtree syrup is sweet enough, with all the honey you use to make it." Managing a wry smile, her indomitable sense of humor gave way to another fit of coughing. The catarrh in her lungs was thick, and Maddy handed her a clean linen handerchief to spit out the green phlegm. When Margaret was able to speak again, she winked, her voice hoarse and soft but clear. "Have ye no sense at all? Give me a draught of good Arrain whiskey, girl."

The door opened and Colin walked in, Geleis behind him. "Mòrai, you are awake! We have brought the bourtree syrup." As he crossed the room, Jennet turned to him, widening her eyes to shush him and inclining her head toward their grandmother.

"Our patient is impossible. Mòrai has made it clear that she wants no more herbs and palliatives but prefers a *beag drama seo càin spiorad*!"

Geleis was back within minutes with the decanter from downstairs and several copper cups. He took a place beside Colin on one side of the bed.

Margaret glanced at him approvingly. "That's right, Geleis, a wee dram for everyone. We are celebrating."

When five cups had been poured, Margaret held hers up with a shaking hand. "I celebrate you all, and the lives you will live. The good deeds you will accomplish." Her voice cracked with the strain of getting the words out, but she continued. "I drink to your health and happiness my loved ones, my dearest and nearest of kin. *Sláinte mhath!*"

Geleis responded, "*Do dheagh shláinte*, Mòrai."

When all had toasted, each one carefully leaning forward over the bed to lightly touch Margaret's cup with theirs, they sipped. Jennet reached to take the cup that had fallen slack in her grandmother's hands. Outside the wind howled and rain pounded the castle walls and the one leaded window of Margaret's room. Through it came a dim grey light that cast little warmth and barely relieved the gloomy shadows of the stone walls and chilly corners. Geleis moved to light several tapers and a sconce, and the chamber was illumined with the glow of their flames as Colin put two more logs upon the fire then stirred its coals to a blaze.

Jennet and Maddy sat quietly beside Margaret's bed as the two men returned to the other side. Colin reached out to take one of her hands in his own. A sense of impending presence was growing in the room and, wordlessly, they glanced from one to the other in the knowledge that Morai was preparing to leave. Her eyes were closed again, and she breathed through her mouth very lightly, her chest barely rising at all. The breath rasped in her throat, and her cheeks burned red from the fever. Suddenly her eyes opened, and she reached for the whiskey cup again. Unable to hold it to her own lips this time, her eyes glanced toward Jennet, who reached forward to help her lift the cup for another sip.

When she had wet her lips and watched as they each sipped their own cup of the fiery spirits, she spoke, struggling a little for breath between the words and phrases. "The door is open. Before this night is over, I will be gone. Let me depart in peace, my dear ones." Looking at each one for a brief moment, she closed her eyes.

No one spoke. Tears cascaded from Jennet's eyes, and she wiped them away with strong, capable hands. Geleis and Colin were calm and steady, as men often are, and yet their eyes glistened in the half light. Geleis reached over to place a hand on Margaret's arm, and as he did, her eyes opened to meet and then linger on his. Seeing this, Jennet motioned to the others that they should leave Geleis alone with her. They walked through the door to the small sitting room adjoining the hallway leading to the other bedrooms on the second floor wing of the castle.

"We can take turns sitting with her, so each of us has time to say goodbye. Whether we speak or no doesna matter at all." Jennet's gray eyes searched from one to the other.

"I have tended to many a person's death these past years, and I suspect that Mòrai will go deep within herself soon, to prepare for her journey, as I have seen many do. She has asked us to let her go, but she must also let us go, so let us not try to draw her back from the door she seeks."

Colin built up the fire in the sitting room to a roar. Outside the sun was setting unseen, hidden behind indigo cloud mountains and shifting mists, which moved fast across a thick blanket of grey that poured down in a relentless curtain of rain. Jennet lit the candelabras and sconces and Kenna arrived with a large tray laden with platters of food, bowls, linen napkins, and spoons.

Setting down the tray, she looked around at them, quickly surmising the purpose of their vigil. With a hesitant smile, Kenna ventured, "May I stay, to keep watch with you? I can run errands should you need…"

"Of course, Kenna. You are part of our family. You love Mòrai well—as she loves you. She has told us she will pass away this night." He gestured toward a low couch near the fire and the maid took a seat there, smoothing back her hair and apron.

"We should all eat a little something," Maddy urged, over the roasted lamb and hot oat cakes that Kenna had slathered with butter.

"Yes," Jennet returned in quiet agreement. "If Mòrai goes tonight, as she said she will, or during the early hours of morning, we will need to be strong and clear to prepare her and sit for the wake. And besides, Kenna has gone to some trouble to bring this food for us." She smiled at the younger girl, covering her hand with one of her own.

Just then Geleis appeared at the door and, seeing Kenna, gestured to her.

"Tis good you are here, Kenna. She has asked for you." He smiled, ushering the girl in to Lady Margaret. Some minutes later they re-emerged and Geleis looked to Maddy.

Colin's gray eyes, so like Jennet and Margaret, met Maddy's as she rose from her seat that was then taken by Geleis. As Maddy walked to the door, Colin chuckled, "Mòrai will have her way about things to the very end."

Jennet's turn came next, on the half hour. Ten minutes had passed when Jennet opened the door and looked at Colin.

"She asks for you, now, *bràthair*."

Colin closed the door behind him and moved silently to Margaret's bedside. His hand was warm as he reached out to gently take Mòrai's hand, feeling her bones move, delicate as a small bird, and touching the translucent skin and blue veins with tender fingertips. He looked at his grandmother with awe and gratitude—here was the woman who had raised him, who had sheltered his spirit even as she molded the man he would become, who had sent him to Glastonbury Abbey, blessed his marriage and his destiny. She had been beside him through it all, supporting, guiding, an ever-present refuge in the storm. Now he gazed upon her with love pouring from the cracks in his heart.

"Mòrai." His voice broke despite his best efforts to keep it even. "Mòrai, what will I do without you?" The words rushed out and he gasped in surprise.

A tiny smile stretched her lips. "You will do well, my *duine làidir breagha*." She met his eyes and held them with her own. "You have always been the child of my heart. Promise you will celebrate my passing. It is natural for the old ones to go and the young ones to carry on."

He leaned down to kiss her cheek then bowed his head over her hand.

"I live on in you, Colin," she whispered, "and in Maddy. You, my son, must keep the faith. Now, stay a while."

An hour passed in a timeless communion of the heart that needed no words. Her breathing became more labored as she seemed to recede further within herself. At the same time, Colin sensed a golden presence that grew stronger and stronger, until a moment came when Margaret breathed a sharp breath and her mouth worked as if she tried to speak.

He leaned close to listen as she mouthed with the barest wisp of sound, "Tis beautiful, beautiful! A light shining!"

With a delicate hand raised, as if she greeted a beloved friend, her face was transfigured with joy as she panted softly, eyes fixed upon the invisible world. Her whisper was barely audible, and Colin leaned his ear close to her lips.

"They come for me," the sibilant words tumbled out, "I am eager to go." Her head fell back upon the pillow, eyes half closed. Within seconds she stopped breathing and he knew she was gone. He sat at her side for some moments, marveling at the smile that slowly appeared upon her lips.

When Colin emerged from the bedroom, he was met by the anxious faces of those who had waited for over an hour while he sat at Margaret's side. Seeing that his face was bright as the sun, their expressions turned to wonder.

"She has left," he said. "A great peace and happiness descended upon her. Come, and pay respects..."

Memories of Mòrai's passing swirled in Magdalyne's mind as the faint light of dawn seeped in and she watched the familiar shapes of the kitchen emerge from night's anonymity. They had buried Morai's body a half-mile west of Kildonan castle on the hillside overlooking the tiny islet of Pladda, or Seal Rock, which Margaret had loved so dearly for its sleek and fat seals that lived and played there.

With a smile and a prayer for Margaret Hamilton—benefactor, wise guide, grandmother, and friend—Maddy's mind returned to the dream that she had waited for these past weeks, which had finally come this morning. She marveled as she recalled the vivid clarity of the image of a small woman with long, tangled hair of burnished copper and catlike smoky eyes. She wore a long red robe with a cloak of white fox fur, and she carried a staff, carved from an apple tree limb, with which she beckoned to Maddy. They walked together through a forest of trees with gilded leaves of silver and gold, across a grassy plain as green as emerald. Overhead the sky was spotless and blue as a robin's egg. A gentle breeze pattered among the leaves as the woman turned to her and spoke in a language unknown but familiar, which Maddy somehow understood with uncanny clarity, as if each word rang forth from a delicate crystalline bell.

"You know who I am." The woman's voice was resonant with the simplicity of utter conviction.

Maddy answered, "You are Morgan, the Lady of the Lake." With a smile, Morgan enjoined her to walk with her, and they moved arm in arm—or so it seemed to Maddy—as Morgan revealed the scenes of a story that unfolded before Maddy's dreaming eyes. Allowing the images and memories of the dream to scroll through her mind and body, she knew that the answer to her question lay within the story.

After sunrise, Maddy spent the morning in the library by the window, writing feverishly. Now and then Colin came to the desk and raised the dark wings of his brows in question. She had told him that the dream had come but nothing more. In the late afternoon she returned to the library to read, in the last of the day's light, what she had written down. After starting a small fire, she settled in at the desk and was still there when Colin walked in just before sunset carrying two cups of ale.

He chuckled, "If Mòrai was here, she would say, 'Tis time for a wee *drama,* lassie!' But instead, we have ale this afternoon." Placing the cups on the desk, he turned to stir the fire in the hearth and add a log to the blaze.

Putting down the quill and pushing away the ink pot, Maddy laughed. "You are right, as you usually are, husband. Your company is most welcome, and good timing as well, but I'll decline the lovely ale you have brought, *cariad.*"

"No ale for ye?" His gray eyes sparkled with warmth as he pulled up a chair and reached out to touch her auburn hair. "The fine middle path of abstinence, is it?" When she said nothing but looked at him with a somber but mysterious smile, he frowned. "Does something trouble you, Maddy? Are ye well?"

"Nothing troubles me. It's just that," she touched her belly gently with one hand, "now I must also think of the babe."

Colin's mouth fell open in surprise, then turned up in sheer delight.

"*Mo ghràidh*! Maddy!" Joy spread across his face like morning light across the moors. "I...dinna ken! But I should have."

Then she was enveloped in his arms as he lifted her up from the chair and pressed against the length of her body.

"*A chiall mo chridhe,*" he breathed into her ear, "you said once that you mean to make me yours in every way. Bonnie Magdalyne..." Taking her face between his palms, he kissed her sweetly, then again, deeply, wrapping his arms around her waist and pulling her tight and warm against him.

"Yes, I do mean to make you mine in every way, Colin Thorne." She smiled into his eyes. "Do not forget it, for I wager there is yet more to come on that account!" They laughed and held each other close, feeling the way their hearts beat together.

"Aye, Maddy, I should have known, because of what Mòrai said to me just before she died. She said, 'I will live on in you and in Maddy.' I suppose at the time I thought it was poetic or, you know, symbolic."

Maddy smiled. "In fact Mòrai knew. She guessed it, though I was not yet sure myself."

"What did she not know?" Colin laughed with delight. "'Tis soon time to gather for supper, Maddy. Shall we tell them the news?" A sunburst of a smile lit her face. "Good! But I think it is also time to call together the Company of Avalon, to hear your dream, *mo ghràidh.*"

A week later they planned to come together for a festive supper at Kildonan on the Feast of Saint Brigit, which the island villagers just as often referred to as Imbolc. Kenna had spent three days cleaning and scouring with her helpers, as had all the housewives in the village. New rushes were placed upon the stone floors of the keep, and fresh greenery—mistletoe, rowan berries, hawthorne and holly—decorated the doorways and the hearths of the great room. Tallow tapers and even beeswax candles were freshly placed upon tables and mantle, and the hearth was well-stocked with firewood.

That afternoon Maddy and Colin walked down the path from the castle to the shore. It was the first of February, and the rising hillocks beyond the shore were verdant with growing things, even though the trees had not yet unfurled in the delicate pale green that would come soon. Sea grasses and sedge grew tall in dull greens and browns, the new leaves of dark green dock curled, last summer's tall seed-spires rising up in rusty clusters of brown seed that would soon be released on the spring winds.

Standing below Kildonan Castle on the strand they could hear the shouts and joyous calls of Imbolc revelers who combed the beaches for driftwood to pile up with dried seaweed and wood cut from the hills for bonfires that would burn all night during their celebration of Imbolc, when the ewes begin to give milk once again. Father Gordon would mingle easily with them that night, weaving together their faith in the ancient Goddess with his prayers to Saint Brigit, Holy Mary, and Lord Jesus.

As they walked hand in hand, Maddy pointed out the mustard yellow and orange lichen that grew on rocks piled or scattered helter skelter, as if strewn by a giant along the shoreline, interspersed among the long stretches of pale sand.

"This always amazes me, the way it glows." She touched a finger to a patch of orange lichen.

Colin stooped down for a moment to examine the strange growths. "It has a magic of its own, does it not, here among the rocks and tidal pools? Look." He pointed to the chaotic wreckage of seaweed strewn in myriads of shape and color from black to golden brown to green.

"Tis otherworldly, is it not?" He stood up, then turned to catch her about the waist and pull her close for a kiss. They stood together for a moment, then walked on, hands clasped. It was a rare day of sunshine, and a smooth, round rock that sparkled in the sand caught Maddy's eye. She picked it up and slipped it into her pocket then gazed out over the sea—the water was gray with shimmers of green in the shallows and blue in the deeps further out. Fluffy mountains of clouds were banked on the mainland, across the blue water at Ayr.

"The beauty of this place never ceases to move my heart." He tossed a rock out toward the surf, accenting his wistful remark as they strolled along.

"What are your thoughts about the dream?" Colin asked, glancing down at Maddy.

"It was...extraordinary. So real, so vivid! And, what is most strange is that even as the Lady walked with me, I knew I was dreaming." She shook her head in awe. "It seemed to me that she communicated directly from her mind to mine—as if her thoughts were transferred directly to me."

Squinting at the sun that hovered above the western horizon of the sea, Colin stopped, raising one hand to shield his eyes. After a moment he mused, "Do ye believe that we live many lives Maddy, as the ancient Celts did?"

Her gaze followed his across the water. "I do, Colin. There was a time, when I was in the monastery in Bruges, when I struggled inwardly over this question, because this belief is not part of our Christian faith. But when I returned to England, I began to listen in a new way to Uncle Richard. With all he shared with us of his own life and his faith, there is a clarity that has dawned within me. And, after all we have lived through, I know in my heart that we will once again see your parents and Mòrai and our uncles, John and Richard, and perhaps dear Roger as well as many others, not only in a place we call heaven, but in this world. I feel we are not finished, somehow. I sense that the events of our lives are intricately interwoven with events and lifetimes we have lived in the past."

She paused, bending down to pick up another rock and hold it up to the sun, then continued. "And after the amazing things we have seen and experienced in this great quest with the relics—the secrets of the king and the queen and their first knight, and now my dream—how can I not know that somehow, in some way, Arthur, Gwenivere, and Lancelot are still seeking each other? They are not finished either. Their love is alive. It burns and moves and flows, it continues to reach into our hearts to touch us. They have something to tell us. The question I ask now is: What is their message?"

Colin listened, turning to face her. He brushed the strands of auburn hair back from her face and kissed her cheek. "I ken verra well what you say, Maddy, and I know it too. But most of all, *mo ghràidh,* when you and I are parted in this life, whether you are first or tis me, my deepest wish will be to see you again. Here, in the paradise of this world, despite all the horrors and the wrong-doings and inequities, Maddy, I wish to look into your shining eyes, to be with you here, where there is tender love, a sweetness that that moves in the deepest recesses of this life and canna be named.

"I wish to gaze upon you and kiss you again and again, for I believe this is how we worship God. And in this knowledge, my heart tells me that Jesus and Blessed Mary and Mother Mary smile down upon us."

His words had come out in a passionate tumble, a necklace of pearl that hung, vibrating, between them. Facing the east and the mainland of Scotland, they stood arm in arm, looking out over the water while the sun shone upon their backs and the wind gently moved the grasses. Time seemed to stand still, and they were suspended in a vast flow of holy love that moved in and through them, weaving them together with everything that had occurred and would occur and sweeping them along in a grand design of divine purpose.

"We should go back to the castle, Maddy." Colin squeezed her hand lightly. "Sunset comes early still, and our guests will soon arrive. I ken Angus and William have arrived already, and, with Jennet, they have everything ready for our celebration of Brighid."

By dusk the flames of bonfires leapt high outside the castle doors and down along the shoreline by the village. The music of lutes and pipes and drums could be heard sailing into the coming night, clear for a rare evening of stars that scattered, a glittering array in the dark vault of the sky. The ocean was restless and immense, an endless dark and heaving presence that swooshed upon the shore in rhythmic waves upon the white sands of Kildonan.

The magic of the place permeated even the stone walls of the castle. The cheerful gold of candlelight made rainbow aureoles in the air as Anne and Ben burst through the door with the four monks of Glastonbury, spirits high with the happiness of reunion. Within moments cloaks were shed and taken by Kenna to be hung in the hallway. Bidding them to be comfortable beside the long hearth, the laird of Kildonan sat upon the chair that Margaret Hamilton Thorne had always taken—now it belonged to Colin. Geleis stood at his side, ready to pour libations and host the companions.

After they had feasted on the sumptuous table of Kildonan Castle, they gathered around the fireplace. A joyous clamor rang out as Colin swelled with pride at the telling of their good news—a child would be born at the end of the next summer, lending all the more enthusiasm to their praise and prayers for the coming of spring and the renewal of life. Jennet had prepared their own Imbolc offering of seeds and milk and cream and whiskey, which she offered into the fire, singing an ancient song for the Goddess. With Father Gordon down in the village, it was William who said the prayer to Saint Brigit, and when both the goddess Brighid and Saint Brigit were pleased with the offerings, Anne turned to Maddy with a hint of impatience.

"Cousin, do not keep us in this terrible suspense! Now," she urged, "will you tell us the dream?"

Maddy blushed, flashing a glance toward Colin, who encouraged her with a nod as she unfolded the parchments held in her hand. "I have written it all down, as I wish to relay it with that strange lucid clarity, as it was given to me in both pictures and words."

She began with a storyteller's finesse, describing the appearance of Morgan le Fay, and how they had walked together through the supernal beauty of the forest and moors they traversed while the Lady of the Lake unfolded before the dreamer's eyes a tale of grave consequence, of nobility and eternal love, of betrayal and heartbreak. As Maddy read the words she had written, they became absorbed, their faces rapt with listening.

"And Morgan said, 'History did not remember us kindly. The bards sang of the glory of Arthur Pendragon, the great battle leader, while they sang of infidelity and betrayal by Gwenhyfar and Lancelot. It may seem there is no justice in this, as they were not the ones who betrayed but were betrayed themselves. And yet, over eons of time, destiny weaves its mysteries. The story of Arthur, Gwenhyfar, and Lancelot is not to be judged; it must told, time and time again, to witness the truth of how it really was.' "

Morgan then relayed to Maddy the true tale of the greatest lovers in history. When she was finished, Maddy heaved a sigh.

"At this point, the dream faded. Her last words were, 'Do not fear. You will be guided on the right path. You will find the answers you seek in a small book, *The Histoire of Tammas Pender*. Look in the small chest you have kept secret on the mountain these years.'"

Maddy stopped reading and folded the parchments in her hands. Like the dream, Maddy's voice dissipated in the rarified atmosphere of the room. Looking up from the parchments, her eyes went to Colin, then searched to connect with each one who sat wide-eyed and still—Geleis, Anne, Ben, the two monks William and Angus. She looked to Jennet and Broderick and then, finally, to Ambrose and Rowland.

No one spoke for a long time, until Geleis broke the spell that had been cast by the dream, lifting his glass halfway to his lips then pausing to muse.

"An ancient history, written by someone named Tammas Pender. It must be a text hidden in one of the small chests brought from Glastonbury, and now hidden in the cairn on Goatfell Mountain."

Maddy nodded her head thoughtfully. "That was exactly my thought, upon waking."

"Well now, clearly we must go and retrieve it," Geleis chuckled.

A rare spirit animated their discussion as they began to talk all at once, making plans for a trek to Goatfell to retrieve the relic. Colin, Geleis, and Broderick would leave within the week. Then, looking around at the companions, Colin ventured. "Well, does anyone else think of Iona, the Holy Isle, as the new home of the relics, upon hearing of this dream?"

Geleis murmured, "Certainly, I had the same thought." Angus and William both nodded in thoughtful assent while Broderick poured another round of spirits.

Ambrose moved to a place by the fire. "Iona is a tiny place. It is three miles long and half that wide, so I have heard. Of course it is well known among monks as the place of Saint Columba—where it is said Christianity met the Scottish tribes—the wild Pictish people. Saint Columba built the first monastery there in 563, just after Arthur's time on earth. It's possible that the queen, her first knight, and their companions were still alive at that time."

Angus stirred from his hassock, his face lit with inspiration. "In the dream, the Lady of the Lake said that they were helped by the monks of Ynis Witrin. It boggles the mind, that we monks of Glastonbury Abbey have been woven together in this tapestry with Arthur, Gwenivere, and Lancelot over centuries of time."

William and Rowland murmured in agreement. Ben shifted in his seat, putting an arm around Anne, while Maddy rose to stand beside Colin. She warmed her hands before the fire.

"We have other important news to share this night as well," Colin interrupted their reflections. "Maddy and I will move before summer to Edinborough, where I will resume my studies. I plan to earn my doctorate. This is a decision we talked over with Mòrai this past fall, before she left us. When my studies are finished, we will move to the Hamilton estate south of Glasgow, which she has bequeathed to us. It is a beautiful place to raise children. We will be joined, in a few years, by Jennet and Broderick. I hope to teach in the university there. Geleis will carry on here as regent, and we will visit in the summers, as often as we can."

Maddy's smile was as infectious as joy carried her words. "Hopefully our children will enjoy Kildonan as their summer adventure, just as we did, and as our uncles did so many years ago when they were students at Oxford. And we will see you all often."

Delight and surprise moved across Anne's face. "This is wonderful news, though we will miss you sorely. There is so much to take in! My head is spinning with it all. Like Angus, I am still pondering your dream, Maddy. How extraordinary that our lives—nay, our destinies—have been entwined with the king and queen and their first knight. Does it occur to you, as it does to me, that a strange magnetism draws us together with them?"

Looking from Geleis to William to Angus and Ambrose, Colin moved his head slowly from side to side, digesting it all. "So," he concluded, "what of moving the relics? Is it to be Iona, then? Or somewhere else?"

As one, the Company of Avalon turned and looked at him, their faces bright with beginnings, with springtime, new life, and the vast empty canvas of what was yet to come.

End Note

Long ago I read Marion Zimmer Bradley's extraordinary masterpiece, *The Mists of Avalon*, which brings the Arthurian legend to life in a brilliant retelling of an ancient story that has captivated readers for centuries. Inspired by the book's rich mythic underpinnings and vivid characters, in 2012 I made a pilgrimage to the Tor and its holy springs in Glastonbury with a friend. Exploring the village, we walked across lush green grounds toward the stone remnants of a once-imposing cathedral, Glastonbury Abbey, located less than a mile from the Tor. I was aware of a palpable sense of the sacred, coupled with the dawning awareness that a terrible tragedy—and a great wrong—had been committed there. The feeling lingered, coming into focus as I stood looking down at a bronze plaque, almost hidden in thick grass, that marked the place where King Arthur's bones had been buried "on the Isle of Avalon," as it said, during the centuries when the cathedral thrived.

Intrigued, I worked my way through the impressive, large visitor center at the site of the cathedral ruin, stopping to learn about Richard Whiting, the last abbot of the monastery. His story immediately captured me, and as I stood there reading, it was as if the "true" story of what had really happened was "downloaded" to me from an invisible source. Now rather awed and even enthralled, that night in our hotel room in Bath, my friend and I got our laptops out and began to Google research Glastonbury Abbey and its last abbot. The story teemed with numinous threads that interwove with my longtime passionate study of the life of Mary Magdalene, revealing a potent tapestry of history and mythology that spanned a thousand years in the Summer Country of ancient England. I had the unmistakable feeling that, unbeknownst, I had stumbled into an epic tale that would not let me go until it was written.

As time went on, the adventure of research and writing revealed the interconnected threads of not just one book but three, each one demanding a deep dive—one I've been happy to make. Weaving together strands of fact and imagination came in an effortless flow of historical and fictional characters who called me to revisit beloved places in Scotland and England (the lands of my ancestors) as well as many pilgrimage sites associated with Mary Magdalene in the south of France. When it became clear that the bones of Arthur and his queen (supposedly Guinevere, but you'll have to read *The Queen's Tale* to get that twist in the story) would make their way to the Isle of Arran (today's spelling), I made another pilgrimage, going back to Scotland in 2017, where I researched historical details of language, culture, traditions, place, landscape, plants, animals, and trees.

One of the great joys of writing historical fiction, for me, is that unexpected serendipities show up. For example, arriving on the Isle of Arran, we disembarked from the ferry in "Whiting Bay"—the actual name of the waters where the ferry lands daily from mainland Scotland! At the ruins of Kildonan Castle, perched on the edge of the island and gazing southward out over the sea, I discovered a bronze plaque about the history of the castle. It relayed the fact that the Earl of Sussex returned to Kildonan around 1558, when he ransacked and destroyed the place, tearing it down stone by stone, leaving only a few thick walls—for reasons that are lost to the mists of time. I was taken aback by how much the castle remnants reminded me of the stark stone ruin of Glastonbury Abbey.

Readers may be interested to know that Richard Whiting did have a family in Exeter and a great-niece named Jane in the monastery of Bruges. However, Maddy and Colin and their family and friends in Scotland are fictional characters. The many historical characters that come to life in *The Company of Avalon* can be easily found in a plethora of factual accounts (both in books and in online documents) of the Dissolution of the Monasteries, the reign of Henry VIII, the lives of Thomas Cromwell and other political and religious figures of the Reform—and, of course, in existing detailed accounts of the destruction of Glastonbury Abbey and the brutal deaths of Richard Whiting, John Thorne, and Roger James.

And so, *The Company of Avalon* came to life in a timeless story that continued to intrigue, delight, sadden, and outrage me. I learned that when Henry VIII became king in 1509 there were more than eight hundred and fifty religious houses in England: abbeys, friaries, priories (nunneries), and monasteries. By 1540, over eight hundred monasteries had been dissolved. The main thrust of Henry's war on the monasteries occurred in the last four years of that time, with Glastonbury Abbey being the most famous and tragic example. Henry put to death over two hundred of his people, some in positions of religious or secular power, and others who had simply protested his new religious laws, his frontal attack on their faith, and his regime of oppression and madness.

The events of 1539 at Glastonbury is a tragedy whose reverberations were made all the more poignant to me when I visited the magnificent, ancient cathedral of nearby Wells, which was converted by its abbot to Henry's new religion in 1539. It was an act that saved their lives and preserved the gorgeous old cathedral, gardens and vast grounds from the destruction that was wreaked upon Glastonbury Abbey. Of course, the Anglican Church shares deeds of atrocity in common with all the major organized religions of the world, not only Christianity. History is riddled with recurring horrors, perpetrated in God's name—religious war, genocide, violent intrigue, sexual abuse, wanton murder, greed, and abuse of power upon ordinary people for thousands of years. However, all religions carry universal truths and have hidden saints of true spiritual realization and genuine humanity residing within them. Richard Whiting was beatified in 1895 by the Catholic Church, but what is truly significant about his story transcends religion, politics, sects, and creeds. It is a tale of our shared humanity, of great-hearted courage and integrity, of being true to one's deepest convictions when pitted against terrible forces and facing a certain death.

Today Glastonbury Abbey is a national shrine of England. What happened to the abbey's secret treasures remains an unsolved mystery. The Company of Avalon lives on, in a way, in the extraordinary legends and mythology that surround Glastonbury and the Tor. To learn more of the fascinating history surrounding mythical Somerset, read the prequels that make up my trilogy, *The Summer Country: The Queen's Tale* (available now) and *When Swans Fly* (coming soon). For more about the process of writing historical fiction, visit my website at maryangelonyoung.com.